THE TRAIL OFTEN CROSSED

BAKER OAKS
BOOK 2

AMBAR CORDOVA

AUTHOR'S NOTE

Hi friend,

I am so excited you picked up my book today. I hope you love it as much as I do, and that Santiago and Roe will stay close to your heart forever. There is so much I could say about this book, but I just hope you give it the chance. Also, I would love to hear from you. Feel free to message me on social media or shoot me an email. I love to chat!

The Trail Often Crossed is a contemporary romance, with some on-page topics that may cause discomfort for the reader. I will list them at the bottom of this page as they may be spoilers, and I want to allow those of you who may not be sensitive to skip them if you wish. If you want to know what they are, just keep reading and you will see them soon. I will also list them on my website to keep them up to date.

This is a stand-alone and can be read as such, but it will give you more depth if you read The Truth Never Spoken first. If you have and you're wondering what the timeline is for this book, The Trail Often Crossed takes place the August before Allie gets to Baker Oaks. There will be a crossover, and the timelines will catch up. The Trail Often Crossed also has an element of suspense.

If you read The Truth Never Spoken, you might be familiar with my open-door symbol. I went back and forth on whether I should include the same symbol for this book, but I decided against it. The growth and development these characters go through and the pieces of themselves they share during the intimate scenes are an incredibly huge part of the plot. In this case, skipping the spice would affect the plot and it wouldn't be fair to the story or the characters. So instead, I am opting for a spice guide in the back of the book to give you a heads up when it will be happening.

The Trail Often Crossed is a fictional story and although Roe has a very real diagnosis of ADHD and Sensory Processing Disorder (SPD), no two cases are the same. You may not see the same symptoms in her as in people you know who may have ADHD and SPD. There's Spanish on-page without translation, except for words and phrases that might need interpretation and those are included in the footnotes. If you're reading digitally, you can also use the translation feature.

Now for the reader precaution themes. They might have spoilers so if you want to skip the next part, you can. There will be profanity, on-page descriptions of explicit sex with power play, death of parents, death of a child (off-page), breaking and entering, keeping someone against their will, cancer diagnosis, and mental health struggles.

Thank you again for giving this book a chance.

143,

Ambar.

PLAYLIST

I've curated a playlist but there are no rules on how to listen to this. For the playlist to enhance the reading experience, some chapters have song titles that match the overall feel of that chapter. Feel free to listen to them after you read the chapter (or during if your brain will let you do that ♡) for a multi-sensory approach to reading the book. You can listen to the playlists on Spotify and Apple Music. Both include an instrumental version as well.

•Prologue: Not About Angels - Birdy

1. A Bar Song (Tipsy) - Shaboozey
2. Fire For You - Cannons
3. Alive and Unwell - Leah Kate
4. Fast Car - Boyce Avenue
5. Training Season - Dua Lipa
6. I Did Something Bad - Taylor Swift
7. The Chain (The Voice Performance) - Girl Named Tom
8. Gravity - Alex & Sierra

9. Into You - Ariana Grande
10. Misery Business - Paramore
11. I'm a Mess - Ed Sheeran
12. Let It Go - James Bay
13. Ojitos Lindos - Bad Bunny & Bomba Estereo
14. Lose Control - Missy Elliott feat. Ciara & Fatman Scoop
15. Kissin' When We're Mad - We Three
16. Midnight Rain - Taylor Swift
17. imgonnagetyouback - Taylor Swift
18. Tattoo - Rauw Alejandro & Camilo
19. Skin - Rihanna
20. Pretty Little Poison - Warren Zaiders
21. Photograph - Ed Sheeran
22. To Love Someone - Benson Boone
23. Out of The Woods (Taylor's Version) - Taylor Swift
24. Collide - Howie Day
25. Me Quiero Enamorar - Jesse & Joy
26. Breathe Me - Sia (for emotional) or Shit Show - Leah Kate (for upbeat)
27. Loco Contigo - J. Balvin
28. Peer Pressure - James Bay Ft. Mia Michaels
29. Play with Fire - Sam Tinnesz
30. Sweet but Psycho - Ava Max
31. Love Lies - Khalid Ft. Normani
32. Unravel Me - Sabrina Claudio
33. CONTIGO - Karol G & Tiesto
34. Rewrite the Stars - James Arthur & Anne-Marie
35. When September Ends - Green Day
36. Let Me Love You - Glee Cast
37. Yellow - Kinna Grannis
38. die first - Nessa Barrett

39. The Cello Song - The Piano Guys
40. 9 Crimes - Damien Rice
41. Little Bit Better - Caleb Hearn & ROSIE
42. Thunderstruck - AC/DC

Epilogue: Everything - Lifehouse

Scan here for Itunes:

Scan here for spotify:

DEDICATION

To those who look fragile on the outside but are unapologetically themselves and will kick some ass when they need to. May you find a tall, broody, protective partner who appreciates every single part of you, especially the chaos.

... AND TO ADRIANA, *because you let me live in delusion and dream big without making me feel like I don't deserve to. Everyone needs a Roe in their lives. Here's to you, keep being a badass.*

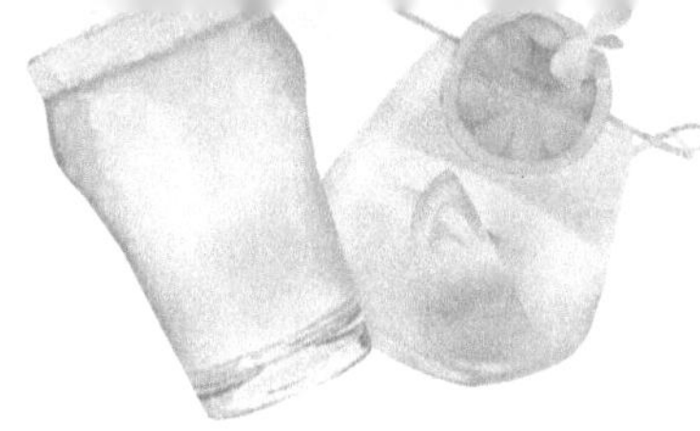

PROLOGUE

NOT ABOUT ANGELS, *Birdy*

ROE, *sixteen years old*

"I'M GOING to give you two some privacy," the nurse says before touching my shoulder and walking out of the room. It feels more like a coffin than a hospital room. She slides the door shut, and with a click she seals us in here, in this state of reality and hell.

"Daddy, please don't leave me," I say, my voice breaking into a silent sob. My head rests on his hand but it's not enough. I climb up onto the bed and lay my body next to him. My arms are around his waist and my head is on his chest. With every passing minute, his breathing slows and my heart weakens. I can feel it breaking into more pieces.

Is there anything that I could've done to stop this from happening? To stop me being an orphan at sixteen? What was the last thing I said or did that was truly good? Truly deserving of having my parents with me? The slower beeps of the machine in the frigid room remind me: not enough. All that is left is anger and sadness. Because yes, I know I acted like a spoiled brat and maybe that didn't win me any points in the lottery of life. It didn't win me any siblings, or any family to rely on.

Tears slip down my face, tears that I've been afraid to let go because it makes it all real. Am I ever going to hear his voice again? *How am I even going to talk to him now?* Who's going to understand all the fucking pain and the sorrow I've been drowning in for the past eight years? God, I just want him to stay. Maybe I should try to do that. I should try to pray.

"I don't know if you're up there, or if you even exist, but God, if you're a thing, would you please let me keep him? Please, don't take him away from me. I'll pray more. I swear I'll be good. I will do as I'm told. I will—" My voice paralyzes in utter fear when he lets out a breath and his eyes open.

Did it work? Oh my God. I'll behave, I promise. I promise I will. I close my eyes tight and open them again, making sure I didn't just imagine that and making sure that it is my dad's beautiful blue eyes that I see staring back at me.

"Anna," he whispers, or I think that's what he says.

Maybe I'm imagining things but in this case he did say *Anna.* I reply, "No, Daddy, it's me. Mom is not here anymore." Adding insult to injury, he called me by my mom's name.

Do I look like her now that I'm older? I don't want to. Not right now. Not when these may be my last moments with him. I don't want to be anyone else but his little girl. I don't want to remind him of the love of his life who died first. The biggest loss of our lives. I don't want to be sitting here when he wishes I was someone else.

"Daddy?" I ask in a broken plea. Maybe if I ask nicely, he'll stay. Maybe if I promise to behave, something will forgive me and let me have my dad. Maybe they could take me instead?

He holds my gaze and smiles, looking the most at peace I've seen him in a while, and right when I think I can maybe, just maybe, wish the cancer away, he closes his eyes and takes his last breath.

It takes the last grain of hope I had left in me. Because it doesn't matter how much I ask for him to stay, nobody does in the end.

ONE
AT THE BAR, EVERYTHING IS FINE

*A **B**AR **S**ONG **(T**IPSY**)**, **Shaboozey**

ROE, **Twenty Four Years Old**

THERE'S A BACHELOR PARTY TONIGHT. Those are known to drain my fucking soul but fill my pocket. They're fun for everyone, except for the bartenders trying to keep up with demands. Especially when we get misogynist assholes from out of town who want to see *"Real Cowgirls"*. If I had a dollar for every man who comes in here telling me to "ride them" or to "show them what I'm good for," I would be a millionaire by now.

Baker Oaks is a small town, but since it's so close to three big cities, we get plenty of people wanting to live the Nashville experience outside of Tennessee. They think they can get away with a cheaper version of Nashville in this small town in Florida but that's not really it. Yes, Saddlers is a country bar offering line dance classes for free every Saturday. Yes, a lot of people dress up like cowgirls and cowboys. But this town is nothing like Nashville and they're usually in for a surprise when they come. Some like it better, the family feel and all, and some? Well, they act all pissed when a five-foot-four blonde bartender kicks them out of the bar for calling her staff names.

I truly don't hate it here; even though I rant about things I don't like, I've come to love this place. Baker became my home eight years ago when I moved here to live with Grandma. Even after she died, I didn't have it in me to start over somewhere else. So, I just stayed. I love this crazy little town. All the quirks and people make it the place to be.

It just annoys me when the big crowd comes in looking for something they won't find here. This is not a cowboy town nor a bull rider's hang-out spot. Just a small southern town with all the charm.

The bar area is crowded as usual, leaving me hardly enough space to lay out drinks. Some people are pushing in, trying to get closer, and I'm two seconds away from standing on the damn bar and telling everyone to chill or they can get out. And seeing as I own this bitch, I can do whatever I want. Including telling people to watch their tone and the way they behave.

I could sit in the back and handle the business side of owning a bar but what's the fun in that? I can pay someone to do that, and I can be out here using one of my many talents: pairing people with a drink that will change their lives. Sometimes I think that, in another life, I was a witch. Because the way I can pinpoint who needs a dry martini and who needs a Coors Light is unmatched. Or so I've been told.

I scan the bar to make sure everyone is being served when I see a guy sitting by the corner without a drink in front of him. He doesn't seem to have a sense of urgency to order, but his eyes are roaming around the room with an unknown purpose. Heavy eyelids and an intense stare. Maybe he isn't looking for something, but someone. The matching shirts and the pats on the back from the other obnoxious men let me know for sure that he's part of this bachelor party.

The shirts say, 'I'm with stupid' and the groom has one that says, "I'm stupidly in love." *So cheesy.* They all look young, maybe late twenties or early thirties. They all seem to be having the time of their lives—except homeboy at the bar.

He's sitting there looking ready to kill someone or just bored to death. The black t-shirt fits him perfectly and digs into his tattooed arms, showing his muscles. Oh, what a beautiful canvas he is. What I would give to get my hands on his skin and add more ink to that masterpiece. I can't tell from far how the designs were made but I *can* tell he has good taste. His chest is broad, and with how much of himself hovers over the table, I would bet good money he's over six feet tall. He has dark hair and piercing whiskey-colored eyes that are currently watching me ogle him. *Fucking great.*

I walk toward him, tucking my comfort rag on the back pocket of my jean shorts. And yes, I have a comfort rag because sometimes you have to hold on to the things that are constant in your life. I place both hands on the bar right in front of him but before I can ask him anything he says, "Enjoying the view?" with a smug smirk that I want to erase right off his face.

"Nah, I was just wondering why you look so damn miserable. Got dumped and now have to celebrate your buddy getting married?" I nod toward the group of guys who caught the end of my sentence and are shouting behind him. *Children, men are children.* If it wasn't for how much I like dick, I would swear them off. They're all the same, and something tells me this guy is nothing different.

"Not dumped, just annoyed nobody has gotten my order yet. Why don't you be a doll and bring me a drink?"

"Change that *doll* for Roe and I might," I snap back, already annoyed at this man. "I'm not sure how men treat women where you're from but out here, we save the pet names for actual relationships. What do you want, *sunshine?*" I ask sarcastically.

"How about a Miller Light?" he asks, taking the edge off his words.

Miller Light? I did not picture this guy drinking that at all. Usually broody men with square jaws, intense stares, and the whole mysterious vibe this guy is showing ask for liquor, not a beer. My usual beer customers are the ones who are either too young to know what they want, or your typical man who comes to the bar before going home. Instead of asking him if he's sure about it, I just shrug it off and say, "Coming right up."

I walk toward my tap and fill a cup with beer, spilling some everywhere because, even after years of pouring beer, I still make a mess. Before turning back to him, I get an idea. I pour some whiskey—good Old Rip Van Winkle— on the rocks in two short glasses.

Placing both drinks in front of him and looking him dead in the eyes, I chime, "Here, why don't you drink some whiskey, like a man?" and drink one of the glasses in one gulp. "On the house." I wink at him and walk the opposite way, leaving the other one for him to enjoy.

TWO

PIXIE DUST AND LIQUOR

Fire For You, Cannons

SANTIAGO

"HERE, why don't you drink some whiskey, like a man?" the spitfire bartender quips. I have never been more annoyed and turned on in my life by a single statement. This little blonde seemed to be friendly with everyone, especially locals, but then she came over here and gave me a run for my money. Calling her *doll* struck a nerve, but it was the closest thing to what I wanted to call her without sounding insane.

The minute I walked to the bar, my eyes kept drifting toward her. She couldn't be more than five foot three, but she was commanding this whole place like a queen. She's standing behind the bar, wearing jean shorts no longer than the rag she holds in her back pocket, and a black top that looks painted on her body.

She has her blonde hair up in a ponytail and piercing blue eyes—I swear those reached my soul the minute they met mine. She's also wearing checkered Vans. For some reason beyond me, I find it incredibly hot. There's something about someone being so comfortable in their skin they don't need to follow trends or social status that gets to me every time. Like wearing Vans in a country bar. She seems like the type of girl who likes something and goes for it; fuck what everyone else thinks.

I was not expecting that mouth on her, that's for sure. She chugged the whiskey like water and returned to tending to the other people waiting on their drinks.

"Dude, she doesn't play," Joey says, putting his hand over my shoulder with a big chuckle.

"Yeah, yeah, I figured."

"You need to fix this shit. Roe makes the best drinks, and we can't be on her bad side."

"What am I supposed to fix?" I ask, dumbfounded by what he's implying.

"Whatever it was that pissed her off. She usually is pretty nice and sometimes even playful. She didn't even bring you the Roe Flight."

"The Roe Flight?"

"Yeah, every time someone new comes, she reads their 'vibes' – her words not mine. Then she brings six small drinks. You get to try them all and order one of them. It's hard to narrow it down because she's so damn good at the choices she makes for you. We all have a favorite drink here thanks to her," Joey finishes, nodding in her direction and keeping his eyes on her.

I follow his gaze and see her laughing with someone who has a fresh drink in front of them. Her smile is blinding—making me wish I was closer so I could hear her laugh too.

Her lips are full, too; without an ounce of lipstick, I notice. Clearly my dick notices too as it twitches in my pants. Apparently, we like Roe.

With my whiskey in hand, I walk toward the other end of the bar. There's an empty stool by the tap, keeping it partially isolated from the rest of the place. It will give me space to either keep watching her or fucking leave if I can't figure out exactly what I want. I can't stay long considering I have to be at the track bright and early tomorrow to practice. The same reason why I didn't want to drink tonight, but whatever drink this is, I need another one. Maybe her drink-picking superpowers worked for me without giving me a flight. Maybe she somehow knew I hate making choices and it is easier for me to just be given straight answers.

Another bartender approaches, giving me a great smile and pushing her breasts up to show more cleavage. On an ordinary night, this would be something I'd go for, but my eyes are set on the blonde behind her.

"What can I get you, hotshot?" she asks with a sultry tone.

"You can get Roe for me, she's handling my drinks," I reply with a dry tone and serious eyes. I'm not here to flirt with this girl.

"You got it!" She turns around to grab Roe.

Uh? Maybe she wasn't interested after all. I'm getting old and losing all my game.

When the girl reaches Roe and starts talking to her, I can see her visibly stiffen and roll her eyes. *The fucking sass.* It makes me want to turn her around and spank her until she's rolling her eyes for completely different reasons.

She walks to me, hands on her hips, face straight. No smiles for me, that's for sure. Standing in front of me she asks, "What can I get you?"

"I heard there's a secret Roe Flight I was supposed to get."

Now that she's closer, I can see her tattoos even better. I could before, but I didn't take time to appreciate them. She has a full sleeve, a couple kissing her collarbone and little wisps of another one peeking from her shorts. They're stunning. The designs are incredible and seem to fit together. I would pay good money to whoever did those to get some on me. I bet they look even better in the daylight.

"Yeah, but then you ordered a Miller Light and there's only so much I can do for plain beer people." She crosses her arms over her chest and looks me dead in the eyes like she didn't just try to insult me.

"Mm, something tells me we started on the wrong foot. Let me try again. Hi, I'm new here, what do you recommend?" I reply with a smile. Her eyes dip to my lips and I know I've got her right where I want her.

"Fine," she replies, stomping to the wall behind the bar and grabbing different bottles.

She returns with six tall shot glasses, all different colors. They all seem like liquor. *Interesting.* I ordered a beer and she decided I'm more of a liquor guy. The funny thing is, she isn't wrong. Usually when I go out, I opt for liquor. But when I go to a new place, I prefer playing it safe, and beer typically tastes the same regardless of where I am. So, beer was the easy choice tonight.

She keeps her eyes on me while her hands rest on top of the bar. I raise an eyebrow at her stance in wonder.

"I need to study your expression to know what to get you next. So, get to it, I don't have all night." The music is loud, and people are dancing around. I could easily shift my eyes from her but it's impossible when she looks at me so attentively.

Me cago en la madre[1]. This girl and her attitude. I usually don't give into the chase of women who are not interested. It's one thing to have back and forth banter with someone, and then there's blatantly showing you're not interested in someone. In this case, I'm not sure this is either. I feel a pulse. I might not be the only one interested here and this is more than physical attraction. She's hot. Actually no, she's more than that. She's stunning, and her sass might be a turn-off sometimes, but in this instance, it adds to the appeal. This girl can hold her ground. She's acting like she's unimpressed or like my purpose here today is to annoy her. Makes me want to prove a point and find out if she's truly indifferent to me or if she's as intrigued as I am.

Game on.

I try the drinks and they're all fantastic. I opt for the dark-colored one and she nods. She walks back and brings me another short glass with ice and whatever liquor it is.

"I was right the first time. Smooth whiskey is your drink."

"Would you pour one for yourself too?" I ask, lifting my glass to her in invitation. Offering her an olive branch. "Have a drink with me," I add, smiling at her while refusing to break eye contact.

She scans me, up and down, stopping at my lips while licking hers. "Nah, I had my fill already. You enjoy, alright?" She tries to walk away, but I get up, quickly reaching over the bar and grabbing her hand. Electricity courses through us instantly, making us both look at where our skin is connected. She lifts her eyes slowly and when her gaze

---

1. Me cago en la madre: I'ts a saying that can mean many things, in this case it's like fuck my life.

meets mine, I recognize the lust in her eyes, the same way I'm sure mine look too.

She pulls her hand away and walks around the bar to where I'm sitting. I assume she'll get security or something because I crossed the bar line and touched her, usually a big no with female bartenders. But she does the last thing I expect.

She stops before the hallway that seems to be leading to the back of the bar, turns around to look at me, and asks, "Are you coming?"

Holy shit.

I walk toward her confidently, whiskey in hand, and smirk knowingly. For someone so small, she walks damn fast. The hallway has three doors. Two bathrooms across from each other with 'gals' and 'pals' written on the door in gold. The door at the end doesn't have a sign showing what's behind it and looks different than the other two. It also has a scanner by the handle. I assume you need some sort of key to get in.

Roe stops in front of the door and turns her body around to look at me, her back pressed against the door and her eyes full of mischief. I place my hand above her head on the door, leaning forward and closing the space between us. She has long thick lashes that she peers up at me through, her light blue eyes darkening with desire before placing her hands on my chest.

I lower my head to her ear, my other hand brushing her neck, and whisper, "Lead the way, doll," thinking that will piss her off more and give me some light on what the fuck is happening here, but it doesn't. She just grabs my hand and pulls me through the door.

I was not expecting that. Again.

The room is dark with only a small lamp in the corner,

allowing me to see bits and pieces. The dim light illuminates a desk full of papers and dark shelves around it. The floor is checkered, unlike the dark wood that covers the rest of the bar, and there are plants hanging. Dropping my hand the minute we're inside, she shuts the door behind her and pulls me toward her by my shirt, placing herself between me and the door. Her pouty lip is between her teeth and her eyes are blazing fire on mine. *Oh shit.*

I stare at her, a little shocked at the turn of events but it doesn't take long for me to snap out of it because this gorgeous sassy little thing says, "How about you use that mouth of yours for more than just calling me a doll?"

I give her what she wants and kiss her.

THREE

DIRTY MOUTH AND GOOD HANDS

***Alive and Unwell,* Leah Kate**

ROE

THIS GUY, who I don't even know, *not that it matters*, is kissing me without reservation. Lips on mine, hand behind my neck and the other one on the door, framing my face. I open to him and he slides his tongue in without hesitation. If the assumption that tattooed, good-looking men know how to kiss was a doubt, it's a confirmation now. This man knows what he's doing, with his hands, his lips, *his tongue.*

Usually I'm attracted to all the bad boys, the walking red flags, and this guy is no different. There is something about the broodiness and the back-and-forth banter that gets me going every time. His dark caramel eyes and strong arms had me more distracted than I can afford to be, so something had to be done about it.

The bar takes some of my time, but in between racing

moto this season and all the unknowns about which class I'm racing, I have some pent-up energy that needs to be released. One-night stands often do it for me. They might not get me off in the moment, but they get me going. Then I can go home and bust one off, think of it like foreplay for a solo event.

"Where did you go, little doll?" he asks with confusion in his eyes. I guess I was lost in thought. When I look at him and don't say anything, he smirks and adds, "I must be doing something wrong if I can't keep your attention with my tongue."

Ouch. This guy speaks his mind even when it won't earn him brownie points. My thoughts do wander sometimes. But if he knew I was thinking about how I need a release and he's the vessel getting me there, he might appreciate it. Most guys are happy to get an easy lay. I don't require much to pretend I'm done. And I never ask for any form of contact. Easy. No mess.

"If you wanted to get me naked, you just needed to ask. No need to act all tough," he says looking at me expectantly. When I stay quiet, he asks, "Where did the sass go? Did I leave you speechless?"

"How about you kiss me and show me how my sass made you feel?"

"There she is," he says, before sealing my mouth with a kiss.

His lips are on mine and his hands are everywhere on my body. I try to get closer to him but he's like a damn tree, and I practically have to stand on my tiptoes to reach him. His head is lowered, and he must sense me struggling because his hands go under my ass and he lifts me up, pressing me against the door. My legs wrap around him, making me feel all of him against me. The way he holds me against the door is effortless.

My hands roam his hard chest, going lower until they're under his shirt. I pull it up to try and take it off but he stops me. He breaks the kiss momentarily to take it all the way off. Removing the shirt with just one hand, he lets me lean against the door giving me time to appreciate his upper body. He's hot, I'll give him that.

He catches me staring and says with a smirk, "Like what you see, little doll?"

"I'm nobody's doll," I sass back.

"Mm, we'll see about that," he growls before pulling my tank top up.

I usually don't wear bras, so my breasts are out the moment he takes my shirt off. I grew up hating my body. Too small, too skinny, not enough curves, you name it. But I have worked hard to love every inch of me so I don't cover myself. In fact, I lower my hands from his neck and touch myself, going from my neck down my breasts, to my belly. He still keeps my body between himself and the door. He looks down and mutters something in another language that I cannot pick out before letting his mouth get back on mine hungrily.

His body is rock hard against me and the way he's kissing me is causing me to make indecent sounds. My hands go back to his neck, lacing my fingers behind his head. I pull him closer to me, opening my mouth to allow him more access and moaning against his lips. I'm so lost in the kiss that I almost miss the sounds of the door lock system and I freeze.

A couple of my employees have a key fob to get into the office, but they usually only come in if I'm needed on the floor. The bar is busy but I'm fully staffed tonight so it shouldn't be an issue. Our heavy breathing sounds even louder in the quiet space alongside the rattling of the handle. We don't speak; we don't move but Whiskey Guy keeps the door shut with his hands.

"Roe? Are you there?" Jackson asks while pounding on the door.

I open my mouth to reply but this guy shakes his head *no* while putting a finger on my lips, silently hushing me.

"Roe, if you're in there, we need you out here now. There's a fight," he adds before letting go of the handle.

Fuck my life.

"I have to go," I say to this guy, wiggling so he can put me down. He does and squats down to grab my tank top and hand it to me. I put it on and look at him. He's standing there, a little dumbfounded and shirtless. His chest is broad, with tattoos spreading across his pecs, sternum, and ribs. I admire how good they look and my hands itch to add more ink to them. So many pieces I could work with on his skin, but I don't have time for that right now. I need to go figure out what the fuck is happening out there.

"It's a shame. You look like you would've been fun for a minute," I add before winking at him and slipping out the door.

FOUR
SMX

Fast Car, _Boyce Avenue_

SANTIAGO

I WAKE up at the crack of dawn with a FaceTime call from Marco. I don't answer and take it for what it is. He's canceling our riding session again. When I decided to move to Baker Oaks to be closer to the motocross track, my friend Marco started making plans for our Sunday riding sessions. The big issue? He doesn't take riding seriously. He wants to, but his health conditions make it easier for him to be more of a leisure rider. He likes the look of riding a dirt bike and the camaraderie, but the hard work it takes to make this into a semi-career is too much for him. He knows it and his parents know it too.

Nobody thinks that at thirty we would make a career out of our hobby, but to get sponsors and gear deals to offset the cost of this expensive pastime, you need to be more than good at this. You need to be outstanding. How often you ride is usually a good indicator of how well you will perform in races. Marco tries hard to be the best he can be, but other riders with more seat time will typically beat him in the race. This is the first season he feels better enough to practice almost as often as I do, and he has made everyone aware that he's coming for first place.

I moved to Baker Oaks to be closer to the best motocross track in the south, Shoals Motocross. SMX is about a twenty-minute ride from Baker, making it a perfect place to live. I had been online looking for a job no farther than an hour away when I ran into Baker Auto.

Tinkering with cars has always been a passion. When they posted the position for a part-time mechanic with the possibility of extra hours, I jumped at the opportunity. It helped having a close friend already living here, making my transition easier. Marco, who has been a family friend for years, had an extra room in his house and needed a room-mate so it was a win-win situation.

Marco's friend Joey—I guess you could say my friend too—is another rider and he's getting married in a couple of weeks. When he heard I was moving to town, he invited me to the bachelor party last night. I had been exhausted from interviewing, moving, and organizing all my stuff but I still made it happen. *Tienes que mostrarle a los demas lo bueno que eres. You have to let others see how good you are.* I remember my mom's saying all too well. So, I went and tried to be social. I tried to push through the discomfort of being in a sea of people I didn't know. In a new town, two days before starting a new job. I was about to leave the bar, but I couldn't keep my eyes off of her. I couldn't keep my eyes off *Roe*. Her name, sweet on my tongue. Because of her, I stayed and well, the rest is a blur.

I made it home, and after the longest and coldest shower of my life, I was able to fall asleep. I set my alarm for five in the morning to give me enough time to get up, go for a run, eat breakfast, pack the trailer, and make it to SMX before the 8:00am practice.

It's hotter-than-hell outside on this early May morning in Florida. The humidity is making my shirt stick to my chest, and I haven't even started running. I don't know the town well enough, so I find a running path on the trails app on my phone and head that way, stretching while I walk. I'm usually good with directions and don't need much to get around; however, being unprepared is how bad shit happens so I like to have all my i's dotted and all my t's crossed. By the time I make it to the beginning of the trail, my shirt is slick with sweat, so I take it off and drop it by a rock, making a mental note to pick it up later. Running my hands through my thick dark hair, I set the timer on my watch to thirty minutes and start running. I don't know how long it will take me to run the full trail, but I need to be back in an hour so at the thirty-minute mark, I'll turn around.

Most people run with headphones on; I like to be present with my surroundings. I like to hear the sounds of nature. Feel the air on my face and connect to whatever is happening around me. Life is too fleeting to pass by without noticing the little things. Ana used to call those *glimmers*. The opposite of triggers. *You're so worried about what you need to do, big bro, that you ignore all the glimmers around you,* she would say. And oh, she was right. She deserved to live her whole life full of glimmers but in the end, her days were cut short. Forever dimming the light she brought into the world. I promised her before she died that I would try to find glimmers every day for the rest of my life. I won't break that promise.

I run through the trail and all the way back home without seeing another soul. I'm guessing everyone sleeps until it's time for church in this town. It's quiet; only birds chirping and a distant train passing. The sunrise peeks behind the Southern Yellow pine trees, painting the town hues of purple, blue, and pink, making it today's first glimmer. This type of sunrise reminds me that you can always start over, even when you think there is no end in sight. The sun always rises.

I walk into the house and, to my surprise, Marco is awake waiting at the breakfast table, sipping on coffee and reading the newspaper. The only person under thirty who still reads the newspaper. "I thought you were canceling on me," I say while opening the fridge to grab a water bottle.

"Nah, I FaceTimed on accident. I was trying to text you to ask if you were going running first." He doesn't look up from the newspaper while he sips his coffee.

"I did. My bad if you wanted to come. Next time."

"Not running anymore but I made a list of good running areas. Here." He hands me a piece of paper with a list. He's also the only guy under thirty who uses pen and paper for reminders and notes. "Where did you go?" he asks.

"I found this trail today." I show him the trail on my phone with the distance I covered. "It's called St. Mary's Trail. It was good but I only made it three miles in before I had to turn around. I'm sure I'll be back in a couple of days."

"That's a good one! You can go in different ways too, making it a new experience every time."

I pat him on the back and say, "I'm going to shower and get dressed. Give me ten."

I walk into the room, strip off my clothes, and hop into the shower to quickly rinse off. I get dressed in my riding clothes: shorts, a dry-fit shirt, tennis shoes, and my Baseball Classic cap worn backward. I run outside and after loading everything up, we head to SMX. The clock on the truck reads 7:20am. *Right on track.*

We park the truck and exit into humid hot air. I can feel droplets of moisture on my skin like I'm getting out of the shower, except I'm standing fully clothed in the morning sunshine.

The track is packed, which doesn't surprise me: round one of The Trail Riders starts in a couple of weeks. People are parked all through the pit area, unloading their bikes and gear, and getting ready for TTR.

Most riders are men, but I've heard about this rider, A. Sorelle, who is supposed to be one badass woman. She trains here and I have been wanting to see what all the fuss is about. Her online videos are what legends are about but there's very little information about who she is. The word on the street is that she doesn't socialize much. She supposedly intimidates the crap out of people. She also doesn't go by her first name which makes it harder to find. Too many A. Sorelles out there.

We've been out here for a good thirty minutes and are ready to go. There's a line waiting for the gates to drop so we can all ride; a sea of riders and their dirt bikes. The sound of revving and the smell of burning oil from the two-stroke engine reminds me of why I'm here and why I like this sport.

We still have ten minutes before the gate drops when we hear a loud vehicle pulling up. I turn to see what the commotion is all about. A shiny black Jeep enters, blasting a song that sounds like it could be Miley Cyrus from the speakers. It parks right by the gate entrance where we are waiting, and when the engine stops and the door opens, I can see thin legs and checkered Vans peeking from under the door. The person jumps down and slams the door shut. It's the feisty, sexy bartender from last night.

FIVE
SAFETY IS OVERRATED

TRAINING SEASON*, *Dua Lipa

ROE

AS USUAL, arriving at the track causes more ruckus than anything I have ever seen; as if seeing a woman in a man-led field is an anomaly in the 21st century. Mostly helmeted heads turn my way – I can't see most of their faces, except for some boys in the back row. I recognize a couple of them but there is one face in particular drawing my attention.

Standing at the back of the lineup, helmet on top of his gorgeous YZ-250, is the guy from last night. He's wearing full gear matching with his blue, white, and red bike. He also has a chest protector on, which is a shock because most guys hate wearing it. Yet this broody, tall as fuck, half-scary guy wears it loud and proud. Safety first, I guess.

I've been so preoccupied looking at his bike and setup that I completely miss him walking my way until he's standing right in front of me. He stands there, looking delicious and with a know-it-all smirk on his face.

"Hey little doll, didn't get enough of this last night?" he asks, his hands on his hips and his eyes drinking me in. *Cocky asshole.*

I step forward, crossing my arms over my chest, and look up. Showing him that his height doesn't intimidate me. "Oh, pretty boy, you thought that I came here for you?"

"Why else would you? This is not the place for a doll like you." He pulls on one of my French braids, my signature hairstyle for track days, and I pull back, rolling my eyes.

While I was distracted by this banter and his stupid handsome face, the gates dropped and practice started. Most bikes are on the track and the remaining few are getting ready to start. I look at this guy again; "Cruz", according to his bike's tag. Smiling devilishly at him, I run past him and to his bike. I grab his helmet and pull it right over my head, leaving the straps loose because if I stop to buckle them, he might reach me and stop me from doing what I'm about to do. Guys don't like other people riding their babies. And by babies, I mean their vehicles. Cars, trucks, bikes, you name it. I hop on the bike, pull the kick starter open, hold the clutch, and kick hard to start this bitch. It roars to life and I head into the track—not giving two fucks about wearing any gear. Safety is overrated. My parents were safe and died anyway. Just like everyone around me does.

I rode my first dirt bike at seventeen, when a friend dared me to it. It took me two tries to learn how to ride the beast and I've never been able to get off one since. It's a way for me to release anger, sadness, and expectations. Is it dangerous? Sometimes. But teetering between life and death is where I feel most alive. It's the only thing that makes me feel free.

SMX is my favorite track. As a trail rider, I struggle to find anywhere to practice offering more than singles with mild jumps and less supercross-style tracks. SMX has more turns, and the ground is less prepped than other ones, making it ideal to practice in a controlled place without the risk of running smack into a tree without anyone knowing where you are. I go as fast as I can, taking sharp turns and jumping, clearing the tabletop. Some people pass me, putting their boots down between me and their bike, marking distance, and balancing on their bikes. Others I pass, giving them the same treatment.

I finish my lap, exhausted since this bike is a lot heavier than mine, but fuck if I'm showing him that. I stop right next to my Jeep, where Cruz stands, arms crossed and lips tight. I turn off the bike and swing my leg over, walking to him. I remove his helmet, grab a braid and with a smile on my face, I hand the helmet to him.

"Nice ride, but to answer your question, I had no clue you were going to be here, pretty boy. I'm a rider myself." Looking over my shoulder I see some guys covering their mouths and cackling behind me.

His eyebrows practically twitch. His jaw is tense and his dark whiskey eyes look like asteroids. Heated and deadly.

"Relax. Not my first time on a two-stroke. Not my first time at the track either, in case it wasn't obvious," I add.

He was definitely mouthier yesterday, so he's either not a morning person or he's pissed at me.

"Well, if you excuse me, I'd like to ride my own bike now." I start walking toward the back of my Jeep when he grabs me by the wrist. Again. Twice in twenty-four hours, this man has grabbed me and both times he's had the same effect. Shivers run down my spine, and I feel a primal need to climb him like a tree.

"It's not very nice to ride other people's bikes without permission," he snarls as seriously as he possibly can.

"It's also not very nice to assume that your almost-bar-hook-up was going to show up at the race track like a stalker. I didn't even know you were a rider, Cruz."

"Not my name, doll," he adds, acting unimpressed.

"Already told you mine is Roe, not doll. How about you tell me yours so I can stop calling you pain-in-my-ass in my head?" I sass back.

He shakes and lowers his head in a futile attempt to cover his smile but fails miserably. He rubs his chin and takes a deep breath. He holds his helmet in his hand, and leans against my Jeep, crossing one foot in front of the other and his eyes take me head to toe.

"There hasn't been one single thing about you that doesn't surprise me, Roe."

Roe. My name on his lips is music to my ears and I am annoyed at myself for letting this guy have such a big effect on me. My insides are humming at having this much of his attention directed my way. It's almost like the rest of the track ceases to exist around us. "Stick around and I am sure I'll surprise you some more."

He stretches his hand forward and says, "Santiago."

I place my hand firmly in his and shake without taking my eyes off him. "We have to stop meeting like this, pretty boy." If I did serious relationships, I'm sure I could get lost in this man. But since that's not my MO, maybe I can get lost in him for one day. I'm ready to offer to leave this place with me when I hear a golf cart pulling up behind me.

Allen, the owner of the track and the true pain of my

existence, jumps down with papers in hand and a mean look on his face. *Shit, shit, shit.* Here we go again.

"Allen, my man. Happy Sunday! What a beautiful day at the track it is," I call in the chirpiest tone I can muster.

"Aurora, how many times do I need to tell you not to ride my track without signing the waiver or without gear?! You're going to get yourself hurt and make me go broke paying for a lawsuit. Stop riding without the waiver." He acts like a grumpy grandpa more than a business owner.

"Okay, okay. My bad. Here, let me sign your little paper. You know I'm going to be here on Sundays, just forge my signature next week." I sign my name on the line and flash him a big smile that he won't buy. He's over my bullshit but I'm a loyal rider so he can't say much. Also, his wife loves me, and she was friends with Grandma.

"Please put some gear on." He looks at Santiago and adds, "I hope she's not causing you much chaos, Mr. Cruz, but if she is, don't take it personally. Chaos should be her middle name." He steps away, climbing back into the golf cart shouting, "Don't ride without gear on in my track, Aurora!"

"Aurora?" Santiago asks with a confused look.

"Nobody calls me that, except the old people. I go by Roe."

"Huh? Aurora doesn't fit you so I can see why you wouldn't like to use it."

"Why doesn't it fit me, pretty boy?"

"Because Aurora is such a princess name, and you're more like a brat."

"Ooh, I can be on board with being a brat sometimes." I close the space between us, so close that if I were taller, we could kiss. "Would you spank me like one too?" His eyes grow wide, and he shakes his head mumbling something in what seems like Spanish. "What's the matter, pretty boy, can't handle spanking a little spoiled brat? Maybe you just need to go back to your Disney princess movies."

I step back, pulling both braids forward over my chest. "Enough talking. I'm going to ride." I open the back door of my Jeep, grab my bike stand, and place it on the ground. I walk around to grab my bike from the small trailer hooked to my hitch. I start removing the straps so I can get it down when Santiago speaks again.

"Let me help you get that down." He's reaching for my bike before I can say anything, but I block him with my small frame.

"Bite me, pretty boy. I'm not a damsel in distress and I've been doing this for too long without any man pretending I need their help." I pull the bike down, walk it toward the stand, and place it on top. I may be 110 pounds soaking wet, but I can definitely carry my own damn bike.

I continue, finding my gear and getting ready to ride without uttering another word to him. He gets the hint and goes back to his own bike. I finish by pulling up my black and hot pink gear. I snap my helmet in place and ride my bike to the gate. Ready to take on the day, I leave Santiago Cruz in a cloud of smoke behind me.

SIX

RIVALS

I Did Something Bad, Taylor Swift

SANTIAGO

THIS GIRL IS GIVING me whiplash and I am not even trying to chase her. I'm too old for this. I'm thirty, for fuck's sake, but there is definitely something about her. I can't help but feel a pull to her. Maybe it's the fearless way she talks or her perfect crystal blue eyes.

I can't believe that she rides. I actually *can* believe it because I just watched her steal my bike. I don't know why I'm surprised. I know nothing about her. What I still can't believe is that the tiny thing could ride my beast of a bike like it was nothing. Pretty badass, actually. I shake my head and put my helmet on, wiping the smile off my face so I can go ride.

We've been riding for hours, just taking water breaks every now and then. During a race, I can't just stop in the middle of the trail so I try to treat practice the same way. We realize we won't make it all day with the temperatures, so we decide to call it and start loading up.

I haven't seen Roe all day. Unless you count the spark of pink and black gear as she blazes around the track. It's almost impossible to miss anyone out here in general so she either hasn't taken any breaks from the heat, or she left while I was still riding laps. I need to stop worrying about her and focus on me if I want to be successful this round. This is my year; I feel it in my bones.

The trailer is packed, bikes secured, and our gear is off and hanging from the railings inside the trailer. Marco ran inside the office. While I wait for him, I lean against my truck's door, eyes on the track trying to find Roe. I was so astonished seeing her here that I didn't even notice her number. Marco says he's never seen her here before but from the looks of it, she doesn't mingle much. Maybe she just comes to ride and leaves, but her Jeep is still here so she's either riding or hiding. I don't take her as a hiding kind of girl, so riding it must be.

"Lose something, Saint?" I hear her voice from behind me, so I turn and see her walking toward me. Her face is covered in sand, especially around her cheeks and nose, typical for an open-faced helmet like the one she uses. Her braids, which were previously pulled perfectly tight, are now loose with strands of gold flowing around her face. Her black jersey covers most of her body and has the number 114 in sparkly pink, front and center.

"Saint?" I raise my eyebrow at her.

"Apparently nobody has anything negative to say about you, and that doesn't happen around here, so you must be exactly that: a Saint. It also happens to fit your name."

"I just moved here, that's why. There's plenty of bad in

me, I can assure you." I wink at her and that earns me the sassiest eye roll I have ever seen. *There she is.*

"Santiago Cruz, twenty-eight, YZ-250, two-stroke. Likable with good sportsmanship. Refuses to work with brands that are not transparent and helps kids get started in the sport when possible," she adds, as if she was reciting my stats from the Trail Riders website.

"Did you Google me?" I ask with a broad smile on my face.

"I did, the minute I saw you and I were racing in the same category in a month. I needed to find out how big my competition is this season since I'm moving up classes. And to my surprise, my competition seems to be you, Saint."

"Are you riding The Trail Riders?"

"Yeap." Roe pops her 'p' as if she's a toddler being inconvenienced by my mere existence. *The brat.* "I rode last season too but I was in the women's class. We both know that class is more recreational and I'm looking for more. This industry, at least in TTR, advertises the women's class as a pastime. I won every time, but I'm ready to compete with people who are actually racing, not out there frolicking through the meadows."

"Hold up, hold up," I choke out, trying to gather my thoughts because my chuckles won't let me form a coherent sentence. "You rode last year, won every round, and somehow that's a bad thing?" *This woman is something else.*

"Am I speaking in a different language here? Yes, that's what I said. That's not the point. The point is, it seems like you and a couple other riders will be the biggest pain-in-my-ass, but neither of them ride at SMX, only you apparently." Her hands go up to her hips before adding, "This is my track. If we are going to share it, we need to lay down some rules."

"Your track? What the hell are you talking about?" I'm still reeling from the fact that we will be racing together soon but she keeps spitting out facts left and right without giving me the chance to gather my thoughts.

"This is where I train. This is my safe space. I don't need to be on high alert here, too. Worrying that you might be messing with me to get me disqualified."

"Roe, it's just a race. Nobody is that evil," I urge.

"Actually, people are. But you, with your Saint complex, wouldn't know. I've worked too hard to make it where I am. I don't own the track so it's not like I can forbid you from coming, and Allen is too damn nice to take my side. So, here's how it's going to work."

I have reached my damn limit with this woman. Before she can give me more ultimatums, I pull her by her wrist, turn her body and lean her by the truck. My hand caging her in, and my body pinning her to the truck. I lower my face next to her ear and I can hear the gasp she tried to hide. We have chemistry, so I'm using it to my advantage. "Here's the deal, Aurora. Nobody sets rules for me. Nobody tells me what to do. And if you're going to act like a spoiled little brat, at least let me use that to my advantage. Because believe me when I say, I can teach you a lesson on how to be a good girl." My finger traces her chin. "I get that this is your space and I am new or whatever, but I am not out here to make you my enemy. If what you're saying is true, then we are rivals. Big fucking deal. The track is big enough for the two of us, just like the trail is. Stay in your lane and I'll stay in mine."

My hand slides lower, tapping her neck and collarbone slightly and her skin breaks into goosebumps right under my fingertips. "I would never do anything to get a competitor out of my way. When I win—make sure you hear this loud and clear because I *will* win— it will be fair and square. You're just going to have to deal with it." I run my finger back up her neck and pull back, leaving some space between us so I can see her face. She looks at me partially in shock. Like nobody has ever cut her off and put her in her place before. I touch her bottom lip lightly and the little minx barely parts her lips. And before I can do anything about it, she bites me. Hard.

"Fuck," I curse.

"Stay out of my way, Saint and we'll be fine." She tries to push away from me but when I won't budge, she hits me with her dainty fists right on the chest.

I grab them both and say, "Whatever you say, Princesa." I move out of her way and let her walk past me. She keeps walking without turning around, leaving me in the dust twice in one day. This time I keep my eyes locked on her and see the name right above the number on her back, in big sparkly letters, A. Sorelle. *Fuck me.*

SEVEN

HERO COMPLEX

The Chain (The Voice Performance), Girl Named Tom

ROE

GOING HOME yesterday after the track proved to be the wrong move. I should've gone to Saddlers or at the very least for a run. My brain wouldn't settle, and the quietness of the house just made it easier for me to replay the events of this afternoon over and over again. I felt like an entitled bitch all afternoon and then couldn't sleep at night, completely restless. Not being able to shut my brain off must be the most annoying part of having ADHD. I can hyperfocus on something and be fine with it most days, but sometimes I just wish I could shut it all off and drift.

If you had told me that I was going to go from happy that the racing season is almost back, to utterly annoyed at the fact that I have to share the track with him, I would have called you a liar. If you had added that riding all afternoon was not going to be enough to get my body past the point of exhaustion, I would have said you've got jokes. And, if on top of that, you would have told me that I would be up and running at 5:00 am on a Monday, I would have straight up laughed in your face. Yet, here we are.

If I can't sleep, there's no point in staying in bed doing nothing when I can be training, doodling, or reading. With the first race right around the corner, going for a run sounded like a good idea. Baker Oaks has so many hidden trails and small areas to run that you rarely see other people, especially this early in the morning. Some people may find that creepy or unsafe, but this little town is nothing like that. I also enjoy the quiet of being outside before the sun rises. My parents always used to wake up before the sun; 'miracles happen every day Roe, you just need to find them,' they would say. This is the closest I feel to them. Early in the morning, before the light filters through the clouds, it's like I can almost hear them.

The air is humid, making my hair stick to the back of my neck. The ground is soft with tiny drops of dew and the pounding of We Three is playing in my earbuds. I'm taking it all in, breathing through my discomfort, and singing softly to the lyrics of the song. That's when I notice that there is someone else running. From here I can tell that it's a man—broad shoulders and tall. He's not wearing a shirt, and his eyes are looking down, so he doesn't see me right away. I stop running as he gets closer to me, and I notice it's Santiago. *Again.*

He keeps jogging and when he looks up, he sees me and his eyes lock on mine. I have mastered the 'back off' stare, but his gaze has nothing on mine. His eyes are dark— piercing mine with an intense stare that freezes me in place.

I remove my Air Pods as he stops in front of me. His skin's glistening and the tattoos I noticed before keep my eyes on his damn body. My mind spirals in contemplation of how I can add more to the beautiful canvas that is his golden skin.

"Roe?" he asks tentatively. Not like the confident man that I met this weekend. His voice is tender like he's sleepy or sad. His eyes roam my body and his eyebrows slash into a frown.

"You forgot about me so quickly, Saint?" I sass, waiting for his face to relax but it doesn't.

"Why are you out here by yourself? It's dark," he deadpans.

"Why are *you* out here by yourself?" I ask. If he's going to say something all alpha man and shit, I'm going to lose it.

"Roe, it's not safe. Anything could happen. Women get taken from trails like this every day. I'm sure you can protect yourself, but the truth is that any man can take you out with some force."

"You're right about one thing. I do know how to protect myself." I get my knife out of my necklace and show it to him. This little knife clips on it, making it look like a shark's tooth. It's one of my favorite tools because it's not flashy and I learned how to use it quickly. Then, I square him up and signal him to come near me with my empty hand.

He raises his eyebrow at me and says, "Roe."

"Come on, let me show you I *do* know how to defend myself, Saint." I smile big at him, testing the waters and his patience. He clearly has none because in three seconds flat, he has me in a lockdown that I can't get out of, and I don't even know where my knife went.

"See, here's the thing. No matter how prepared you think you're, you're what? Five-foot-two? Three? On top of that, you're thin. You can have all the reflexes you think you have, which are not much considering I took your knife and you didn't even notice it, but the truth is that I have more pounds and muscle on you. And you knew I was coming."

He lets go and I snatch my arm from him. He stands in front of me with both arms crossed over his naked chest-and *fuck*! I should not be paying attention to the way his forearms flex or the way his sweat glistens over his pecs. His hair also has tiny beads of sweat dripping onto his shoulders. His eyes darken and he raises his eyebrows. *Shit.* He just caught me ogling him, *again.*

"Make no mistake, princesa. I can teach you how to better protect yourself, but your height and size are a disadvantage. Running by yourself, in the forest, in the middle of the night is another disadvantage."

"If I cut your dick off, who would be at a disadvantage?" I threaten almost breathless.

"You need to get to it first. Now, let's stop this fucking nonsense and tell me what you're doing here at this time of day."

"Running, jackass. Same as you. I've lived in this town for years. No bad shit happens here, and when it does, it's not usually on this trail. People are terrified of bobcats, so they stay out of here. Actually, you're the first person I've seen on this trail in probably months, especially at this time of day."

"What if I was here to hurt you? Who would have heard you scream?"

"Oh, Saint. So cute of you to think I'm a screamer. I'm going. Leave me the fuck alone," I snap and I'm about to run back the way I came from, when he steps closer and blocks me.

He steps around me and grabs both my wrists. He turns me and pulls me close to his chest. No, not close--

completely against him. His mouth drops next to my ear, his hot breath caresses my neck as he whispers, "I'm sure I can make you scream, princesa. Not by scaring you, but by showing you so many things. If you say you're not a screamer, then nobody has given you anything to scream about." He licks his lips; the sound alone has me salivating and nearly turned on. *And I. Hate. It.*

"I really don't give a shit what you do with your life, but my mamá raised me to look out for people. And there's no way I'm letting a woman put herself in danger by doing something as careless as running by herself in the middle of a fucking national forest. I knew in two seconds you had nothing more than this dainty knife on you. Anyone could have known that." He takes the knife and clips it back into the string hanging from my neck. *Clearly, I did not learn how to use this well enough.*

"Do me a favor and let me run back with you," he insists, letting go of me and leaving me breathless for the second time this morning.

"No, Saint. You may not. First of all, it's not the middle of the night; it's morning and the sun will rise in no time. Second, I'm not a fucking damsel in distress. I told you this yesterday, and I'm telling you again now." I am annoyed and I sure as hell let him see it. Both my hands are on my hips and my stare is deadly. "I'm going to run back home, and you're not coming with me. If you do, I will make sure people know you're a fucking stalker. You won't like it. Trust me. Go away with your hero complex and go be someone else's saint."

I turn around, clicking my Air Pods on, and I let the music drown my thoughts all the way home.

EIGHT
GRAVITY

GRAVITY, *Alex & Sierra*

SANTIAGO

THIS IS the third day in a row I've been left in shambles by this woman. *I can protect myself—* my ass. I know women need to work hard to prove their worth and to show that they are equal to men, but fuck, the whole movement has put more women in harm's way. I'm all for empowerment so long as you're prepared for it.

I come from a family with many strong, independent women. Hell, I'm more terrified of my mom and little sisters than all the grown men I know. I still would say something about them running in this trail by themselves, especially in the dark. My mom taught me that women are strong and can do anything they set their minds to, but she also raised me to be a gentleman and a protector.

Additionally, she taught me consent and that *no* is a

complete sentence. Which is why I'm following Roe back out of this trail without her noticing me. Am I honoring her request? No, but she doesn't need to know that.

Her music was loud when she left; I could hear the bass from where I was standing, so I knew she was not listening to her surroundings. Another fucking risk. So, I waited until she ran around a big yellow pine and then followed her, keeping my distance.

I'm sure I came across as an asshole. But for some reason, I feel the primal need to protect her. To shield her from whatever is eating at her from the inside. I see she has a wall up, and it makes her seem abrasive and headstrong. But it's there for a reason. I know it all too well. But her reason? That, I don't know. I barely know her and the way my body reacts to her is new to me. It doesn't help that she has the prettiest set of crystal-clear blue eyes I have ever seen. Her dark lashes frame her doe eyes and the contrast of her lashes, light eyes, and blonde hair make the blue pop even more. She truly looks like a damn princess. A sassy-mouthed sailor of a princess.

She's independent and doesn't need a man. It's clear as day. The way she carries herself is hot as fuck, too. She doesn't care about what others think. She's comfortable in her skin, but it doesn't take away from the fact that my skin prickles at the thought of anyone putting themselves in harm's way willingly. Especially her.

I continue following her, keeping distance between us until we are out through the trailhead, and I see a small street in the distance. This is not the way I came in, but Marco did say there were different entrances to the trails. The sun is rising behind some of the houses and with it, the heat. Roe continues jogging, but quickly slows down and starts to walk. Her head is bobbing side to side, and she does some sort of drumming on her hips before stopping in front of a house and walking in, without even using a key. *She doesn't lock the door.* Fuck.

You know what? Not my problem. She's home, she's safe. I don't even know this girl and what was it that she said I had? A hero complex? There's not much I can do if someone doesn't want to save themselves.

I turn around and run back to my house.

THE WEEK WENT BY FAST. Starting at Baker Auto went better than I expected. I've already fallen into a routine: wake up, run, shower, eat breakfast, work, relax, sleep, and repeat. My boxes are unpacked, and my things are put away. I've barely seen Marco all week because he's working nights, so it's quiet by the time I'm ready to settle down.

Although I have not seen Roe since Monday, I can't get her out of my mind. I kept using the same trail from when I followed her home to see if I would run into her again, but no luck. I have considered going to Saddlers to see if she's working but that would make me look like a lunatic.

My work schedule is flexible. This week, I took the day shift so that I have the weekend off. The weather is supposed to be great, so I want to ride the trails or the track. It's Friday morning and I decided to venture out and see more of this small town. Everyone I've met is friendly and there are a couple of businesses I've been meaning to check out, starting with Ronnie's Kitchen.

I walk across 6th Street, the hot air whipping against my face and making me wish I was already inside. Walking through the heavy doors, I can see a few people inside turn their heads my way after the bell rings. The sweat instantly starts to dry as I walk to the warmly lit space to find a seat in one of the booths in the back.

"Hi there. Welcome to Ronnie's. What can I get you?" the friendly waitress with the million-dollar smile asks. She has this girl-next-door vibe going on and it works great for her. I would probably let her sell me anything she wanted because I wouldn't want to say no to her. I'm sure it's great for business.

"Hi, can I start with coffee and milk?" I ask politely.

"Cream or milk?" she asks.

"No, I mean milk. I know, I know, cream is the usual but please, just bring me a side of milk and hot coffee."

She doesn't say anything else for a second, but she looks at me up and down and writes the order on her worn-out spiral notebook, before saying, "Sure thing, coming right up."

She walks away and my eyes follow her. Something about her commands the space like the best friend we all wish we had. Not exactly the same as what has me watching a certain little blonde, but definitely something. I can't stop thinking about Roe's feisty little mouth and her sassy attitude. She commands a different kind of attention that has me itching to find out more. It's like my brain wants to find ways to connect with her and it won't let me forget that she exists.

Growing up so closely with my sisters meant I was always surrounded by girls. At some point, I'm sure I was the annoying big brother, but generally speaking, we were all friends. When I started racing, it seemed natural to gravitate toward the female riders. But seeing as most were moms and wives, it made sense why their husbands wouldn't want a tatted stranger trying to start a conversation. It also didn't help that I quickly moved up the racing ranks, causing me to constantly have to start over socially. Marco and I met through one of my sister's friends. It's been so long at this point, he's basically a brother to me, and our families get along as well. His parents are uptight and don't understand his racing life, mostly because of health issues. They are allowing him this season to prove he's serious about the sport before forcing their hand and making him go to work for them. Other than my family and Marco, I don't have many people close to me; in reality, that's another reason why moving to Baker Oaks was easy.

The waitress comes back with my coffee and the glass of milk. After placing them on the table in front of me, she stands back and waits. Stirring the coffee and adding in the sugar, I pour the milk slowly until it turns a shade of brown that mimics sand on a sunny day. I put the spoon down and bring the mug to my lips. She's still standing there, arms crossed over her chest and eyebrow cocked high.

"Mm, want some?" I ask with a smirk after sipping the warm liquid and closing my eyes in satisfaction at the perfect taste.

"I only know one other person who takes regular coffee with milk. I wanted to see if you do it the same way. Weird. But sorry, staring is rude," she says while fumbling with her hands. "Apparently, I lost all my manners today. My name is Cara and I'm here if you need anything. Can I grab you something else or do you need a few more minutes to look at the menu?"

"Thank you, Cara. How about your breakfast sampler?"

"You got it. Coming right up." She walks away again, heading toward the back where the kitchen is. Before I can focus on anything else, the door opens. In strolls a beautiful, blue-eyed, tattoo-covered, dirt bike rider, smiling from ear-to-ear as she heads straight toward the back. *Roe.*

She walks past a few empty tables, holding a checkered flag backpack with little smiley faces, and slides into the back corner booth. She pulls out an iPad and a small bag, setting them both on the table before smiling at Cara and placing her order without even glancing at the menu. Her eyes roam the restaurant, and just like gravity, they land straight on mine. There's a slight surprise at first, quickly replaced by what seems like annoyance, but the surprise was there. I smile and nod at her, but she looks down, grabs her iPad and buries herself into the corner of the booth. I don't know what annoys me more, the fact that she chose to ignore me or the fact that I don't want her to.

I don't play games. I don't fall into the whole cat-and-mouse chase. If I'm sure I want something I go after it. And when it comes to women, I have never been one to follow someone who doesn't seem interested. Women have fallen at my feet since I was young; something about the accent and skin tone, or so I've been told. But none of it has ever been a turn-on. Neither has chasing someone who doesn't want to be caught. But there is just something about her that has my feet itching to get up and go to her.

My eyes keep going up to look at Roe, but she doesn't look my way once. Annoying beyond measure. She's just sitting there, peacefully sipping on what seems to be hot cocoa, and either writing or drawing on her iPad. Her lower lip is trapped between her teeth and her long blonde hair falls around her face. I continue to stare at her like a damn stalker —twice in one week—when I see her fidgeting and frowning. She starts looking for something inside her backpack, and she has almost half her head inside it before sitting back and pulling out something to tie her hair up into a high ponytail. She then pulls her legs to her chest and closes her eyes, sipping from the straw in her cup.

"Take a picture, it lasts longer," I hear someone say, making me snap out of the trance. *Coño*[1]. I look up to see Cara holding two plates of food, just standing there with a knowing smile. *I'm so busted.*

"What?" I ask, trying to recover.

She doesn't let me escape the conversation, lifting her eyebrows before saying, "Don't waste your time. That one is a bobcat; there's no taming her."

"Who? Roe?" I ask.

"Oh, you've met her already. Poor boy, are you under her spell already? Don't get me wrong, I love Roe, as does half of this town. But like my bestie says, *love doesn't take away knowledge.* And the truth is, she burns everything in her path, especially boys." She places the plates on my table after offering way more information than I would have liked but shedding a little light into the mystery of Roe.

"Good thing I'm not a boy," I add nonchalantly.

"Oh sweet boy, it doesn't matter. She will eat you alive. Trust me, don't fall for the pretty face and the small size. She's vicious. She's a great friend and I would go to bat for her, but I would hate to be the new guy to get caught in that trap. Or, how about I just tell you the same thing I tell everyone who asks about her? Because trust me, you're not the first and you won't be the last intrigued by her— approach at your own risk." She winks and adds, "Enjoy your meal," before walking away.

---

1. Coño: Damn or shit

NINE

EVERYTHING I TOUCH

Into You, Ariana Grande

ROE

CARA, *babe, why are you talking to Saint?*

The fact that my brain is going haywire over Cara talking to this guy is fucking with my life more than I would like to admit. The fact that I keep calling him Saint in my head is also obnoxious. And if I'm being completely honest, I am also irritated at the fact that—for some unknown reason—I can't seem to shake the feeling that he is watching me. And worse still, I want to keep looking at him.

Cara leaves his table, and he starts eating and not paying any attention to me. Not that I *want* his attention. It feels like he is taking over Baker Oaks. Everywhere I turn he is there, waiting. I have been able to avoid him so far, but he can't take Ronnie's too. The track was enough.

I'm holding my iPad trying to finish drawing some

55

tattoos for today, but I can't focus. My brain is scrambling at the fact that *he* is sitting right there, and I can't stop looking. Almost like that called to him, he looks up and his eyes meet mine. I refuse to look down first, so I don't. We are in the middle of a staring contest now, and if he thinks this will be an indication of the type of racer I will be, game on. I do not give up, I do not back down.

We're in the middle of our staring contest, Saint's eyebrows raised and his eyes not leaving mine when I feel a presence next to me. And I swear, I don't want to look but this is getting to the point of being ridiculous. He won't stop looking at me, and I won't stop either, regardless of who's standing next to me.

"He's a pretty sight, I'll give him that," Cara says with amusement in her voice.

I hate that I am about to lose whatever game we are playing but I have to look up at her. As soon as I move my eyes to hers, I hate it even more, because the smile on her face makes me feel like I was caught red handed, big time.

"I want to murder him with this butter knife, I don't care how pretty he is," I mutter back.

She chuckles and places my plates on the table, adding, "And what did that handsome boy do to you for you to want to kill him? Do I need to add him to my shit list?" She sits across from me, placing her hands under her chin and giving me her full attention.

Cara is one of the kindest people I've met here. She comes back to town during the summers in order to help her parents, who own Ronnie's. I don't think she works much when I'm here though. I'm a huge distraction and we just have girl talk. I wish she could live here full-time because I think we would be closer friends. But I get to enjoy her for the time she's here.

She's not only hilarious, but she's also kind and truly cares about others. Hell, about everyone. She's good company and I don't say that lightly. I usually hate being around people but there's a handful of tolerable ones and she's one of them. She might be kind, but she also has zero filter and will tell you how shit is without concern of what others might think.

"Nah, not shitlist. He's just racing against me in the same class this season, and on top of that, he goes to the same track," I say, taking a bite of my biscuit.

"To SMX? How? He's new here."

"The fuck would I know? All I know is that he was at Saddlers on Saturday, at the track Sunday, and on my running path Monday. And now, he's here on Friday."

"Is he stalking you, Roe?" she asks, concern apparent in her eyes.

"No, babe. You should've seen his face when he saw me riding his bike at the track. He was white as a ghost." I giggle, taking a bite of the bacon.

She smiles, wiggling her eyebrows at me. "I bet he wanted you to ride something else, too."

"Shush. I think he sees me more like a fragile little thing —like everyone else—and he pulled the whole broody, big-guy card at me at the trail too. The *you shouldn't be running alone* bullshit," I say, mimicking his voice.

"I mean, he can keep *me* company anytime."

"You can have him. He's all yours," I scoff, waving my hand.

"Nah, hard pass. I'm not in the business of getting in the way of my friends getting laid. And that, right there, is a man that wants to get in your pants. Plus, I'm kinda seeing someone," she adds.

"Who? Please don't tell me you're seeing Cole again,

Cara. That guy is just stringing you along." The look on her face tells me that I hit the nail on the head.

"I'm just here for the summer. We're just having fun. I'd tell you to do the same, but we both know that you're the queen of fun around here," she says sarcastically, getting up and telling me she needs to get back to work.

Why do I have to fuck up everything I touch? I add a note on my iPad to text her later to apologize for not minding my own business when it comes to her and her man. She says they're just having fun, but from what I know, they've been on-and-off since they were in high school. Nothing serious ever comes from it and Cara is older than I am. I can't imagine being intimate with someone for most of your life and still not knowing where they stand, at almost thirty. Reason #250 why I don't do relationships. I don't have time for that when in the end; it's all ashes either way.

I can see the sun shining through the window and the liveliness of the people walking around. It's a perfect summer day. Then why have I been in the crappiest mood since I woke up? I thought the run and comfort food would fix it, but clearly not. I'm running out of options here so maybe banging the brazen hottie looking my way will fix it.

I finish my food, leave cash on the table, and walk over to him as Cara is removing the plates from his table. She eyes me up and down, smiles at me, and winks. Passing me she whispers, "Go get him," hopefully low enough that only I heard her.

I sit across from him, throwing my bag into the corner, and placing my hot cocoa on the table. "Saint," I say, looking at him.

"Couldn't stay away, princesa?" he asks with a grin, and fuck my life, he has a dimple. On top of the gorgeous skin, the tattoos, and the damn dark eyes that pierce straight into my soul, he has a dimple.

"Funny, I was going to say the same about you. It seems like you have taken over my town."

"Your track, your trail, your town. Do you own the bar too?" he tsks, crossing his arms on top of the table and lowering his head so he's eye-to-eye with me.

"Actually, I do." I sip on my hot cocoa without dropping my eyes. "You see, Baker Oaks is a small town and even though I don't own it, or my trail as you so fondly said, I belong here, and you don't. You stick out like a sore thumb." *Shit.* That was harsh, even for me. The whole 'Let me run with you' shit has been messing with my brain more than I care to admit, whether he's doing it on purpose or not. My guard, usually up regardless, is currently sky high, making bitchy Roe come out to play. "I don't understand what brought you here and why you think that you can just take whatever you please."

"What did I take, huh?" *Shit, shit, shit.* He's hurt, I can see it. "All I did was try to exist in your sweet presence. Yeah, maybe I overstepped a little, but I didn't do anything to get this treatment. I'm a gentleman, so I won't fucking snap at you, but how about you just stay in your lane, and I'll stay in mine?" He gets up and walks past me, lowering his voice saying, "Stay away from me, Roe. I mean it."

He leaves Ronnie's and I feel like an enormous bitch. I did not need to say that. Ugh. I drop my head on the table and hear footsteps coming near me. I know it's Cara with her *I told you so face* but I don't want to deal with her right now, so I ignore her.

"You know, just because you don't see me doesn't mean I don't see you. What did you do?"

I mumble that I fucked up under my breath with my face still on my arms.

"Bitch, I can't understand what you're saying. Get your head up and spit it out," she says, tapping my head like an annoying little sister

"I fucked it up, that's what I did," I reply. I look at her and she has the same know-it-all face I was expecting so I don't know why I'm so annoyed by it. "I came over here to try to sass him into leaving with me but instead I was a fucking bitch and he left. Respect to him though for not letting me treat him like shit."

"Stop being hard on yourself, Roe. If you want him, go after him."

"I don't chase men, Cara, and you know it. I also don't think I want him. Do I want to get laid? Yes. Do I think he's easy to look at? Also yes." *Easy to look at?* Just plain delicious but I'm not going to say that. My body has been humming for a week just with the thought of his rough hands on my body last weekend. "But I won't chase him. If I see him again, I might apologize though because I haven't been the mean girl that I just was to him in years and I'm not going to start being her again now."

I stand up, grab my bag, and wave goodbye to Cara. "See you soon, babe."

"See you soon," she replies. She sounds disappointed that I'm not going after him right now, but I can't let myself go down that rabbit hole. What was said was said but I can try to be nicer next time, I guess.

TEN

PAST THE BREAKING POINT

Misery Business*, *Paramore

ROE

HELL. Pure and simple. There is no denying that these past weeks have been hell. I wish I could pinpoint what went wrong but to be honest, everything did. Not one thing went my way, and the impostor syndrome is *loud*. Especially after the way I raced this weekend. I came in fourth place. Fourth! It doesn't really matter that I'm faster than most—if not all— of these men, but my fucking body crashed on me with 24 minutes left. I had two choices: push through at the same pace and finish another full lap, but risk passing out and not finishing at all; or slow down and save my energy. I chose option two because I'd rather finish in fourth place than not finish at all. I need to work on my stamina if I'm ever going to be able to finish a full scramble without feeling like I might pass out.

Hare scrambles are a series of off-road races in which all the riders begin on a single line. It is not about who finishes first, but who does the highest number of laps in the allotted time. They track your speed and movement with a transponder attached to your helmet. If your transponder has not moved for a few minutes, they will send someone to check on you. The races are hard and lengthy. The terrain is not clean like in Supercross or track races, making it more of a workout with harder challenges than other races. It pushes your body to the max; on top of the effort it takes to ride a dirt bike, you also have to balance and maneuver a bike that weighs as much as most riders. Hell, mine weighs more than me. There are ten rounds in a hare scramble series, all at different trails, and the races take place over a few months. The winner has the highest cumulative points from each race at the end of the series. And I already started off on the wrong foot by finishing fourth.

And what's worse than not placing in the top three? Guess who got the second-best score? Santiago Cruz, of course. Agh, I'm over this. I can complain forever, or I can do something about it so I can beat him next time. That includes upping my strength and conditioning and making sure that my body can tolerate the force that is AA class racing. I've been reading about different ways to help me build my stamina, but more than that, helping my body keep its fuel. My training starts today.

After stretching for a few minutes, I bend down to double-tie my shoelaces, blowing the pieces of hair that got out of my ponytail away from my face. I shuffle my playlist, and as soon as I hit play, Misery Business blasts in my ears and I begin to run. The air is crisp, unusual for summers in Baker even in the early morning, but in no time I'm drenched in sweat. The knife necklace thumps on my chest with every step I take as I explore the rough terrain in this trail.

The moonlight casts a low glow over the Southern Yellow pines, making this the most serene time and place to be, away from everything and everyone. The way I always am, alone, just me and my thoughts. I keep my pace steady, sprinting through the shadows and trying to calm my breath. The music pounds in my ears but I'm sure the sounds of my ragged breath and footsteps against the branches on the ground echo through the forest. I feel the air leaving me, my lungs straining, making it harder to breathe, but this is when I should push harder. *You have to push harder after you think you can't do it anymore.* It's something my dad used to say. I just need to push a little harder. I just need to keep going. My vision blurs and when I think I'm going to step again, my legs give out beneath me. As I hit the cold hard ground, I succumb to darkness.

ELEVEN
SKELETONS AND SELTZERS

I'm a Mess, Ed Sheeran

SANTIAGO

WORK, train, race, repeat. That has been my life for the past few weeks, and it's paid off. Top two in overall scores in the AA class should be an accomplishment itself, *and it is,* but it doesn't stop here. This is just the beginning, and I need to keep the momentum going. I have nine more rounds to go before the final score is totaled and I won't back down now.

It is so quiet today. The sun seems to be taking longer than usual to rise through the morning haze, giving the morning an eerie glow. *Increíble.* The little wonders that make each day worthwhile. This might be my glimmer of the day or Ana's way of saying hello to her big brother. Maybe both. My breath matches the whispers of the wind through the lush oaks. The deeper I run into the trail, the darker it feels—making me feel a strange sense of peace in the solitude. In the quietness. Some early birds are chirping, and a distant owl's sound lets me know that the sun will fully rise. Everything will keep going, like it always does, no matter what happened the day before.

I keep my pace, staying aware of my surroundings and still hoping to see Roe. There's a part of me semi-wishing she took my advice and isn't running by herself, but the thought of her with someone else scorches my lungs. I have the urge to be the one running with her, to protect. Why I want this is beyond me—she hasn't once treated me right since we met. Yet I have the feeling she's closed off for a reason. I'd pay good money to know what happened to her.

As I round the bend, I catch a glimpse of something on the ground ahead. Carefully drawing closer, I make sure that whatever it is isn't hurt and is still alive. Doing a double take, I see it's a person. I rush to get to them faster when they sit up. I can tell it's a woman when she holds her head in her hands. *Roe.* It's not even a question, I know it's her. Is she hurt? Who did this to her?

My pulse quickens as I kneel beside her, saying her name softly so I don't scare her. But she seems to be out of it because she doesn't react. The warm dawn hues reveal her soft features; she looks up at the sun and then puts her head back down. She looks a little flushed but there's no blood and nothing else seems to be wrong, so I whisper her name again, this time more certain. "Roe?"

"Ugh, even in my fucking dreams you haunt me," she groans without lifting her head from her hands.

I'm still kneeling beside her, ignoring all the sounds around us and her sassy attitude, trying to assess what the fuck happened here. "Roe, princesa, talk to me. What happened?"

Her head raises and her gaze locks with mine, a look of

confusion flashing over her face before saying, "Ah, I guess you're really here." She reaches her hand and touches me to confirm that she's not imagining me, I guess. "I think I fainted," she adds, trying to get up but losing her strength and sits back down.

"Easy, easy there. Has this happened before?" *This girl.* Running by herself at the crack of dawn and fucking fainting in the middle of the damn forest. Who knows what could've happened?

"Yes, often, but never while running. Never so suddenly."

She's not fighting or sassing me so she must not feel great. I don't have any water on me, but I can help her make it to the end of the trail and grab water from my truck. "Here, let me help you up."

Roe willingly gives me her hand, without hesitation. I help her stand and wrap my arm around her before she loses her footing again. Her long blonde hair dances across my arm as I help her balance, and I want to more than just this. I want to pick her up and roam my hands all over her body. Kiss her until her lips hurt, explore other places until she is putty in my hands.

Snap out of it, Santiago. Today is not the day, and now is not the time. Right now, I need to figure out what happened to her. "Can you walk?" I softly ask.

"Of course I can walk," she snaps, slapping at my hand which is trying to keep her straight. "I already told you; I don't need you or your hero complex saving me."

Her step falters. She's okay, my ass. I do the one thing I know will keep her from trying to walk away from me. I bend down and scoop her up, arms behind her knees, and place her over my shoulder.

Roe yelps in surprise. "Put. Me. Down. You. Big. Dinosaur!"

I laugh, a deep belly laugh. A sound I haven't made in a while. *This fucking girl.* "Big dinosaur, huh?"

"Well, you're acting all neanderthal right now. Put. Me. Down," she quips, kicking her little feet and pounding her fists on my back. Her perfectly round ass is right by my face and it's taking everything in me not to smack it and tell her to be quiet. My dick on the other hand didn't get the memo that we are just helping her out. *Another thing to take care of when I get back.*

Eventually she stops fighting me and stays quiet. So quiet that I think she passed out again. "Roe?"

"What?" she bites back.

There she is.

"How about you tell me what you ate for breakfast today and how far you ran?" I'm trying to keep her talking to me while also trying to figure out why this happened.

"I made toast, eggs, and sausage. A protein shake, a banana, coconut oil, and water. Happy?" I can practically feel her eye roll and I definitely notice the annoyance in her voice even though the fight is gone.

"Are you secretly my mom's child? She's the only person I know who eats coconut oil by itself."

"Stop deflecting, Saint. Are you going to put me down? I'm lightheaded from being upside down."

Shit, I didn't think about that. I lower her slowly until her feet touch the ground, lifting her away from my body so she doesn't think I'm trying to feel her up. She stands in front of me, flustered and sweaty in her black sports bra and tiny shorts that shouldn't be called clothing. Her eyes are so blue, and right now in the early morning light, they look almost crystal-clear. Pure. She has a strand of hair falling loose from her ponytail, so I reach out to brush it away from her face and she flinches. Just a split-second, but I saw it. I take that as a signal that my touch is unwanted and lower my hand, letting her adjust her hair herself. I may have come on too strong. Trying to match her feistiness seems to have backfired on me so I try a different approach.

"Roe, would you please let me walk you home? I don't feel comfortable letting you go back by yourself."

She doesn't answer for a second, then two, and finally she speaks. "Agh, sure," she says, putting her hands on her hips and stomping away. I stand there just staring at her. After a few steps, she turns around and asks, "Well, are you coming?"

I jog slightly to catch up with her and fall into comfortable silence, walking by her.

The walk to her house is serene. We don't see many people, and the only sounds are the wind and the few animals we encounter along the way. Nature surrounds us and the soft orange and pink hues of the morning envelop us in what feels like a hug. We don't talk—we don't even look at each other. We just coexist, feeling minuscule in this broad space.

We make it to her house without concern. Stopping at the door, Roe turns and sighs. "You didn't have to walk me home…but thanks."

"Ooohhh, so you *do* know how to be nice!" I snark. "Good to know that it's just me you hate, and not the rest of the world."

"Are you gonna make me regret being nice, Saint? Or are you gonna appreciate it while it lasts?"

Contestona y respondona[1], *así como me gusta.*[2] "Touché, touché."

We stand in awkward silence, not knowing what to say. At least, I don't know what to say – I doubt Roe says anything she doesn't want to. Opening the door without a key, she steps inside and signals for me to walk in. I hesitate, not knowing what to expect, and questioning this is a genuine invitation. I'm about to turn around and leave when she sighs, "Are you gonna come in or what?"

I raise my eyebrows at her, waiting to see if she's serious.

She groans. "Saint, I don't bite. You're probably thirsty and the least I can do is give you some water. Stop being stubborn and come in."

"But you did bite," I snark, but it may be too soon for jokes because she gives me a side-eye.

She lets me go past her into her house, but before I can get too far, she says, "No shoes in the house."

I turn around and see her removing her shoes and waiting for me to do the same. I don't want her to suddenly change her mind, so I take my shoes off quickly too even if I don't want to. *So damn bossy.* She walks by me, passing the wall full of threaded knick-knacks and Halloween decorations. *Halloween? It's the middle of the summer.*

She looks up and down at me, quietly assessing my movements and when she notices my eyes scanning the Halloween decorations she smirks and says, "Every season is spooky season, come on in and sit down. Stop being nosy."

I laugh again, partially at being caught but mostly at the fact that there are skeletons, cauldrons, and spider webs in

---

1. *Contestona y respondona:* Someone who talks back or sassy.
2. *así como me gusta:* Just how I like it

the middle of a wall with what looks like a beige sun catcher. It must be eighty degrees in here too, which is bizarre.

"Is your AC broken?" I ask before I can stop myself.

"Do you have the habit of being rude in other people's homes?" she deadpans.

I should've known better, truly. "I'm sorry, it's just warm in here."

"I like it warm, anything lower and I have to wear a sweater."

"Oh, okay. It's not too bad, it just took me by surprise." A lot of things about this girl seem to have that effect.

Her kitchen and living room are in the same space. An open concept that gives her house the feel of being huge. Bright and airy, my mother would say. All her furniture is beige, except for a terracotta rug, and there are plants every-where. Vines, tall plants, a little pink one, and even one that looks black. On the table next to a little plant with pink dots sits a plate full of exactly what she said she had for breakfast this morning; even the little container with what I assume is coconut oil.

She follows my eyes to the plate and sighs exasperatedly. She sits on the ground in what feels like one split-second, bringing her knees up and placing her head against them. She shakes her head, and her knuckles turn white from squeezing her thighs so hard. She's leaving marks on her legs, and I am at a loss. Do I sit next to her and hug her? Do I rub her back? Do I leave? I've never second-guessed myself before on how to soothe a woman, but she seems to be apprehensive to my touch and I don't want to make it worse.

She continues sitting in that position, but now she's tapping her fingers in a pattern: thumb, middle finger, index finger two times, ring finger, pinky, repeat. *She's self-soothing.* I give her a few minutes and some space, stepping into her kitchen where I find a cup full of water. I grab it and turn around to find her standing. Her eyes are glossy, like she's holding back tears, and I hope it's not because I'm here. I can leave. I don't want to, but I would.

I walk toward her to give her the water, which she takes, grabs a straw from the countertop, and drinks more than half of it.

"I can leave if it makes you feel more comfortable," I offer, hoping she says I don't have to.

"Nah, it's fine. It looks like I forgot to eat this morning. I clearly made the breakfast but then didn't eat it, which is not uncommon. Then I felt extremely overwhelmed just thinking about how stupid that was and how much worse it could've been if you hadn't found me. I spiraled but I'm fine now, scouts honor. Also, thank you," she says, raising her hand by her face and flashing me a smile. Damn that smile.

"Okay, well then, maybe eat now?"

"No shit, Sherlock. I'll heat it up. Are you hungry? We can split this."

"I'm good, I've overextended my stay. I'm gonna head home," I add calmly.

She nods, grabs her plate, and puts it in the microwave. She walks to the fridge and when she opens it. There's no food in there; just an obscene amount of seltzers, milk and some sports drinks. I raise my eyebrows at her, which feels like all I've done lately.

"What?! I own a bar! I get a lot of free samples. Want one? Or is it too early for you to drink, Saint?" she sasses. I shake my head, so she gets two bottles of water out. She tosses one to me and walks to get her food out of the microwave. She grabs two forks from the drawer and extends one to me in an offering but I gently decline.

"I'm good, really. Are you going to be okay?"

"Yeap," she says, popping the 'p.' "You can go now. You saved me. Thanks, I guess."

I start heading out of her house, but an uneasy feeling stays with me and I can't shake it. As I reach for the handle I turn around and ask, "Hey, Roe?"

"Yeah?" she shouts from the kitchen.

"Can I run with you tomorrow morning?" I am putting myself on the line here. She clearly hates my guts, but I can't leave her feeling like she's putting herself in danger again.

"I don't need saving," she sasses, narrowing her eyes at me.

"So you've said," I add and pause, giving my voice a second to settle and not show my frustration before continuing, "Maybe I want company?"

"From me? You literally could run with anyone else and they'll probably do it gladly."

"I don't know many people here, and the time I like to run doesn't match my friends' schedule, but clearly it matches yours." I let out an exasperated sigh. "Just forget I asked."

I open the door but before I step out, she shouts, "Be here at 4:40am tomorrow."

Check.

TWELVE
MONSTERS IN THE DARK

Let It Go, James Bay

ROE

IT'S 4:30 am and I am scrambling to find things to make for breakfast. There's not much here since I forgot to get groceries and everything is closed—so I guess it will be a PB&J. I went to sleep wearing running shorts with a sports bra, so I only have to put on my running shoes to be ready to go. I never know how my body will react in the morning, so I give myself plenty of time to get ready. Telling Saint to be here early was not that smart after all. *Saint.* I can't make myself call him anything else anymore. Great, now the stupid nickname will stick because my brain refuses to acknowledge anything else.

I truly want to hate him. Every single piece of him. First, for being so damn hot. Second, for the way my body reacts to him. Third, for scoring higher than I did. And fourth, for treating me so kindly even after I have been nothing but a bitch to him. I have been hot and cold toward him like it's my job, and he still finds it in him to be the kindest man. *Agh, I hate it.* Men are supposed to be assholes, but this damn town apparently attracts the good ones.

There's a slight knock on my door that startles me because it's so damn early. Without a second thought I shout, "It's open! Come in!"

Saint walks in, closing the door with his hip. He has a pained expression on his face. I carefully take stock of the rest of him. He's wearing dri-fit shorts and a t-shirt that hugs his chest and arms perfectly. He's also holding two cups and has a bag looped around one of his wrists.

"Good morning, princesa." He places the cups on the table and hands me the bag. *The fuck?!*

"What's this?" I deadpan while pointing at it.

"Breakfast. I brought you a smoothie, too," he answers, pointing to one of the cups. He grabs the other and takes a sip, pulling out one of the chairs and dropping into it. He is so comfortable in his skin; he exudes confidence, even when he's just sitting there.

"Why did you bring me breakfast and a smoothie?" I ask, standing still in the same position.

"*Thank you* would be the proper response when someone brings you breakfast, princesa. Didn't your mom teach you manners?" he asks, unintentionally hitting a nerve.

"Well, she's dead. Whatever manners she taught me went to the grave with her," I snap, placing the bag beside the smoothie on the table. "I don't need breakfast, but thanks."

"Roe, I'm so sorry, I didn't know." His face looks sincere, like he truly does feel sorry for my loss. Not pity behind his eyes—just true understanding. "I know sorry doesn't change the facts but I am," he adds. He's either a big empath or he knows grief too.

"Who did you lose?" I ask, because apparently I have zero self-control when it comes to this man.

He stays quiet for a moment before saying, "My little sister." Time freezes still. What am I supposed to say to that? Do I sit down and unpack all my trauma? Do I open the door for him to share more? No, neither of those are options. I closed the door to my soul years ago and it's sealed shut. So, changing the topic it is.

"Why did you bring me breakfast, Saint?" I ask again, holding his stare.

"You forgot to eat yesterday and fainted while running by yourself in the middle of a dark national forest. You barely had food in your fridge yesterday. This way, I can at least make sure you're fed before we leave," he answers casually, sipping on his smoothie.

I open the bag and see a flaky pastry. It looks absolutely delicious and freshly made.

"Did you make this?" I ask, half shocked and half flattered. Did this man cook something for me?

"Sure did," he replies with a smug grin.

I smell it and quickly take a bite, closing my eyes and practically moaning into the crunchy dough. "Oh my God, this is heaven. Thank you I add, tasting the explosion of flavors in my mouth and he laughs. "What is this?" I say in between bites of what seems like cheese. It's still warm, like he just made it before he came here.

"It's an empanada. My mom's recipe." He winks and holy shit, he just got even hotter. A man that looks like that – tall with perfectly sun-kissed skin, square jaw, mysterious tattoos, and with eyes like the blazing sun, who is respectful and a gentleman and cooks like this – how the hell is he not taken? He looks at me with contentment and smiles softly.

I finish eating the empanada, making obnoxious sounds, and throw the bag away. I take a few sips of the smoothie he made—also fucking fantastic—and put the rest in the fridge for when we get back. If I eat anything else I won't be able to move. I take my spoonful of coconut oil and watch him practically gag. I motion for him to get up and we walk to the door. We are heading out when he grabs my arm, stopping me from going further, and I turn to look at him.

"Are you going to lock up?" he asks with concern in his eyes.

"Nah, I never do. It'll be fine," I say.

"Roe," he replies, softening his eyes on me.

"Saint," I sass, snatching my arm from him.

"You can't leave your house unlocked. Was it unlocked all night? Is that why it was open when I got here?" he asks incredulously.

"You seriously need to drop the habit of telling people what to do. I'm a big girl, Saint. I don't have to be afraid of monsters in the dark."

He closes the space between us. He smells like the ocean, salty and fresh. His essence engulfs me and my whole body is practically humming. And the man is not even touching me.

"It seems like you are used to living in this bubble where nothing bad happens, but there are a lot of monsters out there, princesa, and I don't mean just the ones in fairytales. Lock your doors."

"You can't tell me what to do, pretty boy. Are you here to act like my dad or are we going for a run?" I start jogging down the street, trying to hide how his presence affects me. Damn him.

He falls in step next to me, looking forward while completely ignoring me. We stay quiet for the whole trail run and all the way back. Six miles of pure silence and complete peace somehow. This is the first time in a long time that my brain is fully present and not juggling a million things. The only things on my mind are *why do I find his presence comforting* and *how do I get over this?*

THIRTEEN

CUTE FEISTY LITTLE MONKEY

Ojitos Lindos, _Bad Bunny_ & _Bomba Estereo_

SANTIAGO

FIVE DAYS. I've been running every morning with this infuriating, gorgeous woman for five days. Five days that I've had to remind my dick to behave every time I open her door and see that she's wearing the perfect clothes to accentuate her body. Five days of me telling her to lock her damn door, and five days of her not listening. She doesn't even answer me anymore when I bring it up. Yet here I am on day six at 4:20 am on the way to her house.

This has become a routine of sorts. I show up with food because she forgets to eat, and at least this way I can guarantee she does. She has loved every single thing I've brought. And for someone as small as her, she sure eats plenty. Today I have pastelitos, a similar but smaller version of empanadas, and croquetas.

My mom grew up cooking with her mom. She dreamed of having a daughter so she could teach her the same skills, but she had a son instead. For years I got all the cooking lessons, and then I got sisters. My dad didn't love the idea of me being in the kitchen. *La cocina es para mujeres, Adela. Cooking is for women, Adela.* He would always complain to her, but she didn't care. She said that she was raising her son to be the man of someone's dreams. By the time my first sister was born, I knew how to cook, clean, do laundry, and even sew. I learned at an early age that I like working with my hands, and she put that to good use. When Ana's health started deteriorating, it came in handy because my parents could focus on her, and I could take care of the house and the other girls.

Living away from my family is definitely hard, but I needed a little space from that town and from them. Especially if I am ever going to find myself and my own happiness. I'm still close with my mom and we talk every day. She's the first person I want to talk to when something good or bad happens.

I come from a big family. My mom is one of five and my dad is one of four. All my aunts and uncles have so many kids that we lost count of the cousins. There are five of us in my family. Now, I guess just four. My parents had me and then couldn't have kids for a while. I was eight when Anabella was born, and she was my very own living doll. I learned how to take care of babies quickly because it wasn't long before my mom was pregnant again with Daniella. And in less than a year after, mom was delivering Isabella. The year I turned sixteen, my mom had my youngest sister, Gabriella. I went from being an only child to the oldest of five. I helped take care of whoever needed it the most at the moment because there was always a diaper to change, food to put on the table, or someone who needed to go to dance class. I helped as much as I could and I loved taking care of all of them, but that also meant that I never got to experience my own childhood. Bringing Roe things to eat has reminded me that people still need others to take care of them, even if they're grown and grouchy.

I knock on the door because no matter how many times she tells me she won't lock it, I still can't fathom walking into someone's house without letting them know I'm there first. To my surprise, Roe opens the door before I finish knocking, taking the bag of food from my hand, and making a sweet little squeak. She rushes back in, plops herself on the ground, and digs into the bag. Seeing her reaction to whatever I made for her has become my favorite thing this week. The girl lives for food, and I find myself cooking for her just so I can see her enjoy it. My glimmer of the day for sure.

Roe's eyes grow wide when she sees the little snacks. She takes a bite of a croqueta and moans. Those little sounds are my undoing; I must be a masochist because I want to hear all of them knowing I can't do anything about it. Instead of running, I want to find out what else I could do so she would make those sounds for me. Her eyes are closed, and she's enjoying every single bite without looking my way. I just stand there, staring at her and taking it all in. It's ridiculous how much I enjoy being in her presence regardless of how little we talk or how murderous she looks every time I bring up the race.

Round two is this weekend, and she hasn't talked to me about it. Actually, she hasn't talked to me about much at all. I know she isn't quiet; she has no issue telling me how it is when she's mad or annoyed. But I don't think Roe opens up about her personal life easily, especially after the way she reacted when I mentioned her mom. I'm fine with the silence; I have no problem spending time with her until she's ready to give me a chance. To let me in. Why, I'm not sure...but there's something about her that I can't put my finger on. It goes beyond the way she looks—don't get me wrong, she's perfect. I keep thinking about our kiss from the night we met. I can't stop the way my body reacts to even the smallest of touches from her, or the zing of electricity that races through me whenever her eyes meet mine. It's as if my soul is drawn to hers; magnetic, she's absolutely magnetic.

"Ready?" I say, snapping out of whatever spell she has me under.

"Can we change the routine today?" she asks.

"What's on your mind?"

"Let's go lift weights today," she suggests, taking the trash from breakfast and throwing it in the bin next to me. Her lavender scent lingers in the air after she walks away.

"I didn't know you lifted," I say, utterly confused.

"Ha, I don't! But I was watching all of these routines that riders have before races, and they all lift so I want to try that."

"Roe, you don't start a new workout routine days before a race. If anything, we should take things slower today and rest tomorrow."

"Easy for you to say; you placed in the top three. I didn't. I need to do everything I can to match you guys," she adds, putting her hands on her hips and looking at me with those piercing blue eyes.

"Lifting weights is not going to help you this close to the race. It will hinder you."

"Or are you hindering me? Are you purposefully holding me back so I don't beat you this weekend?" she fires back. "You know what? Forget it, I'll go by myself. Have a good day." She walks toward the door, opens it, and leaves the house with me inside.

I run out behind her. I've been doing the same thing every day this week, chasing her like a damn shot of whiskey.

"Roe!" I shout. She doesn't slow down so I just speed up to catch her.

"For someone who hates being called princesa, you sure act like one at every single inconvenience."

"You made it clear you're not helping. Go away, Saint," she snaps, slowing down her pace.

"You don't mean that," I snap back. "I'm trying to help you. To protect you. To protect your body."

She stops dead in her tracks before saying, "You don't need to protect me. I'm a big girl. It's been a pleasure, now if you will, leave me alone." She glares at me and I see the turmoil behind her eyes but before I can say anything else, she turns and runs.

What am I supposed to do? Take her no for an answer and not chase her? Let her try something she's never done by herself days before the race? Why am I even worrying about this girl? *Because I can't pull myself away, that's why.* I'll follow her wherever she goes—even if it means running after her when she doesn't want me to.

I fall into an even pace next to her and we walk into the gym together. The gym is empty and the lights are dimmed. The darkness outside gives the entrance an eerie look. In the time that it takes me to fill the paperwork and pay the drop-in fee, she walks to the back and immediately starts lifting five-pound weights with each hand while bobbing her head. There's soft music playing in the background, but it doesn't seem to be what she's listening to. *Earbuds for sure.*

Walking to the back of the gym, I decide to do some lat

pull-downs. Adjusting the weights before sitting, I realize this gives me a perfect view of Roe as she continues her work with the free weights. Before I can even start, she racks her weights and moves to the pull-up bar. I inwardly snort as I realize she's too short to reach the bar, and I wonder what her plan will be. Can she even do a pull-up? Roe stands beneath the bar, hands on her hips and she scans the room, surely trying to find something to use as leverage to grab the bar. With her hair braided back, I get a clear view of her pouty lips when she can't figure it out. I think she's going to let it go, but I'm surprised when she walks toward me with determined steps and an ever-present eye roll.

She taps her earbud when she's standing in front of me. "Since you're here already, why don't you come help me?" I can tell that she struggles to ask for help so the fact that she did, even after she told me not to come with her, makes me want to smile. Big. I couldn't stop the grin from spreading if I tried.

"Cocky asshole," she snaps, walking back toward the bar.

Roe stands beneath the bar, glaring at me and huffing like a toddler. I can't erase the smile from my lips because I just realized this girl is the challenge I *want* to take. The electricity pulses between us; I know she feels it too. I want to explore the charge; see where this could lead, or if it's simply crazy sexual tension that will disappear after one night. Either way, I want to find out. She wants to act tough and uninterested? *Game on, princesa.*

I put my hands on her small waist and lift her up so she can reach the bar. She grabs it with both hands and I let go, leaving her dangling. She looks up and makes an effort to pull herself up, doing two reps before she lets go and hits the floor. I can see how frustrated she is right now, and I get it.

Pull-ups are hard and it takes time to learn to do them right. She's strong, though. She managed to pull herself up twice even with poor form.

"Again," she says in an assertive tone.

"Sí, princesa[1]," I reply, grabbing her waist again and lifting her above my shoulders toward the bar.

She grabs the bar with determination, but after she attempts to do one and fails, she lets go and drops down with a huff. Her skin is flushed, both from pushing herself and from frustration. Now it's my turn to say, "Again," as I help her back up. This time I jump up, grabbing the bar outside of her hands and facing her.

"What are you doing?" she asks, her breath minty and warm right against my lips. We are so close, and her eyes are practically sparkling. She has tiny flecks of gold and silver in the light blue of her eyes that I can see perfectly now.

"Helping you. Wrap your legs around me," I command and she rolls her eyes. *Brat.* "I have all day, Roe. I can hang for as long as I want, but I don't know how long you can last. Wrap. Your. Legs. Around. Me. NOW!" I demand again and this time she does. It's scary how perfectly her body fits against mine. I get goosebumps up my back as her legs tighten around me and her face hovers close to mine.

"Now, engage your core and use your back muscles too. Let's do it together."

She starts pulling herself up and I help by giving her a small boost while I do a pull-up myself. I try to not assist her too much so she can still feel the burn, like she is doing most of the work, while providing the support she needs so she can learn this movement. Our bodies are covered in sweat now; her skin is glowing with tiny drops, leaving a trail down

---

1. Sí, princesa: Yes, princess

her neck and getting lost in her sports bra. I bring my eyes back up to her face and realize that her eyes are closed, her long full lashes brushing against her cheeks.

"Two more," I urge, continuing to pull us up, both of our chins clearing the bar. She lets out an exasperated sound on our last one before dropping her hands from the bar and draping her whole body around me, like a little monkey. A cute, feisty little monkey.

I drop from the bar, bringing my hands under her ass to support her as she whispers a soft *thank you* against my ears. She pushes slightly against me, looking at me with an emotion I can't pinpoint.

"You're so strong, princesa, but it takes time to learn some of these things. I can teach you if you're interested but not right before a big race, okay?" A glint of pride shows in her face, and she nods before dropping her head back to the crook of my neck. She fits perfectly right here in my arms, our bodies molded to one another and completely in sync. She has shown so much aversion to me touching her that this catches me off guard.

Outside, the sky is radiant as swirls of purple, blue, and pink dance with the clouds. The soft morning sun illuminates the road and the gym, chasing away the eeriness from before. "Are you ready to go back?" I ask her and she just nods. I hook my hands together under her, and walk us back to her house in silence, with her fast asleep in my arms.

FOURTEEN

THE CHERRY ON TOP

***Lose Control*, Teddy Swims**

ROE

IT'S RACE DAY, and I'm at the front of a sea of bikes. Everyone is uniformly lined up all the way back to the starting grid, but I'm struggling to keep my eyes on my own bike. I'm entirely too aware of Saint's presence. The fucker stood his bike right next to mine and now we are stuck together on the starting line.

He's hot, and I hate it. It's unfair how he looks wearing his gear, or anything else for that matter. His navy jersey with red and white accents is completely fitted against his chest protector and arms, and it's doing more for me than any Calvin Klein model could. And I don't even want to talk about the pants or the boots. Maybe for most people, good boots are not a turn-on, but there's something about high-quality protective gear that tugs at not just my heartstrings.

The cherry on top? He looks even more intriguing with his helmet on. I can see tips of his tattoos trailing his neck in the space between his jersey and helmet.

He knows how hot he is, too. It's the way he carries himself, the way he stands, and the way I know he's looking at me through his goggles And he knows I'm staring right back at him. I'm not backing down though. Let him know I'm watching; it'll make it even sweeter when I outplace him in this race.

The thirty-second announcement happens, and the bike holders stand tall at the back, grabbing onto the rear fenders to allow space for the riders to run and start the bike when it's time. Allen, the grumpy pain-in-my-ass owner of the track, is holding mine. When you are an orphaned only child and not the most extroverted person out there, you take what you can get. His eyes are on mine, and when I look back at him, he nods at the same moment as the ten-second announcement. My hands are sweating in my gloves and I can hear my heart thumping in my ears. *Your fears don't control you. You control them. You've got this.* I say this to myself over and over again, narrowing my eyes and repeating the steps I need to take. *Run to the bike on the left side, swing my leg over, hold the handlebars, kick start the bike, hit the throttle, and leave everyone behind.*

I choose to believe that life is meant to be lived as if today was your last day. It allows me to be fearless, ready to take on any new challenge. But this doesn't erase the fact that my sensory processing difficulties often give me a run for my money. That's why I've adopted this cognitive training skill. Fear is all in your head – I can work with that. Overstimulation? Not so much; that's where the repetition of new language comes into play. There's no room for over-thinking if I tell my body *exactly* what to do.

The horn goes off with a low and heavy honk. I start running toward my bike, but Santiago Cruz runs on the same side as me, making me fumble a little and second-guess what I'm doing. What the fuck? This asshole runs on the right side instead of the left, so we have to share the space. He takes the lead because it caught me off guard and I hear a muffled sound from Allen telling me, "Let's go, let's go, let's go, Aurora."

I shake off the uneasy feeling of sharing space and focus on making it to the bike, running through every step for a perfect start. He uses his lead and leaves me behind but in no time, I'm tailing his bike with only one end in mind. Finish before him even if it's the last thing I do.

I rev my engine, tilt my elbows up, and lower my head. I hold my stance and fly around the bikes in front of me. I'm not in front *yet*, but I *will* be taking the lead. I know it. Adrenaline rushes through my veins as I zoom around the narrow trail through the forest. The trees echo with the collective roar of engines as the other riders try to give it their all. Everyone is jostling to hold their position without crashing into a tree or running off the trail.

This trail is known for being challenging. The terrain is rough. There are no steep inclines in Florida, but a mix of moisture and mud makes it sloppy. Wet palmetto leaves and slippery roots can make or break your performance. Can make or break you. It's good to have some moisture to give traction to the dirt as opposed to the dry patches that are like sugar. *Sugar Sand* is very loose, fine, terrain. It's these areas that are the biggest concerns for slippage and falls. In some trails, you can have one or the other, but here we have both.

I navigate through the trails using all the skills that I've learned through the years. And my fearlessness. A magic combination that my parents left me with. The focus my mom had as an instructor and teacher and the grit my dad had as an athlete. I go over branches and obstacles with precision, lowering my foot from the peg when taking turns in case I slip out, and shifting my weight to leverage against the bike and the conditions.

As the race progresses, I manage to do my best time. And with the oversized gas tank I only had one pit stop, only slowing me down for about thirty seconds. With ten minutes left in the race, I can see two bikes ahead of me, both from my class which probably means that I'm in third. *Fuck that.* One of the bikes is a KTM. It's bright orange and white but I don't remember who races that one. I strategically watch as they lean over a broken branch, and I know I have the possibility of passing if I cut through the narrow edge. And I do just that. Holding my breath and looking right where I want to go, I snatch the handlebars quickly, and twist the throttle. I pass him easily. *One down, one to go.*

I can see the start of the trail, which means we are about to complete another full lap. I glance at my watch quickly and see we have two minutes left. *I want that extra lap and I want that first place.* My legs are shaking and my hands are numb but I'm so close, I'm not giving up now. Maneuvering around the rocks and leaves has me right behind the blue, white, and red bike with 755 on it. *Of-fucking-course.* I follow him as closely as I can but he's fast and skilled.

Up ahead, there's a tree with low branches that I ran into before so I could avoid the sand on the other side of the trail. I have to choose between slipping in the sand or getting hit by the branches. I'm not taking the risk of falling, so I keep following Saint. I plan to go around him on the last turn before the end of the lap. But as he nears the tree, he lifts his hand and grabs the lowest branch. In a split-second, he rips it off and tosses it back. The branch hits the top of my bike and makes me lose my balance for a couple of seconds.

No matter how quickly I react, or how skilled I am, those seconds are valuable, and time is up. I finish second, with Saint finishing first.

FIFTEEN

RIGHT IN FRONT OF ME

*Kissin' **When We're Mad, We Three***

SANTIAGO

"ROE!" I shout but it's useless. She's already slammed her helmet on the ground and pulled the zipper open on her tent. She has a tailgate tent that hooks to the back of her Jeep, providing privacy from the rest of the place but allowing her access to her Jeep quickly. Next to it, she has an open canopy where her bike, and now her helmet, both stand. She tries to zip the tent back up but I'm able to stop her and walk in after her, closing it behind me and leaving us in the comfortable close quarters of it. She's tearing paper into pieces while grunting. Her whole face is red and when her eyes meet mine, I see only anger.

"I had to rip that branch off. It already had scraped me once and I'm sure it could've hurt others. I didn't know you were right behind me."

"You knew I was coming for you. I was right there. I was finishing a round with the best time I've ever had, and you threw a stick at me!" She walks up to me and her fists go straight into my chest. "You. Did. This. On. Purpose," she adds, hitting me with every word. I can see the fury in her eyes and if she weren't a quarter of my size, I would be worried that she might hurt me.

"Why would I throw a branch at you after I spent all week training with you?"

"Because you know that I'm strong and fast and that I can take you down. You know I could've beaten you on that round. Your precious ego couldn't handle a girl winning, could it?"

She hits me again and I grab both of her hands to stop her. She tries to pull them from me, not looking away and not losing her stance.

"Roe, if I knew that branch was going to hit you or your bike, I would've never thrown it. It was a split-second decision. I didn't ruin your score on purpose, and I won fair and square. Now, if I let go of your hands, will you stop hitting me?" She makes a sound similar to a growl and bites her lip. I know that she won't stop hitting me or biting that lip that drives me crazy. I *also* know that I want to be the one biting those lips. Bringing my other hand up, I use one finger to try and pull her lip from her teeth gently. She lets me; once it's under my touch I say, "You have perfect lips. You shouldn't be the one biting them."

My body sparks to life as I become aware of how close we are. I'm pressing her fist into my chest. She won't tear her eyes away from mine and when my fingers touch her lips, I can feel everything changing. *At least on my part.* I don't know how to read this situation, but I would love to fuck the anger out of her right here and now. Our breathing is heavy.

Our bodies are in sync. I rub her lip with my thumb as my fingers curl under her chin. Her skin is sticky with sweat and her eyes are filled with lust. I know she feels this too and I'm finally going to do something about it.

"Your lips really are perfect," I tell her again. "Fucking. Perfect." I drop my mouth to hers, letting go of her fists and sliding my hand to the back of her neck. Her body flush to mine, she wraps her arms around my neck and pulls on my hair, deepening the kiss. Her tongue dances with mine as I swallow her moans; my other hand drifts to her lower back to keep her as close as she'll let me. Roe pulls at my chest protector, pushing me to the tailgate before yanking it off and tugging on my jersey. I pull it over my head one handed, refusing to stop touching her completely. She tugs harder on my hair and instantly my hands drop to her ass to pick her up. I sit back, letting her legs straddle my hips, wrapping around me in a hold that I never want to get out of.

Her eyes dance over my skin and she licks her lips. I know she's seeing the work I put into my body, but this goes beyond lust. I raise my eyebrows at her. and she throws her head back and laughs. She doesn't say anything else; she just pulls her jersey off. She has a black sports bra on that I don't hesitate to take off and her perfect tits bounce. I clasp one in my hand and kiss her. I touch, twist, and rub her nipple, seeing how she responds, never letting her mouth leave mine.

Her back is arching against my chest and her hands come up to touch my body, pulling her braid forward on accident. She tries to push to the side, but her beautiful blonde hair is calling my name. I wrap her braid around my fist and tug gently, but when her hands immediately roam my body and a soft sigh escapes her lips, I know she likes it. Tugging at her braid again, I pinch her nipple which causes this goddess to grind against my cock. I'm about to come in my pants like a teenager trying to get off for the first time. I have zero control when it comes to this woman, especially now that I gave into temptation.

"Do you have a condom?" she asks in between breathy sobs. Her body is so responsive that I would bet all my money she's already soaking wet. I shake my head, because who has condoms in their riding suit? She rolls her eyes and stands up, taking off her boots and pants, and climbs into her Jeep from the back seat. This girl is buck naked, showing me and anyone who might be around her perfect ass, and I can't stop staring.

Roe comes back with two condoms in her hand and a mischievous grin on her face. Stopping right in front of me, she coos, "Drop your pants, pretty boy. I need to see what size fits you better."

"You want to see my cock, princesa?" I tell her, getting up and opening my hands next to my hips. "Then you can come get it yourself."

I stand still, looking at her, and she bites her lip and smiles big before saying, "Make me."

My dick twitches in my pants, and my eyes dart to hers. "On your knees, princesa," I growl. I didn't expect her to obey me so quickly; fuck, I didn't expect her to obey at *all*. She's been calling the shots with everyone around her, but seeing her on her knees with her eyes trained on mine, I know this is when she wants to lose control.

I walk to her but stop halfway, adding, "Be a good girl and crawl to me." She obeys again, ass in the air and her braids swinging in front of her. She stops in front of me and runs her hands up my legs to the clip on my pants. She opens the buckle and pulls my pants down, biting her lip as my cock springs free. She looks up at me with lust in her eyes before licking her lips and taking me in her mouth. "Fuck, Roe," I growl.

I grab her braids in my hand and pull, making her raise her eyes to mine so I can watch my dick go in and out of her mouth. "So fucking hot with my dick in your mouth."

She moans in response. *Praise kink, got it.*

I tighten my grip on her braids and push my dick deeper into her mouth. Tears fall from her eyes as she grunts, licking and twisting around the tip. She grabs my hand and places it behind her head, using it to push her harder against my dick, then drops her hand and grabs my ass. I hold her head steady as she pulls my ass and entire body to her mouth deeper and deeper, making her gag as she takes all of me. I know I'll come in her mouth if she doesn't stop, but I have other plans.

Letting go of her braids, I put my hand around her neck, squeezing lightly, testing the field. I'm making sure this is not going too far and it's what she actually wants. *Fuck, I know it's what I want, but this isn't about me.* Before I can think twice about it, one of her hands disappears between her legs. I can feel little moans against my skin as she grinds against her hand before she stops suddenly. Her eyes roll back, and I see a shudder work down her spine, her ass moving in a slow circle before she drops her hand and lets out the raspiest and dirtiest sound I've ever heard as my cock drops from her lips.

I groan and bit my lip. "You're so fucking hot, princesa. Did you just come right in front of me?"

She looks up and shifts her body so she's laying on her back on the ground. Spreading her legs, she pushes two fingers inside of her sex, takes them out and uses those wet fingers to motion me to come to her. I drop over her, placing my hands next to her face, and take her fingers in my mouth. She tastes fruity and salty at the same time. So fitting for this girl full of contradictions. I swirl my tongue against her fingers and suck—*hard*—making her squirm under me. I grab one of the condoms she dropped earlier and put it on, fitting my dick at her entrance.

"Don't go sweet on me now. You might be my Saint, but I want to be your hell. Fuck me like you hate me, pretty boy. I won't break," she purrs.

Fuck, fuck, fuck. There's no holding back now. Jesus, this girl.

In one move, I thrust inside of her. She squirms and tries to scream but I place my hand over her mouth, muffling her cries. That apparently turns her on even more, because her hands scrape against my back like a feral cat. I drive in, with her hips matching my tempo. I grab one of her feet and place it against my ass. She pushes against me, leveraging herself with her heel. She mumbles something behind my hand as her gaze bores into mine. *It feels so good; too good. Mierda.* She fits her other heel to my ass and drops her head back. I curve up, hitting a spot that makes her whole body tighten around me.

Her hands stretch out on the ground and I grab them over her head. Holding both wrists in one hand, I pin her down. "Así, Roe, is that how you like it?" I ask and when her eyes darken and she licks her lips, I drive in her harder; again and again, until she's twitching and squirming under me. She's close, I can feel it, but she won't let go. Her moans are making me harder than I've ever been in my life, and I need her to come before I do. I place my thumb on her clit, pressing against it while commanding, "Let go, princesa, let me feel your pretty little pussy milk my cock."

That's all it takes for her to explode. Screaming, "God,

yes," her eyes flutter close as her pussy tightens around my cock.

"No, Roe, not God. Saint," growling, still driving into her.

Her glossy eyes open and she looks at me. Her lower lip catches between her teeth and she smiles, whispering, "Yes, Saint, just like that." She bites her lip harder, making little drops of blood bead on her skin. I dip my head and lick it clean, making her shiver. Her wicked smile grows wider and she fights the hold I have on her hands. Useless; there's no way I'm letting her go. Her head comes off the ground to reach my mouth, biting my lip but not as hard as she bit hers. *Coño, this woman will be my undoing.* I kiss her, hard, deep, senseless. She kisses me back and when I'm about to explode, she starts pulsing around me again, making me come undone with her.

MIDNIGHT RAIN*, *Taylor Swift

ROE

THE SUNLIGHT WARMING my face wakes me up from the deepest sleep I've had in years. I don't remember the last time I drifted off to sleep without noticing. Looking around, I suddenly remember where I am. I yawn widely, twisting my body only to realize that there's a warm, hard body under me. I flinch when I see that I was completely draped over and around him. This is when it all hits.

The race.

Santiago.

Last night.

What in the actual fuck was I thinking. and what am I thinking now?

I don't cuddle. I don't hug. I definitely don't snuggle with one-night stands and that's all this can ever be. Is it considered a one-night stand if I already know the guy? Well, either way, this can't happen again. No matter how hot every minute of last night was, I don't have time for this.

His eyes are open and he's eyeing me suspiciously. One hand is under his head and his golden skin practically glows in the sun coming through the small tent window. *Shit, we're at the track, in the middle of the campground.* I don't know what I was thinking. Actually, you know what? I do. I looked at him without a care in the world as I was fuming. Combine that with the need to climb him like a tree every time I see him, I figured one quick fuck could get us out of our misery. It may have backfired because that was the hottest sex of my life.

I look back at him and see his beautiful body and how perfect it looks in this light. The web of ink sprawled over his tan skin speaks to me, each tattoo telling me a story. I trace a few of them with my fingertips and he writhes under my touch. He grabs my hand and raises an eyebrow, murmuring, "Be careful princesa, or I'm going to start thinking you actually like me."

That breaks me from my trance, and I immediately get up, grabbing a gray shirt from a pile in the corner. The shirt is huge; it was my dad's, so it hits me right above the knees, nearly swallowing me whole. "I don't like you, you jerk. I was admiring your tattoos," I snap, crossing my arms over my chest and giving him the death stare.

"I've been meaning to ask you about yours, too," Saint quips. When I raise my eyebrow, he grins. "I need new ink and don't know where to go in Baker." He stands up, nonchalantly showing me every inch of his perfectly sculpted body. With a confident stride he grabs his pants from yesterday and puts them on without a care in the world. "Yours are great—can you recommend an artist?"

Oh fuck me. "There's a couple of places in Baker."

Since when have I ever been shy to tell people that I'm the best tattoo artist they will ever find, or that they should check out my work? It took me years to feel confident enough in my skill to recommend myself when people asked. And I'm damn proud of my accomplishments and my skills.

"Actually," I say, shaking myself out of whatever stupor I was in, "I own a tattoo shop in Baker. Some of these—" I lift my arm and show him "—were done by me."

He raises his eyebrows and stays silent, drinking in every inch of my tatted exposed skin. He doesn't take his eyes away from the swirls and creatures designed on my arm. The elephant and the snake. The tens of butterflies. The dotted lines on my wrist or the little mushroom on my forearm.

I feel a defensive fire leap up my spine. "What? Surprised a girl can do this or that I tattooed myself?"

"Neither, princesa," he replies, stepping forward and bringing his thumb to my cheek. "It's just that you're amazing. Every detail I learn about you makes me realize it even more."

I snap my face away from his touch and take a step back. He flinches in response, and I can see hurt in his eyes. *Too soon for these big feelings.* "You keep getting surprised because you don't know me, Santiago."

"But I *want* to know you. I want to discover more wonderful things about you. If you'd let me." His body is tense, but he doesn't wait for a response before he picks up his jersey and puts it on. "And only my mom calls me Santiago, princesa, so unless you have a mommy kink, I'd rather you call me something else."

"I thought nobody called you Saint either," I add, mostly annoyed at the fact that he can read me so well.

"But you do, and I kinda like that." He picks up his boots, unzips the tent, and is ready to walk away when he stops and turns his body to face me.

"You know, life could be so much better if you'd just open up. There's a whole world of possibility out there and you deserve it. You deserve to live it. But you need to let yourself be vulnerable in order for that to happen."

He rubs his face with his hand and shakes his head. Scoffing, he lifts his eyes to mine, staring straight into my soul. I may have put clothes on but I feel bare in front of him. Like he can see every single flaw. Like he can feel the unseen scars. The ones I bury deep for nobody to find. The scars that are known only to my demons and haunted by ghosts of the past.

His voice is low and warm as he continues, "I enjoy your company. God only knows why because you keep giving me whiplash. But I'm here, willing to get to know you if you'd let me. When you're ready, come find me. In the meantime, what happened last night can't happen again."

"Last night was fun and you can't deny that," I say, surprising even myself because I'm usually a one-and-done kinda girl. So why am I saying it now? Actually, this is the first time I've woken up next to someone. "We don't need to talk to keep each other company, especially *that* kind of company." I lift the oversized shirt over my head and drop it to the floor as ammunition. He is stripping me bare to my soul so I might as well defend myself the only way I know how—with my body.

He looks me up and down, his eyes darkening and I think that I'm about to get everything I want. To stop him from thinking. To stop him from telling me more truths that I did not ask for and don't want. He closes his hands around his thumbs, his knuckles turning white before he shakes his head and says, "A taste of you is not enough. I need more. But until you're willing to let me try, whatever this is—" he moves his hand between us "—won't happen again. See you around, Roe."

Roe. My name on his lips feels like a curse. Like I don't deserve his warmth. I didn't know how much I liked him calling me princesa until he called me something else. My name has never sounded more like a punishment than at this moment. He turns around and leaves like nothing happened, like he didn't just throw a grenade at me and walk away with the pin.

SEVENTEEN
LESS BROKEN

I Like Me Better When I'm With You, Lauv

ROE

> Me: When are you leaving? I want to see
> you before you go. This whole waiting a full
> school year to see you is for the birds.

Cara🔍: I have three more shifts before I go.
I'm in today if you want to come.

Cara🔍: And you know, you can always call
me, Roe. We don't have to not talk for ten
months.

> Me: Where's the fun in that?

Cara🔍: Bitch, your life is so much better
when I'm in it and you know it. Come in
soon so we can talk before it gets busy.

Me: Word. I'll be in after my shower.

Cara🔍: YASSSSSS

CARA'S about to leave again to spend the school year in Chicago. That girl is such a gentle soul and even though she says that she comes here so she can *stay away from the children*, I think that's just something she adds to go with her personality. In reality, I don't think anyone else was born to be a teacher more than her.

She's chaotic but in a vastly different way than I am. She's more of a 'ray of sunshine' girl than a 'fucked up by life circumstances' girl like myself. She's fun, dependable, and a good friend. Everyone in town loves her. And the girl is stunning. Put that together with her personality and body, and she's a total smoke show. Why she has been strung along by that jackass of a man that she sometimes calls her boyfriend is beyond me.

In the summer, I usually spend my mornings at Ronnie's after my run; second breakfast if you will. But since Saint was feeding me breakfast all of last week, I didn't see her at all. I only get her for two months so I try to make the best of it. I may not have a lot of friends, but I prioritize the ones I do have, even if I do keep them at arms' length.

Speaking of Saint, he didn't show up today. Not that I miss him or anything, but it was definitely an inconvenience having to make myself something to eat. I went on my run with just peanut butter crackers and half a banana in my stomach which made me feel queasy, so I only ran three miles. My whole body still aches from this weekend and maybe it was dumb of me to push some more but I was so close to winning, I can't back down now.

After I shower, I make my way to Ronnie's and claim my

usual table. I order the same thing I've ordered for as long as I can remember: perfect French toast bites, biscuits, bacon, and eggs. Cara always hands me the menu like I'm going to change my mind, but I won't. Why fix something that's not broken? I never finish the entire meal, but it's the perfect mix of flavors to keep my happy and doing my food dance while I nibble on it throughout the day.

"Your food will be right up, babe. Want some coffee?" Cara asks, placing a cup of water on the table and tossing me two straws.

"When do I ever drink coffee, Cara?"

"I know, I know. One of these days, I'll convert you. It doesn't hurt to ask." She walks away after she blows me a kiss. I shake my head. Nobody should be that cheerful this early.

I pull out my iPad from my backpack, unhooking the pen and swinging my feet onto the bench. Art has always been an outlet for me. As a child, part of my therapy was to use creativity to show my feelings. Very early on I learned that words weren't going to get me anywhere, but maybe art would. Drawing, painting, thrifting to renovate, sewing… all of it makes me feel more whole. Less broken.

When my grandma died, and I was left all of her money, I knew I never wanted to work for someone else. I already loved bartending so it was easy to figure out that I wanted a bar. Just like that, Saddlers was born. This tiny ass town was giving me hell because I was barely twenty-one, but it really wasn't up to them. It was legal, I had the money and the means, so I opened a bar. But I needed something else to do. I got bored quickly and I felt like my fingers were itching to have an artistic outlet. I went to a tattoo convention, connected with people, and a year later I became a tattoo artist.

I still didn't want to work for someone else so I opened my own shop. The town again had issues with what I wanted to do. I really just wish they would leave me alone. But no, they had to say something about my tattoo shop, too. Thankfully, it's working and running smoothly. And now it's my favorite place.

As I work on some doodles on the iPad, my body tingles with awareness. When I look up, I find midnight eyes staring at me. My body hums just looking at him. I can't help remembering all the ways he made me feel this weekend. I wish I could quiet the noise in my head and tell my body to get a grip. I tried so many times yesterday to make myself forget about his hands and tongue all over my body and the way he fucked me to oblivion but it was futile. No man has ever made me feel like that. Usually, I have to help myself to finish if I even climax at all. Not with this man. And now, *apparently*, I'm broken.

Cara catches her ponytail and talks to him cheerfully, touching his hand lightly and making him smile wide at her. He gives her his full attention, and she just laughs before walking him toward the back in my direction. I lower my gaze because I almost got caught watching them with a deadly stare. I can hear Cara telling him to take his time with the menu. Her voice is way closer than I'd like and when I look up, I see her standing by the booth next to mine. I look at her but I can't find it in me to smile. She winks and turns around, walking toward the kitchen as she leaves me looking at a deliciously hot Santiago. He's sitting directly across from me, holding my stare.

He smiles at me before looking down at the menu and suddenly I feel like the shittiest person on the planet. Grabbing my stuff, I walk to his table and sit across from him. He doesn't look up from the menu and that stings more than anything. Because once you know what it's like to have his attention solely on you, like you're the last drop of water in a drought, you don't want anything less.

"I can feel you staring at me, Roe," he says with annoyance in his voice.

"I figured you could use some of your own medicine," I snap back at him.

"And what is that?" he asks, not looking up once.

"You know, just staring, no talking," I reply, taking a sip of my water. *Smooth, Roe, so much for apologizing.*

His brows furrow before closing the menu forcefully. Looking up, his eyes scan me, showing his irritation. He sighs in frustration; his indecision is palpable and I want to flee because being under his scrutiny is impacting me more than it should. I wish there were another way to describe how he's looking at me. His gaze looks hungry and it feels dangerous. I don't know if it's the deeper tan on his skin from the weekend at the track or his onyx eyes that are lighting every inch of my soul on fire. Is it the way the olive Henley accentuates his body? Or is it his hair–dark, shiny, and smooth? The perfect complement to the whole look? This man has a choke hold on me and I want to squirm just looking at him. *I hate it.*

"Roe, did you have something to say? If not, excuse me, I would like to order some breakfast."

"I'm not stopping you, pretty boy, go ahead and order," I snap back. After this weekend, my walls are twenty feet tall. I'm not going to let him see how his mere presence affects me, but for some damn reason, I also can't stay away.

He calls Cara over with a nod and she's there, smiling at us both knowingly. She takes his order and leaves after tracing her fingers over his shoulder. I know she's purposely flirting with him and I'm seething in my seat. I've never been possessive or jealous, especially since I don't go steady with anyone, but every time he smiles at her hair tosses or flirty smirks, it makes me see red.

"Saint," I say, short-fused and irritated.

"Aurora," he replies, short and sweet, sipping on coffee.

"You didn't show up this morning," I growl because I finally was able to pinpoint exactly what has been bothering me. Other than the thought of him with someone else, but that's something to unpack at a different time.

"Oh, is that what this is about? Some expectation you set without telling me?"

"Well, excuse me, you showed up every day last week without me saying anything. So yeah, I was taken aback when you didn't come this morning."

"I thought you said you were independent, princesa. That you didn't need anyone to save you. Isn't that what you said?" he jests, bringing his hands under his chin.

"Agh, you're so difficult," I snap, smacking my open palm on the table. "I'm trying to apologize here."

"Apologies usually begin with a 'sorry'," he says with a smug smirk and the damn dimple appears.

I hate him. "You make it impossible to do so."

"Then don't. I didn't ask for an apology nor did I expect one. Do you even know why you're apologizing?" He takes another sip of his coffee and puts both hands back under his chin. "If you're finding it so hard to do it, surely you don't even—"

"For being a bitch," I interrupt. "I'm sorry, okay? You've been nothing but nice to me and I've been snappy for no real reason. I can see that you didn't try to take me out of the race on purpose."

"I didn't take you out of the race, Roe. You finished

second and I already told you, I didn't know you were behind me. Accidents happen," he replies.

"I know, I know, okay? I'm sorry. I'll try to be more chill from now on and stop snapping at you for every single thing. Truce?" I ask, holding my hand in front of him.

He chuckles and shakes it reluctantly as Cara approaches with our food.

"Sorry it took so long, babe," she says as she places my plate in front of me. "The kitchen was backed up. Enjoy." She skips back to the front of the restaurant, leaving us alone with our breakfast and our thoughts.

Saint has a plate of hash browns, eggs, and—*what the hell? Salad?* "Who eats salad for breakfast?" *Shit, I guess I said that out loud.*

He chuckles, grabbing his fork and knives and cutting his tomatoes into smaller pieces as he answers, "I hate vegetables but if I force myself to eat them in the morning, my body craves them the rest of the day."

"Smart," I say.

"Nah, more like my mom yelled at me enough for not eating my greens that I had to learn a way around it."

"You would think that someone with your body is a health junky." My filter is apparently broken today.

"And you would think that someone as small as you wouldn't eat as much as you do, yet here we are," he says, pointing at the giant breakfast in front of me.

I smirk. "Fast metabolism."

"Good genes," he replies, touching his abs and winking at me. *Instantly wet, great.*

We eat mostly in silence and when it's time to pay, Saint takes both checks from Cara, placing his card on top without looking at her once.

"I can pay for my own food, Saint."

"I know, but that doesn't mean you should," he says.

"Why shouldn't I?" I ask, annoyed because if this jerk is going to talk about this being a date, I might kill him.

"Un caballero siempre paga[1]," he says.

"What does that mean?"

"You'll learn one day." He takes the check back from Cara, signs his name, and gets cash out of his wallet to leave a tip. He thanks Cara and then gets up, stepping back to let me go in front of him. I'm usually all for fucking the patriarchy and ignoring chivalry but these small gestures are making my heart warm in ways that it's never done before. I'm not sure if I love it or hate it.

I walk in front of him and his hand caresses my lower back. I practically jump at the touch. He immediately recoils but is quick to open the door for me, allowing me space. How does this man who barely knows me read my body so well? He knew that his touch was unwelcome and didn't even ask or push it. It's nothing against him but my brain can't handle too much input sometimes, and the way his hand felt over the fabric while applying pressure on my back was not what I wanted at that moment.

"Hey, do you have any plans today?" I ask, trying to offer an olive branch.

"Nah, I'm off today," he replies, standing by me on the sidewalk and putting his hands in his pockets. "What do you have in mind?"

I smile at him and start walking, hoping he follows, and by the beachy smell invading my senses I know he's right next to me.

---

1. Un caballero siempre paga: A gentleman always pays

EIGHTEEN

MAGIC HANDS

Tattoo, *Rauw Alejandro & Camilo*

SANTIAGO

I FOLLOW Roe as we walk down 6th Street. I'm about to tell her that we could've taken my truck when she stops right in front of a quaint shop. It looks like a plant nursery except there's a neon tattoo sign on the front. She unlocks and opens the door with a bounce in her step and ushers me in before closing the door behind her. At least she locks one door.

She tells Alexa to start the opening routine and the whole place lights up in a soft white hue. It's enough for you to see everything around you without being too bright. The plants everywhere combined with the instrumental music and the low light instantly makes me feel at home. This place looks nothing like traditional tattoo shops, which doesn't surprise me after seeing her house.

There are plants hanging and sitting on the floor, burlap on the walls as the background for a collage of art prints, crochet pieces, checkered rugs, and neutral-colored tables. There's an area in the back with a hydraulic chair and a stool next to it where Roe is sitting. Her bag is hanging on a beige hook by a big mirror in the shape of a rainbow. I walk in slowly, taking it all in, imagining her in every space. I notice that this place is somehow making me feel… alive.

She's biting her lower lip and God how I want to be those teeth right now. She's twisting side to side, straddling the stool with both hands in between her legs, pushing against the seat. Suddenly, I wish I were the damn stool. Her oversized overalls and t-shirt she's wearing don't really show her body. But her neckline is completely exposed with her hair pulled back in a high ponytail. This skin is calling my name and I need to stop staring because I don't even know what we're doing here. I clear my throat before asking, "Is this your place?" Pretty obvious it is but I lost my train of thought just imagining how many ways I can bend her over that chair.

"Welcome to Tats and Hips," she says, rolling in a circle with one arm open and her head thrown back.

"*Tats* is for tattoos but what about hips?" I ask. I see the sign on the wall. It's beige and orange with vines and doodles all around it in mural style. Across from it sits another sign, neon pink that says 'Get Ink or Get Out' and both are somehow very fitting to her. Whoever the artist is did a great job with both pieces and I point at them so she knows I saw them.

"Well, when I first opened this place, I wanted to name it Tattoos and Hippies because why not? But this town is full of old hags and they wouldn't let me have the "hippies;" something about hippies being troublemakers or some shit we know isn't true. I shortened it but it wouldn't fit the vibe being Tattoos and Hips so I abbreviated both."

"Genius," I reply, because there's not much more I could say. Every time she opens her mouth, I'm impressed by either her witty comebacks, the way she reacts to situations, or how creative she is. It doesn't surprise me one bit that she's a tattoo artist. You can see the creative wheels clicking in her head when she looks at something, and this place is also a good example. She has an eclectic style that mixes some of that boho-chic, whatever girls are always talking about, and the fun of a six-year-old race car fanatic's room.

"Gotta play the system," she says, looking around and crossing one foot under the other leg.

"Are you working today?" I ask.

"No, I don't usually open on Mondays. Saddlers is closed too so I take the time to chill and decompress at the beginning of the week."

"Which one are we doing?"

She raises an eyebrow. "Uh…what?"

"Chilling or decompressing?" I ask, amused by her confusion.

"Neither, take a seat," she instructs, pointing at the chair.

Alright, Roe, let's play.

I sit quietly and wait for her to explain. She reaches for the hook on the wall and grabs her iPad out of her backpack. I notice that the backpack is shaped like a goose so I chuckle. She notices me looking at her bag.

"That's Bruce," she says, completely serious and not a slightly bit amused.

"Bruce?"

"The silly goose, he goes with me wherever I go." Her

voice is peppy as she smiles and flips the cover of her iPad back, clicking and pushing at the screen with a pencil.

"Aurora, you do know you're *not* actually a Disney princess, right?"

"I'm aware, asshole. It's a long story, I'll tell you one day," she adds, looking up before continuing, "So what are we doing today, Saint?"

"I'm waiting for you to tell me," I ask. Now I'm the confused one.

"You said you wanted a new tattoo. I happen to be an amazing tattoo artist and I have time today, so, my question stands: what are we doing today?"

Holy shit. Okay. "Are you serious? How do I even know you're good?"

"Oh, pretty boy, you already know I am." She winks. "What do you want?"

"How much time do you have?" I ask her and her expression is like what you would expect to see on a child when you offer them candy.

She grins, getting up and throwing herself on the deep green couch opposite of where I'm sitting. "For you? I have all day," she says, and if she knew that I would take all day with her in a heartbeat, she wouldn't have said that. So now I guess it's time for me to pick the biggest tattoo I can think of to keep this girl's hands on me, her body near me, and hopefully get her heart to soften for me.

I OPTED for a back tattoo that, according to Roe, will take several sessions so she started outlining today. She spent around an hour drawing and when she showed me what she created, I had to remind myself to close my mouth after dropping it at the sight. This girl is more than an artist—she's a genius. The drawing looks more like a blueprint for a cityscape and my back is about to be her canvas.

Now I'm settled into the chair with a mix of anticipation and excitement coursing through my veins. My chest is flat against the chair, which is reclined into a bench, and my eyes are fixed on the mirror across from us. I can see Roe's reflection. She's focused, with one hand on my back as she wipes the excess ink and blood while she tattoos my skin with the gun in the other. She asked what music I wanted and I pressed play on the Dale playlist on Apple Music. Rauw Alejandro plays in the background and she's occasionally humming to the beat like she knows this song. Her hands, which look so delicate, are moving against my back with purpose and skill. It's so different from the way she softly touched my skin the other night. I'm in awe of how focused she is. Her confidence is sexy as hell, almost like she has an aura around her that captivates me.

The steady buzzing sound of the machine soothes me. Always has, always will. It reminds me of the busy street sounds where we grew up before we moved to the United States. As she taps that needle and dances it across my back, a wave of sensation crosses through me. She's drawing near my ribs. Goosebumps break on my skin immediately, showing her how affected I am by her touch in that sensitive spot. My breath catches and shivers run down my spine. With each stroke closer to my rib cage, I feel a mixture of pleasure, pain, and comfort. Three emotions I've never felt at once before, let alone while getting a tattoo.

"You need to stop moving," she demands in a low whisper, flattening one of her hands on my back and touching my skin again with the needle.

"Can't. Help. It," I grit out.

"Do you want to stop? We're almost done but this is a big piece. I don't want to hurt you."

"I have so many feelings right now, princesa, but I know you won't hurt me. Keep going," I add.

She sighs and gets back to work, adding a few more strokes before she gets up and motions me to move toward the mirror to see what she made.

Emotions swirl within me. Witnessing the transformation to my skin, at the hands of this tiny magical being with a goose backpack and overalls, the mouth of a sailor, and an attitude to last her for days. This permanent mark, etched by her talented hands, is the best thing I've ever seen and it's not even done.

"Roe, this is—" pausing to look at her in the face and not through the mirror "—*increíble*."

We look at each other for a beat – maybe two – holding each other's gaze and sensing the connection between us. I was right, this is more than sex. And if there was any doubt, this moment channeled by ink and sweat has bound us together even more. I know she doesn't welcome touch all the time but right now all I want to do is hug her tight.

"Thanks." It's all I can muster right now.

She nods, grabbing some ointment and rubbing it on my sensitive back. She places some wraps and instructs me to take it off tonight before showering. She heads to the back for a moment and returns holding a bag with aftercare items. I smile at her, walking to grab my shirt from the table, and putting it on. I intend to grab my wallet to pay her, but when I reach for it, Roe's hand goes up, holding my wrist and keeping me from falling under. Falling under her spell. Falling under her touch. Falling under her mercy.

"It's my treat," she says.

"I can't let you."

"You can and you will. This is my shop so it's my rules," she adds. "Besides, I've been itching to get my hands on your skin since I met you."

I raise an eyebrow at her and she giggles. "Get your head out of the gutter. I've been wanting to tattoo you since I met you. Your skin is like a canvas." She lets out a sigh and when I don't say anything, she continues, "Fishing for compliments, Saint?"

"Not sure what you mean," I say, allowing her time to tell me whatever is swirling in her head.

"Your skin tone is the perfect mix of warmth and richness. The tattoos you already have look like your veins are tracing the ink around your skin." She reaches her fingers over my wrist, flipping my hand palm up and tracing my forearm. "These earthy hues are the perfect foundation for a drawing. For art. I knew that ink would love your skin but nothing could've prepared me for the way it blended seamlessly with it."

Her hand keeps going up, touching and tracing the other tattoos on my arm as I swallow harshly and try to think of anything but the way her touch feels on my skin. My heart's racing fast and I pray that she can't tell the effect that just her fingertips touching my skin has on me.

"It's like a dance of colors, tones, and contrast. It's a timeless effect and it's not often I get to lay my hands on smooth, golden skin like yours. So yeah, I should be thanking you." Her cheeks flush, and she removes her hand from my arm, coughing slightly and allowing space between us. I feel the loss of her touch immediately. It's at this moment I realize something major. *I'm in trouble.*

"Well thank you, Roe," I choke out, distracting myself by looking over the aftercare instructions. "Good thing there's not another race until next month or I would be screwed, huh?"

She nods and throws herself on the couch, closing her eyes and raising her feet to dangle them over the armrest. I walk to her and sit beside her, lifting her feet and placing them over my thighs. She doesn't open her eyes, not even when I remove her shoes or when I take her socks off.

I grab one of her feet in my hand, and massage gently, especially against the arch in the middle of the foot. Hers is a perfectly shaped semicircle, and so soft.

I use my thumbs to massage the bottom of her foot when she moans in response. I work my fingers, kneading away the tension and stress of the day; hell, of the whole weekend. She lets out another moan that makes my dick twitch, and when I look at her, her eyes snap open immediately, creating tension in the air. I continue to massage and with each gentle stroke, a soft moan of pleasure escapes her lips.

"Saint, your hands are magic," she whimpers and I can't help but laugh at that.

"Perks of working with them," I wink at her. This earns me a roll of her eyes. "Just like yours." I wink at her again, and her sass goes away the moment my thumb touches the pad of her foot. She arches off the couch, asking me not to stop. *Mierda*[1].

The room is filled with upbeat reggaeton, punctuated by the rhythmic movements of my hands and her soft sounds. Every gasp is making me go wild. I don't think I'll make it out of this tattoo place in one piece.

I stop massaging, lower her foot, and rest my head back on the couch. I close my eyes and breathe, hoping I can

---

1. Mierda: Shit

calm my erection and my thoughts. Both have been unraveling all day with her proximity and her delicate hands over me. Her lavender scent and her sultry voice are like a damn siren. I can feel her moving next to me and I silently pray to all the angelitos[2] that she doesn't touch me right now because I'm about to lose every ounce of self-control I have left.

"Saint," she whispers breathily, her soft hand touching my elbow and somehow reaching every inch of my body.

Opening my eyes slowly, I tilt my head to look at her, but don't open my mouth to say anything, because truly I can't. If I do, I'll tell her to take her clothes off, and that can't happen here. That can't happen, period.

"I have a proposal," she says, "What if we get out of here, go to my place, and we can have some fun away from this street full of nosy people?"

I stifle a groan, "Roe, I already told you."

"Told me what? That you liked fucking me? That your hands couldn't resist being on my body?" She moves toward me until one leg swings over mine as she straddles me and places her hands on my neck.

"Or that you couldn't contain your demanding voice when you asked me to crawl to you?" She tugs at my hair while pressing her breasts against my chest. "Or the way that you got hard every time I moaned your name?" she adds while grinding her hips on me.

I know deep down I should show self-control. I need to get up and walk away. And if I were a gentleman, I would, but I don't have it in me to deny this girl anything.

"Which one of those things are you talking about, Saint? Or was it that bullshit about not being able to fuck me

____

2. angelitos: little angels

again?" Her fingers are tracing my jaw and she's biting her lower lip. That little move makes me lose it all and I snap. I close the distance between us with a kiss. Swiping my tongue against her lips, she allows me into her mouth, dancing with my tongue and matching my every move.

I reach to tug at her hair, wrapping her ponytail in my fist and pulling back. Her lips leave mine as she arches against me, showing me her perfect neck. I kiss, nip, and bite. One hand tugs harder at her hair while the other holds her flush against me. My dick is hard in my pants and I'm seconds away from turning this couch into a flip and fuck.

With each moment that passes as she grinds her ass against me and her hands tug my hair, the intensity grows and I want nothing more than to get her naked and under me. I let go of her hair, cup her breast and bite down over the fabric and she hisses. "Fuck," I say, unable to form any other coherent thought. Except… we're in her tattoo shop. Her place of work. Sitting near a window that anyone walking by could look in and see. She thinks this town was upset about the name she wanted to give this place? Imagine what they'd say if they find us fucking out here in the open.

"Roe," I whisper, and her bright blue eyes pierce me completely. "We can't do this here. Someone can walk by and you can get in trouble."

"I *know* that you're not using a moral clause on me right now, Saint. You didn't give a shit this weekend when anyone could've walked by and seen or heard us."

She's right, but so am I. The window is behind us and all it would take is someone taking a peek to see her flushed and needy on top of me. I grab her by her ass and pick her up. She wraps her legs around me and her hand touches my back slightly but enough to make me hiss. "Careful, princesa. Your hands may be magic, but I'm still sore as shit, so no touching."

She smiles devilishly before asking, "Where are you taking me?"

"Shh, I have an idea." I kiss her again, this time slower, taking my time tasting her. Memorizing every single curve of her lips on mine. Committing to memory the feel of her soft lips and the way she smells, like lavender and sage, and keeping it under lock and key.

NINETEEN

THE SAHARA

Skin, **Rihanna**

ROE

"TELL her to turn off the lights," Saint says and I tell Alexa exactly that, obeying like I've lost my brain and this man is calling the shots. The room darkens immediately and he continues walking until we are at the tattoo chair. He sets me down, placing my feet on his shoulders and kissing my lips, my neck, and all over my chest while his hands unbuckle my overalls. "Ass up," he adds and when I comply, he pulls them off of me in one swipe.

His hands go back to my body, roaming freely and leaving no inch of skin untouched. As his fingers creep under my tank top and touch the underside of my breast, he finds no bra and his eyes immediately snap to mine. Watching them darken with desire makes me even wetter than I already was. He kisses my navel, letting his calloused hands touch both my nipples. He twists and turns them, making me arch off the chair. One of his hands pins me down while he bites right above my panty line. "Fuck, princesa, how wet are you for me right now?" he growls.

"Dryer than the Sahara," I sass, trying to hide how my body reacts to him.

His nose dips onto my panties and he drags it right in the middle of my pussy, rubbing against it as he looks up and says, "Bullshit. Not only I can practically feel you dripping for me already, I can smell how turned on you are." He digs his fingers into the panty line and pulls them down painfully slowly. "Damn, Roe, you're fucking perfect," he adds, placing my foot on top of his shoulder and using one of his hands to pin me down.

"I thought—" I pant, not finishing my sentence because this man just licked me, flattening his tongue and ensuring I feel every single bit of that touch against my sex.

"No thinking. If you're thinking, I'm doing something wrong, and I know that I'm not." He winks at me before lowering back down to lick me again. I squirm under his touch, to try to get away from this hold. I don't know why I'm trying to escape because this right here is what dreams are made of.

My moans fill the dark tattoo shop as my eyes stare at this man's head between my thighs on the ceiling mirror above us. He licks and nips at my clit while humming in satisfaction every time I moan or say his name. I tighten my legs around his head because this feels like a mixture of too good but also not good enough. "More," I demand, out of breath and with lust in my voice.

He looks up, but he can see that I'm not looking at him, that I'm looking up. He follows my gaze and sees the same view I have: me partially naked, opened to him on the tattoo chair, with him on his knees between my legs. The best fucking reflection on the mirror. "Mierda, Roe. Eres perfecta." He rubs his hands on my thighs, squeezing tightly and bringing his gaze back down to my center. "Fucking perfect," he murmurs before adding two fingers into my pussy, making me see stars.

"Saint," I whisper.

"Tell me, princesa, how do you want to come? All over my fingers while I look at you in the mirror, or with my mouth on your pretty pussy?"

Fuck. "Both," I answer.

"Ask me nicely," he says with a smug grin.

"Make me," I snap back.

"Gladly," he adds before putting his head back down and licking me in the most sensitive spot while pumping his fingers inside of me. The echoes of his movements mixed with my cries are sinful. I watch as his shiny black hair moves with the rhythm that he's licking me while he grabs my waist, putting pressure against my skin to the point that I'm sure it'll have a mark but giving zero fucks about that. He adds another finger, making me drop my knees and open more to him.

He's touching all the right places. He licks and nips while humming against me, making me break out in goosebumps from my head to my toes. His fingers inside of me fill me up and touch every sensitive spot. I'm close; I can feel the warm sensation building in my core, and the fact that this man is about to make me come more times in three days than any other man in my lifetime is impressive. "Ah, Saint, I'm—" I get cut off mid-sentence because this motherfucker lifts his mouth from my pussy and stops moving his fingers. His eyes are molten as he watches my chest rise and fall but he stopped, completely frozen in place. *What the hell?*

"Ask—" He licks one time. "Nicely." And bites my clit. *The fucking asshole.*

"No," I snap, challenging him with my stare. Daring him to do what we both know deep down he wants. His index finger brushes against my clit and I bite my lip, writhing in pleasure. He stops though; he's just giving me enough to make me squirm but not enough to make me finish. He's playing with fire but what he doesn't know is I like to burn. I bring my hand down, touching my chest and tracing the middle of my belly toward my pelvis and coursing straight to my clit. Before I can touch right where I want, he grabs my hand, pinning it next to my head. Grabbing my right hand and placing it with the left, he is now pinning both my wrists in one hand.

He shakes his head with a grimace. "No, princesa. I'm the only one allowed to make you come."

I squirm and twist but he is pinning my hip with one of his giant hands and my hands with his other one. I'm at his mercy, and this is exactly how he wants me. I shouldn't be as turned on as I am right now, but fucking hell, this is so fucking hotter.

"Ask nicely," he commands again, brushing my clit with his thumb.

"No," I fight back.

"I have all day, muñeca[1]." His lips close over my clit again, sucking and flicking his tongue against it. He's driving me wild. Fucking insane. Erasing any desire other than the fact that I want him inside of me. NOW. He grabs my hip, digging in his fingertips while scraping his teeth over my sensitive spot. I'm burning under his touch and then, *mother fucker,* he stops again.

---

1. muñeca: doll

"Agh, stop edging me, you jerk," I sass.

"Ask. Nicely," he replies. His willpower is stronger than I thought. I lift my pelvis, signaling for him to lower his mouth on me again but he doesn't. He waits for me to say something. Again.

"Ask nicely, princesa. Stop being a brat," he says.

And I must be a masochist, because what I really should say to him is *please* but what comes out of my mouth is, "If you think I'm a brat, why don't you spank me then?"

That unleashes the beast that I hoped it would. Demanding his wild, releasing his control. In one quick movement he flips me over, laying me flat on my chest and placing his arm under my pelvis, lifting my ass in the air.

He does exactly what I ask and spanks me on my left cheek, hard. With a loud snap and a sting, I hiss but before I can truly feel the pain, he licks it. His tongue is flat and wet against my ass cheek and I'm about to spiral. "Such a brat. I have no issues showing you that your orgasm is mine. All you need to say is one pretty little word and I'll have you coming on my fingers in seconds," he growls with lust in his voice, his dick pressing hard against my ass.

My pussy is throbbing with need. I wonder if I can manage to touch myself and provide some relief, if he'll let me, but no matter how much I try though, I can't get out of his hold. "No," I say again, but this time it comes out shaky and he laughs—a deep, raspy laugh.

Another smack on the ass, a lick, and a kiss. I can't do it anymore. I'm done acting tough. He bites my ass cheek in the same spot he just spanked it and rubs over my clit with his finger. I've had enough. I wiggle against his face and let out a loud, "Please."

"Please what?" His finger presses harder, his teeth sink deeper, and his tongue touches my skin slightly. *Fuck.*

"Please, make me come." And boom. The magic words were said, and the genie came to play.

He spanks my cheek again, pushing two fingers in me and curving them at the same time that he licks the sensitive spot he just spanked. "Let go," he says and those words finally push me over the edge.

Shaking and twisting on his hand, I come hard as he holds me tight in place. "That's it, princesa," He encourages. But when I stay quiet, he continues. "Don't hold back now, let me hear you scream." His thumb touches the puckered skin between my ass cheeks. I'm officially dead. Limp on his hold, I immediately begin screaming his name over and over again until I collapse over the chair.

I stay here, lifeless, for what feels like hours but in reality, it's probably a couple of minutes. Saint pulls my ass back toward him. "I can't do anything. I'm spent," I whine, earning me a chuckle.

"Tranquila," he says, standing me up and pulling my panties and overalls on me. He snaps the buckles and kisses my forehead. "All set." He walks away from me with his boner in his pants, leaving me confused and mushy.

"Wait, what does that mean?" I ask.

"That you are ready to go," he replies.

"No, not all set. What does that word mean, *tanquina* or something." I feel so stupid but I need to know. I guess I should've paid more attention in Spanish class.

He smiles. "It's pronounced *tranquila*," he says, "and in that context, it means *easy* or *relax*."

"Ah, got it. Thanks. Are you gonna take care of that?" I ask, pointing at his pants.

He adjusts himself and shakes his head. "This," he says while pointing at the chair, and I'm sure my cheeks redden, "was not about me."

He stands there looking at me. One second. Two seconds. Three seconds. My heartbeat drops.

"5:00am tomorrow?" he asks. My eyes open wide in surprise.

"For what?" I ask.

"To train. Adios[2], princesa."

Without uttering another word, he unlocks the door and walks out, leaving me unraveled and sated.

---

2. Adios: Good bye

TWENTY

BARRACUDA

***Pretty Little Poison*, Warren Zaiders**

SANTIAGO

"HEY MAN, HOW'S IT GOING?" I hear Jake, one of the owners of Baker Auto, say as he walks near the car I'm currently working on. Jake owns this shop with his dad. They took it on as a father–son business endeavor but Jake refuses to quit coaching football, which led to them needing help and hiring me. So far I've loved my time here, so I want to continue to prove to them that I'm worth keeping around.

"All good, just working on the 'Cuda now."

"Good," he replies, sitting on a rolling stool and sliding in across from me. "How are you liking Baker Oaks?"

"It's been good. Everyone's friendly and I've found plenty of things to do," I answer, wiping my hands on a hand towel and stepping away from the car. The whole top of the Barracuda's engine is taken apart so the carburetor sits on the table with the intake, next to where Jake is sitting. He comes near the car and looks at it, inspecting the cylinder walls and the pistons. The owner of this car took it racing last weekend and wanted it checked. It's always a good idea after going heavy on the nitrous, because it can melt the piston if you're not careful.

"What are you thinking about for this beautiful beast?" he asks, half his body leaning against the car and his hands and head lost in the engine bay.

"I'm thinking of replacing the head gaskets just to be safe, but other than that, everything looks good to me," I say, confident in my assessment but also a little shaky since Jake and his dad have been the only ones with their hands on this car for years.

"Sounds good, go ahead," he adds, getting a mat to cover the front and checking that the fender protectors are in place. I don't blame him for being doubly cautious. This is an expensive car with years of maintenance and pricey parts in it. From what I know, Joe—Jake's dad—is good friends with the owner. And if Joe wasn't taking a week off on vacation, I highly doubt I would even be the one working on it.

Jake goes back to the rolling chair before saying, "Word on the street is that you're dating Roe Sorelle."

I stop dead in my tracks and look at him with a mix of shock and confusion. "Nah, I wouldn't call it dating. Hell, I wouldn't even call it friendship. The girl is worse than Icy Hot."

I wasn't even able to keep my word and go for the run that I promised her yesterday. I was going to show up but I need to figure out my shit before I spend more time with her, so I just texted her and told her I couldn't make it.

He chuckles to hide the darkening of his features, making me think that they're closer than I realized.

"Shit man, I didn't know you two were a thing," I say quickly.

At this, he laughs harder like I told a fucking joke. I straighten because I feel a ping of jealousy. The feeling is uncalled for because we're really not a thing, but man if that little reaction doesn't pull the caveman out of me.

"Roe and I are not a thing, at all. She's more like a little sister. The girl has gone through so much and this town has her back." He rubs his beard and shakes his head. I can tell he wants to say something else but all he adds is, "Just be patient with her."

"We're not a thing, really. We've hung out a few times, she gave me a tattoo and we race on the same series, nothing else." But somehow, I breathe easier hearing that they've never been a thing. *Little sister* I can do. Boss's ex, not really.

"But she is willingly hanging out with you? That's more than most get, trust me," he replies and my eyes widen. I wasn't wrong; behind the spitfire and take-no-shit personality, a lot is going on that she doesn't show. At least not to me, but clearly people know.

"Can I ask you a question?" I say, leaning against the toolbox and shoving my hands in my Dickies. If he's showing me an olive branch and giving me info on the girl, I'm going to take it. Maybe this way I can get her out of my system. *Or dig her in deeper.*

"Shoot."

"What's her deal? There's something about her that draws me to her but I'm not a kid anymore, Jake. I'm done chasing women."

"I'm not surprised that you see something in her. She's

pretty and anyone with two eyes can see that, but she's truly more than that. She's a remarkable human. It's not up to me to tell you why she acts like she's unbreakable, unstoppable. If she wants to, and if you're lucky," he says, raising one eyebrow at me, "she'll show you the cards life dealt her." He stands up and looks me in the eye with an emotion that I can only describe as pride.

"All I can say is that if you earn her trust, you'll see she's worth all of your time. Trust me." He gives me his hand to shake and when I take it, he says, "Good job on the 'Cuda. I'll see you tomorrow."

He leaves and all my coherent thoughts go with him because now, all I want to do is drive to Roe's house and figure out what makes her tick. What was it that turned this wonderful girl that everyone seems to notice and know and care for, into someone who won't let anyone in.

AFTER CLOSING THE GARAGE, I drive my truck to Saddlers. It's Thursday, which means karaoke night. I'm not personally a fan but it's hilarious to witness others. I'm planning on ordering fried food and drinking. And maybe hoping that a sweet-and-sour blondie will be there, too.

I walk in and sit in one of the small booths to the side where Marco is waiting. I haven't been able to hang out with him for a while, so when I said I was eating dinner out, he said he would meet me here. He likes Saddlers enough; something about it being eclectic speaks to him. It's a country bar with good food and several pool tables. There's a stage at the back with a big red neon sign that flashes every now and then. There's a line on top of the Ds in the name that leads to a cowboy hat, adding to the flair. However, no matter how country it is, you can still find big city drinks and top shelf liquor. If a bar from Miami and a Nashville bar had a baby, that's what Saddler's would be.

The smell of beer and whiskey lingers in the air as soft guitar plays in the background. The girl sitting in the middle of the stage is singing an acoustic cover of a Carrie Underwood song. Why do I know who Carrie Underwood is? Ask one of my little sisters.

"What's up?" I ask Marco when I sit and he raises his beer at me.

"Not much, just waiting for food. You know what you're getting?"

Before I can reply, the bartender from the first night I was here says, "Hi hot shot, how can I help you?"

"My friend needs to order," Marco answers, nodding my way, and the girl rolls her eyes.

"I *was* talking to him, hence the hot shot," she adds.

I don't really have an interest in figuring out what their deal is, so I order. "Whiskey, neat, and a basket of tenders and fries, please."

"You got it! let me know if you need anything else," she says, walking away to put my order in and completely ignoring Marco.

He scoffs. "Women. Always thinking that they're heaven on earth."

We've been friends for a long time but the more I hang out with him in my adult years, the more I realize that we might be drifting apart. The older I grow, the more I realize he still acts like a fifteen-year-old. As teenage boys we often objectified women but my mom put a stop to that the minute she heard me talking out of my ass.

Santiago, te voy a tirar esta chancleta el dia que te escuche hablando de las mujeres asi. Tu tienes hermanas y una mamá, será mejor que respetes.

Something about throwing a shoe at me the day she heard me talking about women like that again. She told me to think of my sisters, to think of her before I spoke. I wouldn't want anyone talking to them like that. I wouldn't want anyone talking *about* them either. Disrespect is not cool.

"Watch it," I warn but he doesn't reply.

The bar is buzzing. Booths and high-top tables are full, and the dance floor is crowded. Not an empty bar stool in sight. The air is thick with excitement and the smell of liquor sticks to your skin. People sway to the music and shout all the familiar lines.

My eyes wander around the packed room, looking for a set of sky-blue eyes and a pretty smile, even if it's never directed at me. I can't seem to find her. Suddenly my skin prickles and I know she's near.

"I thought you said you were a beer guy," Roe snorts, setting down a short glass with whiskey on the rocks and setting a beer in front of Marco. "Do you mind?" she asks, pointing at the seat and when Marco slides over, she takes the spot across from me. She's sipping on a seltzer but she has a shot of something dark in her other hand.

"I ordered a beer that one time, princesa, but apparently nobody in this bar knows how to fill an order," I quip, pointing my head to the glass. "I asked for mine neat." I pick up the glass, swirling the ice around and looking at her.

"Can't even get that right," Marco snaps. I don't know what the hell his issue is, but Roe beats me to the reply.

"Oh hush," she tells him before looking back my way and saying, "I know what you ordered, pretty boy. She tried to bring it to you neat, but something tells me you needed some cooling off today."

I ignore her sassy comment and reach across the table, holding the glass in my left hand and whispering, "Salud," in a low voice. *Cheers.*

She tries to clink her shot glass to mine but I quickly move it away. I tsk before adding, "Left hand. Please."

"Why does it matter?" she asks, scowling at me.

"You should always toast with your heart, and it's connected to the left hand." I bring the glass back and challenge her with my stare. She sighs and finally clinks her glass against mine. She brings her tongue to the rim and practically sucks the caramel liquid out, making all the blood in my brain go straight to my dick. *Jesus santisimo.*

"Ademas, using your right hand means you'll get ten years of bad sex, and we don't want to risk that, do we?" I smirk. She can't hold back the devilish smile on her lips, even though she tries to hide it by sipping her seltzer quickly. *Gotcha.*

"And that's my cue to get out of here. I'll let you two be," Marco groans, and I had forgotten he was even here.

"No need," she adds while sliding out of the booth. She bends over the table and whispers in my ear, "There's no such thing as bad sex, Saint. Just men who don't know how to play." It's low enough that only I can hear her but loud enough for my brain to go haywire.

She stands up straight again, grabbing her drink and biting her lip. "Your food should be right up. In the meantime, enjoy the show." She points toward the stage where two girls have the microphone trying to sing something that's indecipherable because all they're doing is laughing.

"What was that all about?" Marco asks. He also mumbles something about Roe thinking she can do whatever she wants, and I would love to hear exactly what that was about, but maybe I'm imagining it.

"Just Roe being Roe. You racing this weekend?" I ask him, changing the topic instead.

"Nah, I have rehab." Marco has some lung condition that requires him to do rehab every so often which is why he hasn't been able to race consistently. I'm surprised he's even able to race at all. His parents definitely don't think he should race but he got the all-clear from one of his doctors.

"Well, good luck with that, and hope we can race together soon."

The food shows up and it's easy to see that nothing really changes at Saddlers. People sing, others dance, and some drink. Marco talks but his words are muffled because all I can do is look at Roe. My eyes never drift away from her, no matter how hard I try.

I've never considered myself clingy but the more time I spend away from her, the more I feel sick. It doesn't matter that my brain knows only a masochist would pursue this, because my dick has other plans. I've never used my hand thinking about the same person as much as I have since that first night we kissed. It's even more now that I know what she feels like under my touch. What she tastes like on my lips —like sin and hard choices.

Marco leaves and I'm getting ready to do the same. I set cash on the table, and get up, ready to call it a night too, but something keeps pulling me toward Roe. I get a feeling that I shouldn't leave her here alone. She might be surrounded by patrons, but the girl is an island and nobody is allowed near it. I sit by the bar instead, waiting for her to stop doing whatever she is doing in the corner and see if she'll come over to me. Eventually, she does, with her goose crossbody bag around her and her eyes glossy and tired.

"Ready to go?" I ask, putting my tongue in my cheek and hoping that she'll say yes.

"Yeah, but not with you. I drove," she says, walking toward the double doors. She waves goodbye to the bouncer and speed walks to her Jeep. I follow like the lost puppy I am. When she gets to the Jeep, I watch silently as she climbs up, closes the door, turns on the ignition, and drives away. All without looking back at me once.

TWENTY-ONE

BAD WITCHERY

Photograph*, *Ed Sheeran

ROE

IT'S BEEN a long few weeks, but race weekend is finally here. I haven't been able to find my rhythm since the whole tattoo chair shenanigans with Saint. And by 'find my rhythm,' I mean I haven't been able to stop thinking about any of it. I've never experienced anything or anyone getting stuck in my mind this long.

Usually, I hyper-fixate on something for a few days and then move on, but this is beyond that. This is waking up in the middle of the night all hot and bothered thinking about his rough hands against my pussy. This is not being able to run more than a few miles without thinking about how lonely it feels without him. This is me being beyond mad that he didn't show up to run with me or to eat breakfast at Ronnie's. I would know because I went to the diner every day to see if he would. Insane. That's what's going on with me. I'm going crazy because who the fuck gets so infatuated with a man like this? *Someone who's never come that hard at the hands of anyone but herself before, that's who.* I hate that I keep thinking about him, even when it comes to the race. Maybe I'll see him there, I told myself while I was getting ready. *Ridiculous.*

This weekend's race is in Punta Gorda, and even though it's about a four-hour drive from Baker, it takes me almost six because I refuse to drive on the highway. The last time I did, I had to stop because it felt like the world was closing in around me. It feels like a giant rock is on my chest and my breathing slows to the point where I see stars. I hate it. I feel out of control and I can't recover afterward. I would rather be on the road longer than experiencing that, so the backroads it is.

The view is a bonus. Luscious trees color the side of the road in different shades of green contrasting with the blue sky. It doesn't matter that it's hotter than Hades outside, I have the windows down with the wind flowing through the Jeep and Dua Lipa playing on the radio. A girl couldn't ask for more.

I'm shouting to the music as loud as I can because IDGAF is such a bop when I feel the Jeep shake. I lower the volume because I need complete silence to focus, and the vehicle continues vibrating. *Shit, shit shit.* I pull over to the emergency lane just in time for the Jeep to stop completely, and smoke starts rising from the hood.

What in the actual fuckery type of bad witchery is this?

I let out something in between a sigh and a groan. Hitting the steering wheel with my fists and cussing more than I have in a while, I let out all of my frustration before I get out to see what the hell happened. Before I do, I think that maybe it was just a rough patch. I'm hoping that maybe I hit a pothole full of fire or something and the smoke didn't come out of this precious beast. I try to turn the key to see if the Jeep will do anything but it's futile. A small attempt but luck has left me behind.

I roughly open the door and walk to the hood, inspecting for who knows what. I can change a tire, fill my windshield wiper fluid, and pump gas but that's about how far my vehicle expertise comes. I clearly can't tell what happened but I definitely can smell the acidic coolant hitting my nostrils, mixed with what I figure melting metal would smell like. *This can't be good.*

I climb back into the Jeep to get my phone. All I can do now is call a tow truck and kiss my race weekend good-bye. The air that previously brushed my face with tenderness is now a harsh hand wrapping around my throat and cutting off my oxygen now. It's eerily quiet, with just distant birds chirping and not even a breeze to help make this place feel alive. There's nothing around here, other than the Goethe Forest and the quiet state road. I'm completely alone.

I check my phone and there's no signal. But that won't stop me from trying to find some, somewhere. I climb to the top of my Jeep and I'm all but dangling from the roof when I finally get through to roadside assistance. It'll be an hour before they're here so might as well make myself comfortable.

I'm lying in the backseat, feet propped on the window, reading my latest dark romance addiction on my Kindle when a dark shadow looms over me and I jolt. "Fucking shit, you scared me," I shout to the infuriating man standing by my window.

"Then maybe don't get so lost in a book that you can't

hear someone pulling up behind you to possibly kill you," Saint deadpans.

"Have you ever read a book that's so good that the world is better than the one you're living in?" I ask, sitting up and looking at him like he's the last person I want to see, even though all I want is to jump through the window and hug him. The words *comfort* and *safe* pop in my head as soon as I see him, and I don't know if I should flee or fight because it's been so long since I've felt that. "Because until you do, you can't tell me shit about how I choose to read."

"Tranquila, tranquila.[1] I'm just saying, you're on the side of the road, by yourself, in this deserted area and you weren't paying attention to your surroundings. It's not safe," he says. He's standing in front of me looking like a damn snack, wearing a fitted white tee, dark jeans, and black Ray Bans. I can't tell if his gaze is on me or not, which is the most unnerving thing in the world, especially when he's smirking with his full lips and driving me wild.

"Not *that* deserted if you're here, right?" I narrow my eyes at him.

"I was just passing on the way to Punta Gorda and stopped when I saw you." He takes a look at the Jeep's front and then back at me. "You good?"

Letting out a deep breath and dropping myself back on the seat, I reply, "I'm good. Lola, on the other hand? No."

"Who's Lola?" he asks as he leans his beautifully tatted forearms on the window and rests his face on them.

"The one responsible for my transportation," I answer, patting the passenger seat and dropping my arm dramatically.

"What's wrong with it?"

---

1. Tranquila: Easy or relax

"How am I supposed to know? It made some rumbling noises, shut off, and smoke came out," I say, completely annoyed by this whole thing but even more so that Saint has to see me in this situation.

I watch him walk to the driver's side, open the door, and pop the hood. He lifts the hood and starts inspecting the engine like it's his job. I'm sure if you were to look at my face right now, you would see how confused I am. *What is he doing?* I know he has that savior complex of his but I didn't realize it made him stick his nose in everything that goes wrong.

"Roe, when was the last time you took this for maintenance?" he shouts over the open hood and the noise of the birds nearby.

I'm not doing this screaming shit, so I get out and walk around to find him elbows deep into the engine bay. Like he senses my body next to him, he looks up at me, surely waiting for a reply.

"Roe?" he asks.

"I don't know, okay? I think it was on my calendar to go but then I forgot, and I don't think I ever made another appointment."

He shakes his head and closes the hood just as the tow truck pulls up. They talk first and then the driver asks for my information. I walk to Lola to get the papers and by the time I walk back, Saint is walking toward his truck.

We exchange information. He asks me questions and I reply to the best of my ability. What I notice is that he doesn't ask me where he should take Lola. He has me sign this little paper and tells me to give him room to work.

Walking back toward Lola, I notice Santiago is moving my bike and loading it behind his truck. *Holy shit.* I completely missed the gorgeous toy hauler hooked to his truck. It looks new. Shimmering silver edges frame the matte-black trailer that perfectly matches his black truck.

I run toward the back while inspecting the beautiful setup he has going on. This might be more panty-dropping than his smile, and that's saying a lot. But when I get to the open back, I see that the outside has nothing on the beauty of the inside. The ramp is down while he secures my bike to one of the hooks with the wench straps. I can see that the garage side of the trailer is stocked with his bike, gear, helmet, and fuel. It smells like the racetrack, but cleaner. It's pristine in here and the scent of bleach lingers.

I'm so enamored by the trailer that I almost miss Saint walking past me. I turn to face him quickly but he just keeps walking toward my Jeep—which is currently getting loaded onto the tow truck. I'm lost and I wish someone would explain to me what the hell is going on.

"Saint," I shout, practically pouting and crossing my arms like a toddler. Something about my voice stops him dead in his tracks and he turns around to look at me. Frozen in place, he allows me time and space to figure out what the hell I want to say. I walk toward him and lift my sunglasses off my face. "What the hell is going on?"

My voice is on the verge of shaking and he must notice because he walks to me and wraps me in an embrace. Not in a sweet hug; it's more like being compressed. He's squeezing me in a pattern. Squeeze tight. Let go. Squeeze tight two times. Let go.

"Saint," I whisper.

"Shh, listen," he says, continuing to squeeze me. I can feel my breath slowing down and my heart settling. With each squeeze, the hum in my ears lowers and everything around me seems clearer. I can hear the wind and the birds again. I can feel my skin, warm and sticky as he pulls me tighter. "I'm pretty sure you blew up your motor. At least, melted it. I'm assuming you're going to Punta Gorda too since your bike is here and I saw your tent too. There's nothing you can do about the Jeep so they will take it back to Baker and you and I will go to the race."

"No, I'm not going. I need to get my Jeep fixed," I argue, tensing under his touch.

"Who will fix your Jeep?" He lets me go from his embrace, but his hands remain on my shoulders. "You're looking at the one mechanic that can, and I'm not there. Also, you might need a new motor."

"Actually, my friend Jake owns an auto shop, he can fix it," I sass back.

"Yeah, he's my boss. He's also out of town for a work conference and his dad is on vacation."

I stare at him because what else can I do? This man knows so much about my life, and I didn't even know that he works for Jake or that he is a mechanic for that matter. Pretty shitty of me.

"I'm not going to the race with you."

"You are. Grab your bag so I can finish talking to the driver."

Saint walks away from me like he didn't just boss me around and I have the sudden urge to yell, shout, and stomp my feet. I can't even grab my bag because Lola is already up in the monstrosity of the tow truck and I'm not climbing that shit. He wants me to go with him? Fine, but he can grab my stuff.

I stand there, sun bright and warming my body, but also casting a golden light on his bronze skin. He might be talking to the tow truck driver but his gaze is on me. Intense and fixed on my body. I don't know if it's desire, concern, or annoyance but whatever flavor it is, he won't take his eyes off of me.

"Ready?" he huffs, snapping me out of it, again.

"I already told you; I'm not going."

He's not even entertaining my temper tantrum anymore. He climbs on the back of the truck, grabs my goose bag, overnight bag, and helmet and walks them to the trailer. He comes back and grabs the rest of my gear, a scowl painting his stupidly gorgeous face.

"Is there anything else you need in there?" he asks, and when my only reply is recrossing my arms over my chest, he climbs back up, grabs my water cup and my Kindle, and walks toward me.

"I'm. Not. Going." I deadpan and in a split-second, I'm being scooped and carried upside down with my ass in the air by his face and my face next to his ass. Saint's arm wraps around my legs as he walks toward the truck.

"Put me down, you asshole. I said I wasn't going and you can't make me," I shout, kicking and pounding on his ass. He's built like a rock so he doesn't even flinch when I hit him. So, I do the only thing I can think of to shock him. I grab his hips and lower myself even more, until my mouth is hovering over his ass and bite him, hard.

"Did you just bite me, pirañita[2]?" he asks with a low chuckle that sends goosebumps over my skin. I hate that he has that effect on me. Opening the passenger door and setting my ass down on the seat, he smiles at me. He tries to buckle me up but I pull the seat belt from him and do it myself. He hands me my water cup and my Kindle and closes the door before walking to the other side.

He sits next to me, his clean-shaven face on display, the

---

2. Pirañita: Little piranha

tight tee hugging his forearm and showing off some of his tattoos. The leather bracelet on his wrist pulls my attention, and for the first time I notice a small *ella* tattooed just above the band. Before I can think better of it, I grab his hand, pulling it to me and tracing my fingers over the tattoo.

"What does it mean?" I ask.

"It's the ending of all my sisters' names," Saint answers before pulling his hand from me, putting the truck in drive, and heading down the road.

Some sort of Latin music is playing—Bad Bunny, according to the radio screen—but he's quiet. His hand is still resting in my lap from when I pulled it to me earlier.

"How many sisters do you have?" I ask, breaking the silence between us.

"Three on earth, and one in heaven." He pulls his hand from me, turning his arm around to show me four dots and a dash. "Anabella, Isabella, Daniella, Gabriella, and me. The odd one out." *The ending of his sisters' names.*

"They don't go by their full names, unless my mom is yelling at them. Gabby is the youngest and she's a complete mess. We all baby her and she uses it to her advantage. We all know it too and still give in; we don't have a choice, she's too good," he says, smiling and turning the volume down.

"Then there's Dani. Dani is the one that is the most like me. Quiet and moody. She likes to tinker with things, too, and she's a better mechanic than I am. It's scary sometimes how good she is."

I turn my body to face him, giving Saint my full attention as he shares bits of himself with me. I still don't know why, because I've been nothing but a brat to him since we met. He stops talking and I nudge him to continue. "Go on, I'm missing two more, right?"

"Right," he replies. "Isabella is the next one. We called

her Isa growing up, but nowadays she goes by Izzy. She's… well, she's something." Saint shakes his head and laughs, like he thought about something he shouldn't share. He laughs again to himself before speaking, "Let's just say she's a firecracker, and you two would get along well."

He stops talking again, but this time his features turn somber. His shoulders tense and his hand closes into tight fists.

"You said one was in heaven. You don't have to talk about your angel sister, Saint. I know it's hard." I place my hand on top of his and he closes his fingers over mine, holding onto me tightly.

"Actually, it's harder to not talk about her. Ana was everything someone should be. Kind, sweet, smart, beautiful, and good overall. The friend everyone wishes they had, the sister I always wanted, and the best daughter in the world." He lets out a breath and tightens his hold on my hand. "She would be twenty now and I wonder all the time what she would be like. She wanted to be a teacher and I can imagine how many children's lives she would've touched with her light."

I want to ask what happened to her but not everyone morbidly jokes about the death of their loved ones like me, so I stay quiet and adjust my body on the seat. I also want to stay away from talking about dead girls named Ana because it's just our luck that the girls we both lost shared the same name. He lets go of my hand, gripping the steering wheel.

A heartbeat later Saint says, "She was born with the sun in her heart and she shone so brightly, she burned. I just hope that wherever she is, she's bringing all her goodness with her. In the meantime, we miss her down here." He stretches and opens his glove box, pulling out a small tin box and handing it to me.

Opening it carefully, I find polaroid pictures. The first one is a little boy holding a tiny baby with the biggest smile on his face and two dimples framing it. The next one is the same little boy at the same age, with a little girl next to him, old enough to sit but probably not walk, and another chubby baby on his lap. I smile looking at baby Saint, with his huge smile and baby sisters next to him. He looks like the best big brother.

The next picture is him again but older. This time, two little girls are next to him; one draped over him and the other one screaming as a little baby lies on his lap. He's still smiling in this one but definitely less brightly than the other ones. He looks tired and he has little dark circles under his eyes. He couldn't be more than ten or eleven in this picture and he looks worn-out like an adult.

There's a time jump between this picture and the next one because, suddenly, Saint is not a little boy anymore and there are four little girls around him. Everyone smiles at the camera, except for the youngest one who is sucking on her thumb with big bright eyes.

"Don't be going soft on me now," he says with a smirk.

"Shut up, you idiot," I reply, pushing his arm.

I keep going through the pictures, watching Saint grow old under my fingertips. Growing older, wiser, more handsome, and somehow sadder. The girls are also growing up, prettier and wilder. I'm drawn to the one with dark hair and dark eyes, and chubby cheeks that grew to be slim and gorgeous. Her hair gets shorter with every picture, as opposed to the others whose hair got longer.

The setting changes drastically, from a living room to a bedroom, and that same short-haired girl lying on a bed. Still smiling, but not reaching her eyes. Saint sits by her, his eyes on her, not on the camera.

I lift the picture to him and without even looking he says, "Ana."

I nod. I don't want to pry anymore but there's only one picture left. Scared to look at it, I still grab it and see the most beautiful smile I've seen on this man. He's glowing. They're on the beach, Ana is in a wheelchair, wrapped in a blanket smiling. Her lips look grayish but it's a polaroid after all. The other girls are hugging her, all smiling and happy. Saint stands tall above them all, hovering over them. Protective. Proud.

I move my fingers over the picture, caressing this moment among these siblings and feeling a ping in my heart that tells me this was the last time they were all happy together. I would know, because I have my own version of this picture, but I don't keep it close to me. No, I keep it as far away as possible. Out of sight, out of mind. Nothing to remind me that I had happiness once, that I'm not allowed to welcome it again without consequences.

TWENTY-TWO
MASTERPIECE

To Love Someone, Benson Boone

SANTIAGO

OPENING up about Ana is never easy but I would rather talk about her than to let her memory fade away. Not that I could ever forget her. Nobody who met her could, but her essence, her presence, must be carried on regardless of how hard it is for us still living.

I talked about the girls to Roe, but I didn't tell her everything. I didn't share that while Isa might be an absolute terror, spitfire or whatever, she also takes no shit from others. She's the one that would go to bat for all her sisters if needed. She also can throw a football better than any man I know.

What I didn't tell Roe was that even though Dani is the most like me, we don't get along. She was always jealous that

I was older and had more responsibilities and felt that I constantly babied her. *More like parented her.*

And Gabby... Well, even though she's the baby and we all spoil her rotten, not because she's the youngest but because we were all so worried about Ana, we kinda forgot about her. We neglected her. She grew up without the same love and affection that the rest of the girls did. So spoiling her? It's not so much about her being the baby, but about us dealing with our guilt.

What I also didn't tell her was that Ana was more than my little sister, she was my best friend. Yes, I'm eight years older than her but that never stopped her from wanting to hang out with her older brother. Ana always had a million questions for me and others around her. Her brain was always working and she could keep her questions going for hours. But that also meant that she was so interesting to talk to. My little genius sister was the best person to spend hours with, even when she was two and all she wanted to talk about was dinosaur facts. Even when she was nine and the girls around her wanted makeup, she wanted to know how many words she could write in one minute in two languages. Even when she was so sick, she couldn't form whole sentences before sleep took over her. Even now when she can't answer me, she's my favorite person to talk to.

What I didn't tell Roe is that I miss Ana so damn much it hurts. That our family took the hit of her loss deeply and we might never be the same again. What I didn't say is that not a day that goes by where I don't think about my missing sister and how empty life is without her here. What I didn't say is that Ana would have met Roe and fallen in love with her immediately, and I think Roe would've liked her too.

"Why don't you tell me something about yourself?" I

ask, trying to change the topic and hoping for something lighter.

"What do you want to know?"

Everything, I want to say but I control myself. "What's your favorite color?"

"Black, like my soul," she replies, lifting her eyebrows at me and closing the AC vent on her side. "You?"

"It used to be green but now it's blue." *Like your eyes,* I want to say but I keep that to myself. I let the silence cover us for a minute to hide the fact that the more time I spend with her, the more I like her.

Eventually, she looks my way and whispers, "Saint?"

"Si, princesa."

"Thanks," she says before placing her feet on my dashboard and laying her head back. A few minutes pass before her breathing changes, and I'm left in the quiet, alone with my thoughts while she sleeps beside me.

WE ARRIVE at the track and it's already packed. I knew this was a possibility when I decided to take the backroads. I'd rather get somewhere late and enjoy the ride. Everything happens for a reason, and if I would've taken the highway, I would've missed the beautiful and sassy blonde sleeping in my front seat. Roe is cocooned against herself, a tiny ball with her goose backpack on top of her face. It's making me anxious, thinking about her suffocating, but every now and then she moves to stay comfortable so I know she's fine.

I park the truck in the back of the track and start setting up. Bikes are out, gear on a plastic table next to them, and I'm setting up the bed in the trailer's garage when Roe walks in. Stunning and pissed as usual. She has on tiny jean shorts with rips on the front and a black tank top framing her body. She's wearing Converse instead of the Vans that I love on her so much, and socks pulled up higher than her ankles.

I know I'm gawking when her legs appear in my line of sight. I lift my gaze back to her face and smile at her, hoping she'll give me one in return but what I get is her stomping toward me.

"What are we doing here?"

"Hello to you too, princesa," I say, because I know that deep down she melts every time I call her that. "I'm setting up the bed in the back so one of us can sleep here. You're welcome to walk in and see if you want to set up your stuff. The cabinets on the left are empty." I point to the back door of the trailer signaling for her to go inside.

"I'm not staying with you. I have my tent," she says.

"There's plenty of room here. It would've been silly to set it up, especially when you need the back of your Jeep to make it work."

"So you just assumed I would sleep with you?" she snaps, and that makes me chuckle even harder.

"I've got three beds here, and if we're being honest, I'm not sleeping with you. I know how important this race is to you and I don't want you to miss it. I can sleep back here and you can take the main bed."

"Oh, so now you *don't* want to sleep with me?" Fuck, you can't win with this girl.

I walk toward her, backing her against the wall, my hands on each side of her face and my hips framing her tiny body. "Oh, I didn't say I didn't want to," I whisper against her ear. "I said I'm not *going* to. I'm a man of word, Roe. I know there are layers and layers to you, and I will peel them all off. In the meantime, I won't fuck you. I want you to see that there's more that interests me than your body. But let it be clear: your body is a fucking masterpiece. Including that beautiful brain of yours."

I tap her temple and stand there, looming over her with her back pressed against the wall, speechless. *Well, that's a first.* "Learning about you has become my favorite subject. I hope that there's not an inch of doubt in your mind that I'm a good student. I always get straight A's." I wink at her and back away slowly.

I walk out of the trailer, shouting to her, "Going to registration, you coming?" I grab both of our helmets and start walking. Shortly after, Roe's steps catch up to me, and she snatches her helmet from my hands. Chin held high, looking forward like she didn't shatter with my words. It's fine, Roe. Pretend I don't affect you as much as I know I do.

TWENTY-THREE

I HATE THE RAIN

Out of The Woods (Taylor's Version), Taylor Swift

ROE

REGISTRATION WAS A BITCH. There were so many people in line in this hotter-than-hell place, but it's done and we don't have to do it again. Tomorrow is our practice round and then Sunday we race. This is my least favorite track so I'm jittery beyond the norm. Last year, this was the track where I fell crossing the small river and had to wait for shit to work again. I lost ten minutes because I had to turn my bike over to get the spark plug out and let it dry. It didn't matter much then because the other girls were slower and I was able to catch up, but ten minutes in this one could take me from third place to last.

I'm walking around the campground, looking at the setups. Families and their dogs are setting up camp or roasting marshmallows outside. Teenagers are riding One

Wheels and bikes. Not a phone or tablet out, and this is what fills my heart. Nothing against technology, I don't know what I would do without my Kindle or iPad, but it's a breath of fresh air to see so many kids just playing outside.

"Excuse me," a little voice says behind me, and when I turn, I see a little girl who couldn't be more than four or five years old. She's holding something tightly against her chest and her eyes shine under the moonlight. Her parents are standing a few feet behind her, silently watching and with pleading eyes.

I squat down to meet her eye-to-eye and say, "Hi, little babe," offering my hand in case she wants to hold it, but what she does instead is place a photograph on my hand. A photograph of me riding, in the middle of a jump from one of my previous races. My hair is flowing in the wind and the bike is perfectly suspended. It's one of my favorite pictures. "Oh, that's me!" I exclaim, smiling at this little one.

"I know," she adds. "My mommy saw you walking by. You're my favorite rider, Ms. Sorelle. I just started racing and my bike is pink and black, like yours. I was wondering if you would sign my picture?"

Her voice is shaking. I wonder how much courage it took for her to come to talk to me. It's not like me to become a pile of mush over the fact that this little one looks up to me. "Absolutely, do you have a pen?" I ask and she shakes her head. I take off my backpack to pull a marker from it and when she sees the goose, she instantly giggles.

"Do you want to hold Bruce while I sign this?" I ask and she giggles louder.

"Bruce—" she claps "— and Goose," she says, clapping again. "It rhymes," she adds and I just want to pick her up and squeeze her. *Precious.*

"Bruce the silly goose, he's my favorite," I reply, tapping

her button nose and whispering "After you of course." She holds the backpack tight against her chest and looks back to her parents who give her thumbs up. "What's your name, little babe?"

"Emma," she says and I jot it down on her photo.

Show 'em up, Emma. A. Sorelle.

I give the photo back to her and before I grab Bruce, I shout to her parents, "Can I snap a picture with her?" They nod and I grab my Polaroid out of my bag to snap a picture of us. I let it develop to make sure it looks good and give it to her when it's done. She smiles big at me before throwing herself at me and giving me the biggest hug.

"Thank you, Ms. Sorelle," she says in her sweet little voice, full of emotion.

"You can call me Roe, Emma. That's what my friends call me." I wink at her and ruffle her hair. "I'll see you around, okay?" She nods and runs toward her parents who are waving at me with emotion in their eyes. I put the marker and camera back in my backpack and continue my walk.

When Saint showed me the Polaroids, I'm sure he didn't know how much I appreciate pictures. After my parents died, I only had a handful of pictures with them due to a house fire. Now I cherish photos more than anything. When I was fifteen, right before my dad got diagnosed, we had an electric fire start in his closet. We didn't notice until it was too late, and sure, we were fine and we didn't lose the house, but the closet was torched. Burned to ashes with everything that was in there, including all of our family pictures. A house fire because, of course, losing everyone close to me was not enough; I had to lose everything that held meaning too.

When I get back to Saint, he's sitting with his feet up

and his eyes are following my every movement. There's an empty chair next to him. I take it and prop my feet on his lap, secretly wishing he would take my shoes off and massage my feet like the other day.As if he can read my thoughts, he does. He takes off my shoes and socks and uses his hands to massage one foot. I might have hated getting my feet touched before, but now I crave his touch.

His knuckle pressing into the bottom of my foot as he quietly massages every knot he can find is fucking fantastic. I can feel the goosebumps rising from my foot to my back. His touch is pure magic. He's inspecting my foot too and I get the sudden urge to squirm.

"You don't strike me as someone who loves rainy days," he says, touching my tattoo that says I do.

"It's from a book. I hate the rain," I reply, pulling my foot away from him before adding, "I actually don't hate it; I just hate the muggy weather that comes from rain. Humidity and all. Plus, people forget how to drive in Florida when it rains, and I hate that even more."

"What about this one?" he asks, touching the cursive letters that spell my dad's name on the arch of my other foot.

"My dad's signature," I reply in a clipped tone. *No more questions, please.* Reading my mind again, he stops asking personal questions and hits me with a racing one instead.

"How do you feel about Punta Gorda?"

"I hate this fucking trail. Last year I lost because I fell in the water and had to drain my damn bike. If it wasn't for the cumulative points, I would skip this one," I add. It's funny how a month ago, I wouldn't have been able to tell him anything about this trail or how I feel about it. Yet here I am, sharing bits and pieces of me easily.

"I don't like it either. I'll watch your back this weekend,

yeah?" he quips and I nod. He puts my feet down and gets up, walking toward the grill.

He opens the top, grabs two plates from the side of the grill, and places something on them before walking back and handing me one of them—a vegetable blend on one side with a burger on the other. There's a dipping sauce next to it that looks a lot like honey mustard, which is my favorite. But I don't know many people who use it for everything like me, so I assume it's something different.

"You didn't have to cook for me," I huff.

"I know, but I want to make sure you eat. So, eat," he commands, making me feel shitty for not thanking him in the first place.

"Thank you, this looks great." I grab the fork to eat some of the squash and zucchini with the honey mustard and it's fucking delicious. My body hums, igniting with the mix of flavors in my mouth. I look up and catch him looking at me, smiling. "What?" I sass.

"I love that you love my cooking," he murmurs, surprising us both with his honesty.

"I like that you cook for me," I say because I do. And if he's willing to be vulnerable, I can try, too. I can pretend I'm not really dead inside.

"I knew the honey mustard was the way to go," he adds when he sees me dipping a vegetable on it.

"How? How did you know?"

"It was the only thing in your fridge other than your drinks," he answers, smiling at me and going back to his food. He pays attention, I'll give him that.

We eat mostly in silence, but occasionally making comments about the track and the race on Sunday. He stops a few times to look at the sky as it changes color, and closes his eyes before continuing with his food. He does that often;

the stopping, the looking, and the noticing. I wonder what it's about but definitely don't ask him.

I get up, dump the plate in the trash, and climb into the trailer to grab my wallet. Walking back outside, I start to open it to hand him some cash when his hands cover mine, and with a daring stare he asks, "What are you doing?"

"Getting some cash to pay you. You're using your stuff and it's the least I can do."

"I'm not taking your money, princesa. I got this," he says, zipping my wallet back up and walking to toss his trash, too.

He starts tidying up the space and I notice the noise around us has died down. Most people are probably sleeping or getting ready to go to bed. Tomorrow's a long day, we all know it, and part of performing well is taking care of your body, which includes sleep.

"Well, I'm not just squatting in your space, Saint. Let me pay you," I argue.

"I already told you no. I know you're not used to hearing that but hear me now. You're my guest. I dragged you here by my own decision. I always bring extra food and I have the extra space. It's not a big deal." He stops talking for a second, rubs his face and turns to me again. "Marco was supposed to come to this tonight and he didn't last minute, so I already had enough stuff for at least two. He should be here tomorrow but not with enough time to cook and hang out."

"So I'm your sloppy seconds?" I sass back.

"You're nobody's second anything." He pauses, letting that statement simmer before continuing, "Now you can either help me put these things away or you can go inside and make yourself comfortable. Either way works for me."

He turns back to the grill, wiping it down and removing crumbs.

Fine. He wants to waste his things and his time on me, I'll let him. I stomp back to the trailer and change into comfortable clothes. I plop myself on the couch and grab my phone to look up Emma's name to see which class she's racing tomorrow. After I find it, I make a mental note to go see her and grab my Kindle.

IT'S hard to breathe and it feels like I have a hand on my neck cutting off all the air. The overwhelming feeling of helplessness comes and takes me whole in terror. *No, no, no, I don't want to die like this.* I sit up with a gasp, my heart pounding loudly in my chest, making me feel like a trapped animal. It's a never-ending labyrinth of memories and fears. Claws dragging me deep into the middle of my worst years and it's then, hyperventilating on the couch, that I realize it was a nightmare again. I bring my knees up, putting my head between them, and rock back and forth. I can't even focus on where I am or what time it is, trying to control my breathing and lower my heart rate.

I keep rocking until I feel strong arms around me holding me in place. *What the hell?* I try to escape this hold but I can't. Whoever this is, they are strong.

A low voice hums, "Sh, sh, tranquila," bringing me back to reality. *Saint. The race. The trailer. His trailer.* It all comes back to me quickly. He continues to whisper things in Spanish, soothing me and calming my heart, even if I don't really know what he means. His voice alone is getting wired in my brain as comfort. As safety.

Eventually I settle against him, his hand on my temple and the other one rubbing my arm. "It was just a dream," I whisper as he nods against my head.

"A nightmare," he says. "Do you get those often?" he asks, releasing me from his hold and standing up to grab a bottle of water. He opens it and hands it to me. My arm is wrapped around my legs and my head is resting on top of my knees.

"Sometimes," I reply, taking a sip and looking at him, silently thanking him with my eyes. "I usually sleep with a weighted blanket and that helps."

"Like a swaddle," he says and I open my eyes wider.

"Do you have secret kids that I don't know about, Saint?" I sass, trying to break the awkwardness of this moment.

"No, but I helped raise four little girls, remember? Isa needed a swaddle to keep her from waking up a million times in a night. Sounds like that's what you need too."

"I hate being wrapped but the weight of the blanket does help," I add. "I usually don't sleep a lot which is why I run so early in the morning; I might do that now."

"It's not even 11:00pm. You need to go back to sleep," he says with the concerned tone he always seems to use around me, every time he tells me to do something.

Not even 11:00 pm? Did I just fall asleep here? Looking around, I see I'm still on the trailer's living room couch, my Kindle next to me and a blanket draped over the couch that I'm sure was on top of me at some point. I did fall asleep here. Three times now I've fallen asleep out of the blue with Saint. I usually don't do that; I'm too aware of what's happening around me to let go and rest.

"I'm not going back to sleep; I'll take a shower though." I stand up and walk to grab some clothes from my bag but my bag is empty. Before I can say anything, Saint beats me to it.

"Your clothes are in the cabinet by the bed. I didn't go through them so they're not organized, just out of your bag," he says, standing up and putting one hand in the pocket of his sweatpants.

Fuck me slowly, please.

This man wearing sweats and a fitted tee is more than I was ready for. And he's fucking barefoot, too. The contrast between his golden skin and the white shirt is more than anyone can handle, especially not in the middle of the night in a space that smells just like him. Salty like ocean waves and fresh like mandarins.

"Kay, thanks," I say, looking away before his gaze turns me to stone.

I take the quickest shower known to man and grab my pjs, or what I like to call the small piece of shirt and shorts I wear. I get out of the bathroom and back in the living room. I find Saint sitting on the couch, eyes on me, blazing.

"Thanks," I say, plopping on the couch next to him and placing my feet on top of his thighs again.

"What for, princesa?"

"Agh, everything?" I let out a breath and drop my head back onto the headrest of the couch. It definitely feels nice to be able to just relax and have some company. I'm usually alone, which is fine because it's my choice, but being near him makes me feel something that I didn't think I would. He makes me feel at ease, like I can let my guard down and I'm not sure if that terrifies me, electrifies me, or both.

He clears his throat before saying, "I'm going to bed. Let me know if you need anything." He gently moves my feet from his lap and walks toward the trailer's garage. He said I could take the master bed and I guess he meant it. We walk in opposite directions, falling into a silence that haunts me more than the idea of talking to him.

I TOSS and turn all night, or what feels like all night. I can't go to sleep and I'm not sure why. It feels like there's too much space here. I also don't have enough blankets or pillows. I try to make a fort to bury myself in and mimic the pressure of a weighted blanket but it's not working. I'm tired and annoyed and all I want is to fall asleep.

I get a crazy idea and climb out of the bed, walking toward the back of the trailer, dragging two pillows with me. I open the sliding door gently and the movement wakes Saint, making him jolt up. His eyes roam my body and the surroundings, alert and frantic.

"Roe? Everything okay?" he asks, jumping out of bed and pulling me flush against his body. His heartbeat thumps under my ear, and I think I might have scared him.

"I can't sleep so I was going to climb into bed with you, but your reflexes are beyond normal for humans. Are you secretly a werewolf?" I joke, hiding the fact that I had to come get him like a little baby. I've never been the needy girl, never, and yet here I am.

He wraps me up in his arms, lifting me from the ground. I wrap my legs around him and let him drag me to bed but he takes me the opposite way to the master bed. Okay, so he *did* mean it when he said he wouldn't sleep with me. Except when we make it to the bed, he drops me on it and lays next to me, pulling me close to him and draping a leg over me.

"If we're going to share a bed, it might as well be the

comfortable one. Now sleep; it's late and we have a big day tomorrow."

"I'm not a cuddler, Saint," I add but without any attempt of moving away from his hold.

"You said you use a weighted blanket. I don't have one but maybe you can't sleep without it. I'm sure my leg weighs enough."

I freeze because this is the sweetest thing someone has ever done for me. So wholesome.

"Sleep, don't overthink it. We can go back to you hating me tomorrow."

I don't hate you. I want to say but I don't because the alternative is too terrifying. I just close my eyes and drift away.

TWENTY-FOUR

MY FULL TIME JOB

***Collide*, Howie Day**

SANTIAGO

ROE'S ASS is backed up against me and I have to pull my hips away so my boner doesn't poke her. She said she's a morning person and that she can't sleep past 5:00am, but it's seven and she's still out. Deeply asleep. If it wasn't for the fact that I can feel her breathing I would consider shaking her to see if she's even alive.

She softly wiggles a couple of times before her body stiffens beneath mine. "Good morning," I whisper and I sound raspy. My voice is not hiding the need I feel but I try to fix it by removing my leg that has been over her body all night. It's numb, so I sit up and massage it, giving Roe time to recover from whatever she's thinking about.

"What time is it?" is her response, but before I can answer she looks at the time herself. "Shit, Saint, we're late."

She hops off the bed, grabs clothes from the drawer and runs to the bathroom to change. She comes out with a sports bra and running shorts. Her beautiful hair is down and her whole body is on display. Definitely not doing my boner any favors. She runs back to the bathroom and I hear a soft hum, like an electric toothbrush. I take this opportunity to get up and splash some cold water on my face from the kitchen sink in hope that my body gets the memo that we're not touching Roe today.

We're both dressed and out of the camper quickly, with breakfast sandwiches in our hands. I make these and freeze them every month. It pays off when the day after the race my whole body hurts and they are ready to go, or when a certain bossy woman sends us walking out of the camper with zero time to cook. She's almost sprinting toward the peewee track and I have no clue why. She said it herself that she had no other siblings or family.

We make it to the peewee track and she runs toward the front, looking for something. Looking for *someone*. She starts shouting and waving her hands, jumping up and down. When a little girl with big bright blue eyes looks back and waves back at her before sitting on her bike, I know she found who she was looking for. The kid's parents snap on her helmet and the countdown begins. The parents move back from the starting grid and the miniature riders take off.

They do a good job and race for about thirty minutes. All the parents are shouting and clapping as they go by, stopping to pick them up when they fall or helping them off the track once they're exhausted. Roe screams for a little girl—Emma, from what I can tell—every time she goes by us. After her parents and an older sibling who is also already dressed head to toe in gear congratulate her and take pictures, Roe approaches them. I follow along, giving her space.

"Hi, Emma," Roe says approaching the kid who is currently looking at her like she hung the moon.

"Hi Ms. Sorelle," she replies shyly.

"Now what did I say about my friends calling me Roe, little babe?" She ruffles her hair before adding, "You did great out there, way to rip!"

"Thank you, Ms. Roe," she says, getting off of her bike and looking at her parents, silently asking for permission. They nod and she runs to Roe, who's squatting down with open arms. Emma holds her in the tightest hug and she says, "Thank you for coming to see me."

"Are you kidding me? I wouldn't have missed it for the world," Roe exclaims.

They talk for a little bit longer and Emma's parents take a picture of the girls, and they all wish her good luck on her race tomorrow. Emma adds how she will be watching and Roe says that she will win just for her.

We walk back to camp; the distance seems longer now somehow but maybe it's because we're taking our time as opposed to running like gallinitas ciegas[1].

"So who's Emma?" I ask, trying to make conversation and see if I can get more info from her without spooking her again.

"I met her yesterday when I was walking the campgrounds. She had a printed picture of me that she wanted me to sign. It was the sweetest thing. I looked up the peewee riders and saw her name so I wanted to watch her race," she explains and man, I didn't know she liked kids that much.

____

1. Gallinitas ciegas: it's a children's game but in this instance it's used as a reference like running with your head cut off.

"So you like kids?"

"I do, but not enough to raise them," she states matter of factly.

"What do you mean?" I ask, dumbfounded about how honest she is. *Except for when you ask about a topic she doesn't want to talk about.*

"I mean, kids are cool, you know? So pure and wholesome and usually without a care in the world. We need more of that. Gentle souls walking around. But raising them? Raising a good human for this fucked up earth? Nah, I'm not cut out for that. Knowing me, I would fuck them up so badly, they'd be the next serial killer," she says nonchalantly as she keeps walking.

"Okay, so, no kids in your future?"

"None of my own. I always thought I would be the next cool aunt but my lack of friends and siblings proved me wrong on that front." She stops momentarily when we make it to the trailer, grabbing her riding pants and sliding them up her body. She's so confident and gives zero cares about who sees. I kind of like that about her. A lot.

"I bet you want your own soccer team, huh?" she asks. I look at her with confusion on my face. She notices and smirks, saying, "Kids, Saint, kids. I bet you want a bunch of them."

"Are we at that step in our relationship, princesa? Talking about kids?"

"Oh, shut up, you brought it up first."

"Actually, I don't think I want kids," I answer honestly. "I like them but it's a lot of responsibility. I want to be the cool uncle too." I take my shirt off in one quick swoop then drop my shorts. I have impact shorts underneath so I'm not really naked, but by the look on Roe's face, you would think I am.

Her eyes flare as she looks at my body. I'm proud of the body I have, but right now under her gaze, I feel invincible. "Like what you see, princesa?" I ask her with a smirk and she rolls her eyes and puts on her jersey.

Once we're both geared up and ready to grab our bikes, we head to our practice round.

At the grid, I spot Marco but he has no gear on. Makes sense since he said he wasn't racing. He's spotting Joey's bike so I pull up next to them. Marco nods his head at me at the same time that Joey waves to Roe and me. Marco, on the other hand, ignores her completely. She doesn't seem to notice but I do. She might be focused on what we're about to do since this track is challenging.

I hate this track and so does she, so we talk about our plan to try to stick together during practice. I'm surprised she agreed to that and that she shared how much she hates this place. I know that hasn't been easy for her, so I take it. I'll take every second she's willing to be vulnerable. Every second she lets down her guard. Because one of these times, she might not put it back up. Even if she does, I have a feeling I will gladly tear it down.

THE PRACTICE ROUND WAS CHALLENGING. The damp areas felt like clay, making the tires grip to the edges of the tread and flinging chunks of dirt everywhere. Roots were out and raised so lots of people crashed, forcing us to maneuver around them.

We're currently sitting outside; Roe is on her Kindle and I'm cooking dinner. It's hot and humid tonight. The gnats are flying, annoying anything in sight but not Roe. She's just casually sitting there, her hair up in a ponytail, her legs over the armrest and her nose in the Kindle.

"What are you reading?"

"A dark romance," she answers nonchalantly.

"What does that even mean?"

"Mm, antiheroes? Morally gray characters? Heavy topics? And sometimes more."

"Interesting," I reply, still very confused. I don't really know what any of that means but I also don't read fiction at all.

"What about you, Saint, any secret hobbies I need to know about?" she asks, twirling her ponytail around her fingers and looking at me from under her dark lashes.

"No, I like cars so I work on them. I like bikes so I ride them. I like my family so I spend time with them," I say and leave it at that, looking at her and not dropping her gaze.

"What about women?" she asks. "What do you like doing with those?" She puts her Kindle down and her elbows on her lap, smiling at me.

I walk to her slowly, with intention. Showing her that I'm not intimidated by her or her questions. Showing her that I'm here, an open book to her, and she can ask away. I squat down, so my face is level to hers on that stupid tiny chair she's sitting on.

"Women? I can sit here and tell you exactly what I like to do with women because there's not even a slight hesitation in the fact that I *do* add women to my priority list." I swallow and bring my thumb to her chin, swiping gently up to her cheek. "But I don't want to talk about women. Right now, there is one woman in particular getting all my attention. There's one woman who I want to make my sole purpose. Only one who I want to show exactly what I like to do. But leave no doubt behind, princesa, I don't want to make this woman a hobby. I want to make it my full-time job—to know her, to worship her, to adore her, the only way she should be treated." She catches a breath and I let go of her face and grab our dinner from the grill.

Like I said before, *game on, princesa.*

TWENTY-FIVE

PUNTA GORDA

Me Quiero Enamorar, Jesse & Joy

SANTIAGO

"FORTY-FIVE SECONDS."

The announcement blares, carrying the waves of nerves and excitement with it. This is the moment to focus. The moment we block out the surrounding noise and concentrate on exactly what we came here to do. I wipe my hands on my pants and look to my side to see Roe, facing her bike in her running stand. She's ready and she's focused. This morning she was all business, following her racing routine, which is as important as having stamina and good technique.

"Thirty seconds."

My eyes are still on her and it's like she could hear my thoughts because she turns her face and looks at me. I can't see her eyes through her goggles but I'm sure if I could, they would be crystal blue, fire burning behind them.

"Fifteen seconds."

I nod my head at her and she gives me a hand signal before nodding back. She turns to face the track and I do the same because in less than ten seconds, the horn will sound and our race will start. We promised to watch out for each other this morning because on this track winning isn't the most important thing -- it's finishing in one piece. This terrain is gnarly and we need to keep momentum to not lose our spots in the lineup.

The horn goes off and I run to my bike, sweat dripping down my forehead onto my nose, and every ounce of my body vibrating with excitement. Adrenaline rushes through my veins as I swing my leg over the bike and kick start it.

The beginning of Punta Gorda is the easiest part of this whole race. Flat and sandy surfaces with very minimal roots or plants. There's a clear trail of where we are supposed to go and you can see riders on every inch of space, trying to avoid crashes or running people over which usually would cause a domino effect.

Roe's already ahead of me, her tiny frame riding with her ass off the seat as she effortlessly maneuvers her beast of a bike like the damn professional she is. She's majestic to watch; even when I'm trying to find the best path, my eyes keep tracking *her*.

We start going into the trenches. The trail narrows into a single-track lane surrounded by pine trees, leaves, branches, and roots popping out of the ground. I avoid them the best I can but sometimes you just have to push through and go over them. I weave through the lanes, opting to go on the trail as opposed to going on the obstacle course. People fall and tumble through those and the impact can be catastrophic. I'm playing safe and maybe that's why I keep staying behind other bikes. I'm not giving up, but I would rather finish this race in one piece and fourth place than not finish it at all.

Roe's taking the lead and I'm two bikes behind her, chasing their tails and watching this girl dominate the race. I have no doubt in my mind that she's got this track down and that she'll place in the top three.

And one and a half hours later, she finishes first, and my rules of staying away from her won't matter. The only things I feel right now are my chest full of pride and my hands itching to touch her whole body.

"READY?" I ask Roe when she comes back from picking up her plaque from the award ceremony. We parted ways afterward so she could go find Emma and I could get the trailer ready to go. This morning we put all the gear and bikes in the garage and now, all that's left is the mat that's serving as our floor. She seems ready and I get the confirmation I need when she nods and climbs in the truck.

I roll the mat up and shove it in the camper's garage, closing the door with a strong push and run to the driver's side of the truck. My parents only live thirty minutes away and I want to see them before we head back. I hope Roe's on board.

"Hey, are you in a rush to get home?" I ask, blasting the AC on my side while reaching out and closing the vents on hers before her skin breaks into bumps. She's constantly shivering and trying to hide her body from air currents while wearing minimal clothing.

"Nah, I don't work Mondays for this exact reason," she answers, not lifting her eyes from her Kindle. Her hair is pulled to the side over her shoulder, covering part of the design on the black shirt. She's wearing soft leggings and sitting with her feet tucked under her. Her checkered Vans are off and forgotten on the passenger side floor, and her other hand is doing pressure points on the tip of her fingers. She's wearing sunglasses that frame her face and make her look like an angel and her light pink lips are tucked in concentration. *I want to be what she's concentrating on.* Coño, que desastre. *Shit, what a disaster.*

"I was planning on stopping at my parent's house on the way back. It might delay us a few hours but we can leave whenever you want."

"Cool, cool," she says as I pull out and head to the highway. I'm not calling my mom to tell her about bringing Roe in order to avoid them speculating on who she is. I would rather show up. Be the element of surprise.

The ride is quiet. She reads and I drive. I'm playing my 'after race' playlist which consists of Jessie y Joy and Christian Castro, courtesy of growing up surrounded by women. My dad might hate that I don't listen to reggaeton all the time but I do enjoy different types of music, even if it's femenino. Music is music; it shouldn't matter what gender I am, I should be able to listen to whatever I want.

Every so often, I ask Roe a question and she answers without hesitation, which is more that I can ask for. She asks some in return and I hold nothing back. This is a two-way street and I'm here to walk it.

We pull up to my childhood home and Roe's eyes snap up. The well-manicured garden and the yellow accent chairs on the porch makes it look like a picture-perfect house from the outside. There are rocks and small flowers that lead the way from the driveway to the yellow front door. Small daisies in pots next to the door add the perfect touch, or so my mom says.

"What should I expect?" she asks, placing her Kindle in her bag and putting on her shoes.

"Expect the girls to swarm you with questions, my mom to feed you, and for my dad to say nothing at all," I reply, taking the key out of the ignition and hopping out of the truck before walking around to open her door.

"Thanks," she says when I offer my hand and help her down. I'm surprised she even let me do this so I bite my tongue and just nod instead of making a comment about it.

Before we get to the door, Roe steps behind me, shielding her body with mine. She grabs my shirt and tucks herself into my back. I reach my arm behind her, squeezing her arm lightly and turning around to see her face. She's pale as a ghost and she's biting her lip so hard, I'm afraid she'll draw blood.

"What's going on?" I ask with concern in my voice.

I reach out to brush her hair behind her ear, after the wind blew it right across her face, and wait for her to answer my questions. The minute my fingers touch her skin, she sucks in a quick breath.

"Nothing," she answers, avoiding my gaze.

"It has to be something. I can see it written all over your face, princesa. What's going on?" My hand leaves her neck and runs down her arm, all the way to her hand, taking it in mine.

"I'm about to meet your family and I'm not great in social scenarios I can't control," she spits out before tugging her hand out of my grasp and shoving it in her back pocket. She's balancing on her feet, tilting back and forth slightly as her eyes roam over the front porch.

"They're going to love you, Roe. I'm sure of it," I urge, hoping that does the trick to settle her down. However, it seems to do the opposite and she bites her lip harder. I tug the lip out of her teeth with a gentle finger and wrap my other hand around the back of her neck. I want to wrap her completely in my arms and kiss her until all of her worries go away, but I remind myself this is my parents' house and I can't be doing that.

"I know you get overwhelmed sometimes. It's okay; I won't push you. If at any point you want to leave, say the word and we will." I drop my forehead to hers, the lavender scent on her hair invading my senses and her soft skin caressing mine. "I'll follow your lead, I promise."

She closes her eyes and lets out a breath with the wind that effortlessly freezes this moment in time. We're so close we could kiss but I don't want to take advantage of her vulnerability, so I just stay still. Holding her and letting her breathe.

She takes a sudden step back and says, "Okay, let's go before your family thinks I'm a weirdo."

"Chances are they already do. I don't usually bring girls home, so get ready for the trial."

"Trial? How Salem of them. I'll take it, witchcraft and all," she says, walking toward the door with purpose.

God, this girl. Keeping me on my toes. I never know what's gonna come out of her mouth and I am learning more with every interaction, that I really like that.

"Santi, mijo, que bueno verte[1]." I hear from the front door, catching my mom walking toward me, open arms and all smiles. She might be five feet tall but her presence is more like a skyscraper. Her bright red dress makes her gray hair

---

1. Santi, mijo, que bueno verte: *Santi, my son, so good to see you.*

shine white and warms her dark eyes. Think Cruella De Ville but Latina, and not into puppy theft hopefully.

"Hola ma[2]," I say, hugging her and lifting her off the ground. That move earns me a smack on the head with whatever she's holding and we both laugh as she tells me to put her down. I see that this time her weapon of choice is an oven mitt on her hand. "What are you cooking, ma?" I ask, pointing to it.

"¿Porqué me hablas en ingles, mijo? ¿Cuantas veces tengo que decirte que español namas?[3]"

"Because I have a visitor, ma," I add, turning my body so she can see Roe, who is smiling shyly behind me.

My mom lifts her eyebrows at both of us but mostly at me. She hands me the mitt and walks to Roe. As Roe extends her hand, my mom opens her arms and I'm suddenly terrified about how this is going to go. Either Roe is going to freak out and storm back to the truck, or my mom is going to be offended and walk back inside when Roe rejects her hug. To my surprise, neither happens.

My mom embraces Roe in a quick hug that she doesn't return but instead of making it awkward, my mom pats her shoulder and squeezes gently saying, "I'm so sorry sweetie, I have no manners. I'm Santi's mom. Welcome."

Roe smiles and says, "Nice to meet you, Mrs. Cruz. I'm Roe."

Before I can say anything about how much my mom hates that, my mom grabs Roe by the hand, pulls her inside while saying, "None of that nonsense. My suegra[4] is Mrs.

---

2. Hola ma: Hi, mom.
3. ¿Porqué me hablas en ingles, mijo? ¿Cuantas veces tengo que decirte que español namas? *Why are you speaking in English to me, son? How many times do I need to tell you to speak only in Spanish?*
4. suegra: mother in law

Cruz. Call me Adela or Del. Ven, let's go see the girls. They will love to see you."

Family is the strongest foundation there is. I love my parents and my sisters with all my being, and seeing my mom interact with Roe this way means more than I was ready for. Better yet, it might be cementing every feeling I've had about her until this point. I hope my sisters feel the same way and that they don't break my girl with questions.

They walk in and there's nothing to do but to follow them and pray to all los santos [5]that Roe doesn't run away.

---

5. los santos: the saints

TWENTY-SIX

GHOSTS CAN'T TOUCH SHIT

***Breathe Me*, Sia (for an emotional read) or
Shit Show - Leah Kate (for an upbeat read)**

ROE

YOU WOULD THINK the music would overshadow the noise of everyone talking but it just blends into the background between the voices. Saint's mom brought me straight to the kitchen to join the sisters. In between the girls asking me a million questions, their mom finishing dinner, the dog running around, and Saint setting the table, I feel like I haven't had one moment to figure anything out.

So much sensory input at once. I excuse myself to go to the bathroom, wash my face and get back to the kitchen. Saint asks if I'm okay and when I nod and smile, he squeezes my shoulder and gets back to the task at hand.

Everyone in this family is beautifully loud. Full of life and joy. Even though I'm overstimulated, I'm not really overwhelmed. I'm just left wondering—is this what life *should* be like? Is this what true family looks like? It doesn't matter because I will never know.

Everyone sits around the table after the food is set, and I'm about to sit when it gets eerily quiet. I stop from pulling out the chair, and I stare at Saint. He gets up and swaps chairs with me. After we both sit down, his mom says a prayer in Spanish and we start passing the food around.

"So, Roe, have you ever eaten tostones before?" Gabby, his youngest sister asks.

"This?" I ask, holding the plate with round, flat patties. "No, I haven't. What are they?" I pick one up and put it on my plate before passing the tray to Dani who sits right next to me.

"Fried plantains," Gabby says, scooping a type of rice on her plate. "This is called moro. It's rice with *guandules* in it. Not sure how to say that in English," she adds.

"Pigeon peas," Saint says.

I nod and keep shuffling around plates and adding to my own as they take turns explaining what I'm about to eat. My large white plate is full of small mountains of food. I don't like when my food touches and it's definitely a challenge with so many choices.

"Roe, darling, you don't want avocado?"

"No, Mrs. Cruz." To that she raises her eyebrow. "Fuck, I'm sorry. Del. Oh shit, I'm sorry, again," I say when I realize that I just cussed, *and I did it again.* "I'm so sorry, I clearly have no manners." The table erupts in laughter before settling again, allowing Del to talk.

"You get one free pass. No cussing at the table." She looks at her children and smiles. "That goes for all of you, too. Not in English, not in Spanish. ¿De acuerdo?"

"Si," everyone says in unison and we start eating. The

explosion of flavors in my mouth is more than I'm used to but definitely what my body needs.

"I'm sorry your dad is not here to see you, Santi, he has a long surgery today," Del tells Saint before sipping on her beer.

I don't go for beer usually but I'm dying to try this one that everyone but Gabby is drinking, so I grab Saint's and take a sip before giving it back to him. This earns me a laugh from everyone and a chuckle from him when I open my eyes wide.

"You can have one too," Del says.

"I'm usually not a beer drinker but that is delicious."

Everyone says something in Spanish at the same time but before I can ask what it means, Saint translates for me. "Presidente, the cold beer that everyone wants. I'll bring you one, hold on."

He gets up to get one while his sisters ask questions about the race and the plans for the next round. They also give Saint shit when he gets back about losing to a girl, but he replies that I'm a badass girl, not a regular one. His mom pulls his ear over the cuss word and we all laugh.

The hours pass with laughing, joking, questions asked and stories told. When it's time to leave, I feel like I will be empty without days like this afternoon. This was more than nourishing for my body; this day fed my soul and the girl inside who has always craved big family life.

I walk to the truck and give Saint time to say a proper goodbye to his family. His mom tears up as she says goodbye and doesn't move from the door until after Saint is in the truck and we're out of the driveway heading home.

THE DRIVE HOME has been pleasant, all four hours. In between talking and singing, it's been nicer than not. I haven't felt uncomfortable once. My feet are on top of the dashboard and I'm reading on my Kindle. Saint is singing to whatever song is playing. It has an upbeat tempo and two male voices singing in Spanish. It sounds like a bop but I have no clue what it's about.

"Do you like this type of music more than other styles?" I ask, truly curious.

"Music is music. If it can make me feel something, I'll listen to it," he says. "This is my celebration playlist, that's why it's mostly happy music." His eyes wander to mine, smirking he asks, "What about you, princesa? Do you like anything other than Miley Cyrus?"

"Funny, you ass. I'm a rock girl but I listen to pretty much anything, even Taylor Swift," I add. "It took me a while but I even listen to country now."

His eyes grow wide. I knew that would catch him by surprise so I smile and say, "Yee haw." Before I can keep joking around, we pull up to my house. I know something is wrong by the way Saint's shoulders tense right away. I jerk my face toward the door and see that it's wide open. I never lock my house, but the door standing open like this is not normal, unless I somehow forgot to close it.

He parallel parks the truck and opens the door, but before getting out he orders, "Stay in the truck, Roe. I mean it." His voice is sharp, with an edge I've never heard before. There's no thinking on his part, he jumps out and walks in the house, flicking the lights on and walking in.

One minute.

I want to pull out my hair, and I might if he doesn't come out soon and tell me what the hell is going on.

Two minutes pass.

Fuck this shit, I'm going in.

I speed walk toward the house and step in to find Saint about to run into me. His hands come up to grab my shoulders, and he looks as spooked as I felt just seconds ago.

"Roe, can you listen for once in your life?" he groans, annoyed and almost angry but without raising his voice.

"This is my house and if I want to see what's going on, I can," I snap, crossing my arms over my chest. I understand he's being all protective and shit, but he needs to stop hovering and telling me what to do. I've been parenting myself for years; I don't need someone else to try to swoop in and save me.

"Roe, what if there was someone here? You could've put yourself at unnecessary risk."

"Just like you?" I snap. "You think because you're a man, you can just defend against everything and save everyone, don't you?"

"No, but I'm trained in self-defense. I can do a little more than just scare someone." He raises his hand, tucking a piece of my hair behind my ear. "Next time, please listen to me, okay?"

His fingertips graze the side of my face as he pulls back his hand, and a jolt of electricity sparks on my skin. One touch and I'm short-circuiting. I let out a breath and nod. "What's going on in here?"

"Nothing that I can see," he answers, turning his body and looking around. I should be focused on what's happening in my house but all I can see is his shirt fitted tightly around his arms as they flex naturally. I hate that I might be starting to love his protective and borderline overbearing presence. All I can smell is his fresh and salty scent—still can't figure out how he always smells like the beach.

I shake myself out of my stupor and look around. Everything seems normal, except there are a couple plants out of place. I walk around and touch them, remembering exactly where they go. I would never put my Jade so far away from the window, and I never move my snake plant from its precious spot by the door.

I notice my spatulas are out and my cups that usually live on my counter aren't there. I find them on the table. It's not a lot, but definitely enough for me to notice. I look at Saint and whatever he sees on my face alerts him, because he's quickly putting me behind him and walking backward into my room.

"There's nobody here," I say, and for someone so sure of herself, I sure as hell sound shaky. "But someone was," I add.

"What? Did they take something?"

"No," I say, plopping myself on the ground and lying flat with my arms and legs spread wide like a starfish. "They did move shit around though," I add, pointing out the things I noticed out of place.

"Maybe a family member?" he asks.

I laugh and say, "I don't have family, Saint. They are all dead and ghosts can't touch shit."

He looks taken aback by my statement, but somehow, he knows better than to ask more about it. He goes straight to the only other question that makes sense. "Then who?"

I sit up and notice his usually calm eyes are nowhere to be found. I find turmoil and concern instead, maybe even pity, but there's nothing I can do or say to fix this.

"I don't know. But whoever it was, they're gone. I'll get my gear and you can go. I'm sure I can get my bike and shit from you at another time if you don't have time to help." I get up and try to walk past him out of my room but he grabs my arm, stopping me from moving any more. That simple touch wakes every cell in my body and I can't help but be in attention to what he has to say.

"I'll get your stuff; you stay here."

I listen for once and stay put in my room. I change into comfy clothes–boxers that I use as shorts and a tank top. Then I take my pillows and my weighted blanket and walk to the guest room. I couldn't see anything out of place in my room but the feeling that someone might have been in there is too much for me to sleep in there.

"Roe?" Saint asks.

"In here," I shout, hoping he follows my voice because I'm already lying down and I don't want to get back up.

He walks in with his bag and mine, drops them to the floor, and spreads out a blanket on the ground.

"What are you doing?" I ask.

"I'm sleeping here until tomorrow when we can figure out what the hell happened. I was going to sleep on the couch, but it's white, and my mom would disown me if I slept on it. She would ask me if I showered with bleach; if I didn't, then I need to stay off of white couches," he adds.

He stands there looking like a damn snack that I want to devour whole while acting protective but not overbearing. That combination is deadly for me because I get the sudden urge to jump out of bed and climb him like a tree. He already told me several times that he won't lay his hands on me until I open my heart to him. What he doesn't know is that's impossible. It's impossible to let someone in your heart when you don't have one anymore. I was born with a heart, sure, but it was shattered beyond repair. Demolished and decayed, leaving a black empty hole instead.

I do offer him the one thing I can. Folding the blanket back, I pat the empty space on the bed. "You don't have to sleep on the floor, Saint. Come here."

"You sure about that, princesa?" he asks. When I nod, he sighs in agreement, stripping down to his boxers and walking toward me.

He covers us and lays the weighted blanket on top of me before settling down on his side of the bed and keeping to his own side. It's like he's drawn a line down the bed with the promises that he refuses to break. I can feel all the lines that I want to erase that he won't let me bend. His lines are set in stone to divide our lust. The same way that we are split in real life: him full of life and me nothing but empty inside.

Loco Contigo, J. Balvin

SANTIAGO

HOW CAN anyone sleep so peacefully after realizing someone was inside their house? Not me, but the little velcro girl by my side covered in blankets and pillows doesn't have a care in the world. Or at least it seems like it. I've said it once and I'll say it again, for someone who hates physical touch when she's awake, Roe sure as hell loves it when she's asleep. Her body comes to mine naturally. A magnetic force drawing her to me, even if she wants to fight it.

I see an incoming text from Marco which is weird. He usually doesn't text and definitely not in the middle of the night.

Marco: So are you staying over there?

Me: Over where?

Marco: Over at Roe's

Me: Yeah, I said not to wait up. I'll see you tomorrow or something.

The three little dots dance for quite some time but he never replies again. I turn off my recurrent alarm and shut the phone off, setting it on top of the nightstand.

I can only see her dark lashes and eyelids because the rest of her is hidden by the blankets. But it's enough to know that she's peacefully asleep. I know I should be sleeping too, instead of overthinking everything, so I close my eyes, eventually drifting to sleep.

"SAINT," I hear a voice saying. It sounds loud enough that I know it's real but soft enough that I know it must be coming from somewhere nearby. I open my eyes to find Roe standing beside me, wearing almost no clothing, her hair pulled back in a ponytail and her gorgeous blue eyes shining brighter than stars.

Tapping her foot with impatience, she takes a drink from her shaker before asking, "You wanna go for a run?"

I pick up my phone from the nightstand, turn it on and see it's 5:15am. Way too early to be up, especially after a racing weekend. I don't mind waking up early but that means I have to go to bed early too and we definitely did not.

"Roe, it's too early and my body's sore. Come lay back

down," I say, pulling her hand and trying to get her to come back to bed.

"I'm wide awake, Saint. I need to burn some energy or I will combust. Come on, let's go," she says, walking around to the door.

"No, come on. We both have the day off. Let's have an easy morning."

"I already let you sleep an extra hour," she says and lets out a sigh, "Come on, I'm going either way but you're always telling me not to go alone and shit."

I sit up, rub my eyes, and mumble a curse, but get up before she can leave without me. Her devilish smile lets me know that she got exactly what she wanted.

Walking outside, I can feel the immediate change in temperature. No matter how warm she keeps it, it's worse outside. We run for a while in silence, especially while we are setting a pace that's comfortable for both of us.

"Favorite drink?" I ask, adding more to the conversation we started this weekend and never finished.

"Water, seltzers, and hot cocoa," she replies.

"Hot cocoa?"

"Yes, the only hug I need. The one in a cup."

I shake my head and ask another one. "Favorite food?"

"Sushi, you?" she asks.

"My mom's cooking," I reply. It doesn't matter what it is; if my mom cooks it, it will be my favorite.

"Such a mama's boy," she teases.

"Y orgulloso de serlo."

"Does that mean proudly?"

"Yes, it does," I reply before asking, "Favorite place in the world?"

"A hammock in the woods," she says.

"Any woods?"

"Any woods." She slows down and I match her pace, getting closer to the turning point. We stop and she takes this opportunity to ask her first question, "Favorite song."

"How can you just pick one? I would imagine it's like asking you to pick your favorite book," I reply.

"That's fair. What about your favorite singer?"

"Also too hard to pick," I say. "It would depend on my mood and what I want to feel. Music is like a life enhancer. I play different music depending on what's going on and I feel everything intensely," I explain.

She stops running and turns to me, getting closer while she breathes through her mouth. Her breathing is slightly labored and it's doing things to me it shouldn't.

"What would be the soundtrack playing right now?" she asks, eyes attentive on mine and my body sparked with awareness at the way she's looking at me.

"In English or in Spanish?" I ask because this can go two different ways.

"Spanish, por favor," she says, catching me off guard.

"Loco Contigo, J Balvin," I say, grabbing her shoulders and stopping her from getting closer. I'm really close to losing all control and I don't want to, not here in the middle of nowhere.

"What's that song about?" she asks breathily, and now I know she's doing it on purpose because she gets closer.

"What does it make you feel, Saint?" she asks again as her hands slide up my chest and pause right under my neck. My breath catches and she smiles. *Coño.*

"What feeling is it enhancing for you?" She licks her lips. "Intensifying," she adds.

"Aurora," I hiss.

"Don't full-name me, Saintiago. Answer the question," she says with the sultriest tone I've ever heard.

I grab her hand and hold it, staring at her, calling her bluff and trying to think about literally anything but this gorgeous girl in front of me. Begging my dick to calm down so we can continue our run without crossing any lines.

"Come on, Saint, give in," she murmurs, rising on her tippy-toes and getting closer to my mouth. Hovering right there, not closing the distance, she's leaving it up to me.

I grab her chin with two fingers. Her full pink lips part and I can see the tip of her tongue. I bring my arm around her waist to help her balance, my hand touching her sweaty back and pulling her flush to me. Letting her feel every inch of me. She hisses and her lips are so close to mine, all I have to do is reach for her with my tongue and we would be touching.

"I feel a lot when I hear that song, Roe, but I feel even more when you're near me and let me see glimpses of who you are." I turn her face slightly and kiss her cheek, and whisper in her ear, "Let me show you how much there is to feel if you let me in." I kiss her earlobe and she shivers under my touch as I rake her hair back with my other hand. "I could make you feel much more than lust, princesa, if you just let me."

"I'm scared," she whispers.

"You're so brave, Roe." I kiss her temple, her cheek, and her jaw. "Being brave is being scared and doing it anyway. Let me carry you and your fears, princesa."

She grabs my shirt and pulls back slightly, allowing me to see her flushed face. Her eyes are slightly teary and full of concern.

"Can't you see, Saint? I'm dead inside. I don't want my

darkness to take over your light. I'm not afraid of feeling, because I can't feel anything." She drops my shirt and takes a couple of steps back. "I'm not scared of you; I'm scared *for* you." With that, she leaves me standing in the forest and runs back the same way we came. And I run as fast as I can to catch up to her until we make it all the way to her home.

Peer Pressure, James Bay Ft. Mia Michaels

ROE

A WEEK HAS PASSED since the whole "I don't want to taint your light" conversation. Saint is still not taking the hint that I'm broken beyond repair. I know that he's a fixer by nature and by trade. Getting to know more about his job, his life growing up with a sick sibling, and the way he feels like the world is being carried on his shoulders has taught him that he can carry it all and that it's his job to do it.

He's currently working on my Jeep now that the parts have come in, while I sit here and basically stare at him. I'm sitting on top of the tool cabinet, kicking my feet and drawing on my iPad.

"Wanna go to a birthday party with me tomorrow?" he asks, while tinkering with the Jeep.

"I can't. I have work. I have an appointment for a pretty

large tattoo for Jake tomorrow and then I'll be at Saddlers," I reply, showing him the owl I'm supposed to be tattooing on our friend tomorrow.

"How's Jake, by the way? But I think the party is at Saddlers, actually."

"Jake seems happier lately. Rumor on the street is that he has a girl living in his house but nobody really knows much," I say, hopping down from the tool cabinet and pretending I want to inspect what he's doing. He gives me a side-eye and nods toward the spot where I was sitting. I roll my eyes and lean in further. "Is it Nick's party?"

"Yeah, Jake actually told me I should go so I can meet the group of friends," he says, grabbing a towel, wiping his hands and walking toward a fridge on the side of the shop.

Baker Auto is our mom-and-pop auto shop and they do more than just fix things. I don't know how I would survive without Jake or his dad working on Lola. Jake's our town golden boy and high school coach, but he manages the shop in his free time around the school calendar. He's a nice guy and a good friend, but there was some drama with his high school ex a long, long time ago, and then some other drama with another ex, not too long ago, and sometimes I feel like he likes to keep to himself to avoid making it worse.

He brings me a bottle of water, opening his and taking a sip before adding, "I wasn't gonna go but I'm tired of only hanging out with two people in this town. I need to get out more."

"I would be tired of hanging out with two people too if one of them was your annoying roommate," I snap, swiping the pen over the screen.

"What's the deal with you two?" Saint asks.

"There's no deal. He's been acting like I have the plague or something."

"Interesting. Regardless," Saint says, "I wasn't even counting him in the two people. I meant the only two people I know are you and Jake."

"Am I not enough for you, Saint?" I ask, wiggling my brows.

"You are, princesa, but I need to make friends. I'm not really a loner," he adds.

"Shocking. You had me fooled."

"Just because I'm quiet doesn't mean I don't like people. I'm pretty sure you hate people and you're the opposite of quiet," he adds, and when I look at him with intent to kill, he chuckles. "Joking, joking."

He walks back to the Jeep, hands me the keys and says, "Start it for me, would you?"

I hop in, do as he says, and Lola turns on like a champ. I tap the steering wheel, laying my head on the cold leather, and let out a breath. "I've missed you, girl," I whisper, but clearly not low enough because Saint smirks at me.

"Are you done falling in love with the Jeep?"

"Bold of you to assume that I don't already love her," I tell him, putting my glasses on and putting it in drive. "Come on, Saint. Let's go for a ride."

"I'm not done with work," he replies, but it's not lost on me that he's walking around to the passenger seat.

"Live a little. Stop being so good all the time," I reply.

He climbs up on the front seat, filling the space with his ocean scent and my brain with doubts on whether I deserve to spend time with him, knowing how good he is and how fucked up I am.

APPARENTLY, calling him out on being good all the time was what he needed to let loose and break some rules. He called Jake and told him he finished early today and that he would be back tomorrow. He also called Marco and told him to pack the bikes and meet us at SMX's back trail for some evening riding. I hope Marco stops acting like a total weirdo so we can all actually have a good time. We get my bike and gear up. I'm ready to try a challenge with new riders. Again, I'm the only girl, but I'm ready to show them that I ride like them or better.

"What's taking you guys so long?" I ask, impatiently waiting while fully geared up so Allen doesn't have a coronary next to my bike. We have an hour of riding before we get kicked out since you're not allowed to ride after dark at SMX.

"What? Can't wait to see our tails while we leave you behind, Roe?" Marco asks and I swear I want to punch him straight in the face. He gives me weird vibes and I've never been able to pinpoint why. The fact that he's friends with Saint surprises me too because they're nothing alike. Even at Saddlers, he acts like he's above it all and we're all mere mortals next to him, especially the girl bartenders.

I catch Saint looking at me and he stops me with a slight shake of his head. The fact that this man knows that I was about to go crazy on his friend makes me want to shiver. *He knows you, Roe. You let him in.* His eyes darken under his visor and when he faces forward and nods toward the trail, I know what he wants me to do and it's what I should do too. Focus on what I came here for.

"Marco, watch it," Saint says but Marco waves him off, turning to talk to some of the other riders that joined.

We called Allen on the way here and asked him to hide sixteen flags for us to find. We are splitting into three teams and meeting back here in an hour. Whoever collects the most flags wins. I wish I knew all these people's names but my lack of interest in making friends betrays me. I know Joey, the guy from the bachelor party and the night I met Saint. Marco is here, unfortunately. Saint, and some other people. I think one of them might be Gus, but I could be wrong. All men but me. Bring it.

Marco catches Saint looking at me and frowns, scowling before saying, "Alright, let's do this." Allen also left a number written under a rock. We'll say numbers and whoever's closest gets to pick their teammate first.

We all pick our numbers, say them out loud, and wait for someone to lift the rock. Joey lifts the rock and reads off the number eight, which means Saint is picking first because his number was seven.

"I pick Roe," Saint says without hesitation.

"Are you sure, man?" Marco asks, side eyeing me before adding, "You're picking this girl first?"

Saint looks like he's going to ignore him but then he stands in front of him and growls, "What is your fucking issue? Her name is Roe, not this girl, show some respect."

Marco puts his hands up and says, "Easy, easy. It's your team either way, do whatever you want."

"Are we going to ride or are we in a macho match?" one of the guys asks.

Saint walks away toward his bike and says, "Let's go, Roe, we have a game to win."

"Wait, asshole, we're all leaving at the same time," Marco says, and we wait for everyone to pick teams and line up on our bikes.

Kickstarting these beasts is always a little impressive. You can hear the thump of the compression, like a loud bang as the ignition sparks, and see the sand fly off the back tire with the twist of the throttle. We stop, look at each other, and with Saint's nod, we all twist our throttles. The revving gets louder. My focus goes to the task at hand like in-race, even if we're just playing. Every second on the bike is like that for me, and with the second twist, my elbows go up and my head tucks down. With the final rev, we take off and head to the trails.

I take the lead since I know these trails better than Saint and after an immediate left, we find the first flag. I signal to it and stop, letting Saint run to grab it. He twists the fabric off the stick it was on, zip ties it to his bike and we continue.

Thirty minutes later and we've found six flags but we're running out of places to look for more. I take the back trail that leads to a smaller section, not known to a lot of riders because of how tricky it is to maneuver through the trees and branches, twisting and turning with the path until it opens up. I slide my ass off the seat to balance on my bike by standing on the pegs. I'm able to move swiftly with the bike this way, waltzing and following its lead while holding on strong to the handlebars. Saint follows close behind, keeping up with my tempo.

I have to lower my head in certain sections to avoid branches, but eventually we make out into the clearing I was looking for. Big pine trees mark the way to an opening at the top of a small hill. From the top, you can see the St. Mary's River and a small area by the riverbank. The thick bushes surrounding the ending of the trail before the river could be a great place to hide more flags, so I follow the trail all the way down.

I stop my bike on the riverbank, turn it off, and put my foot down, holding the weight of the bike while looking around. I sip water from my Camelback and take my helmet off, hanging it from the handlebars. Saint follows suit and just stands there, straddling his bike and taking it all in. His eyes are closed, his dust-covered eyelashes kissing the top of his cheeks and the soft breeze blowing through his hair. It's a picture-perfect moment.

He catches me staring, his eyes fixed on mine but he doesn't utter a word. Instead, he lifts his hand and motions for me to come to him. I get off my bike, pressing the kickstand down, and walk to him. I stand next to him, my elbow on his handlebars and my eyes on him. *I'm not backing out, Saint.*

"You like the view?" I ask, with a smirk on my face.

"I always do, you know that," he nudges me and opens his hand. When I place mine in his, he pulls me closer to him. The space between us is suddenly gone and the breeze ceases to exist, leaving both of us desperate for air.

"If you take a picture, it'll last longer," I add to try to diffuse the tension and lower the desire that is clearly here.

"I don't need a picture, princesa." He tucks a piece of my hair behind my ear and keeps his hand on my cheek. "I already think about you all the damn time; you're completely imprinted on my skin, like one of these tattoos your hands make magic with. Then you have to go and be an incredible rider too, which just adds to the whole package. Yeah, Roe, I don't need a picture." His finger traces my jaw and stops under my lip.

I catch my breath after his words leave me speechless. My lips part slightly and when his eyes look at my lips, I whisper, "Saint."

"You're committed to memory and I'm done fighting this."

With those words, he pulls me to him and his lips crash into mine. One hand is on my neck and the other on my lower back, sparking a fire within me that only his touch can ignite. This kiss is not careful but it's not rushed either. It has intention and purpose. With every nip and swipe of his tongue, he lets me know how much he's been wanting this. A small moan escapes my lips and he swallows it, deepening the kiss.

My hands roam his torso, thinking to myself how lucky I am he didn't wear his chest protector so I can touch his body freely, but the damn bike is in the way. I push him back so he sits on the tail of the bike, while I swing my leg over and straddle it. I bring my gaze to his chest, going up and down rapidly as I touch his stomach freely. Now that there's nothing between us, my hands roam and explore, reaching up to his chest. He hisses and brings his hands to my face, holding me tightly and breaking the kiss. His forehead touches mine, eyes closed, and he brushes his nose against mine.

"Roe," he breathes, my name a whisper on his lips.

"I thought you were done fighting this," I say, pulling him closer by his jersey and biting his neck. "Are you going to let me corrupt you a little, *Saint?*" I add, while I wrap my legs around his hips. He has no choice but to scoot forward, keeping me flushed to him.

He closes his eyes and whispers in my ear, "Be careful what you wish for, Roe."

At those words, I lick his neck just above his collarbone. You would think his skin would be rough from the sand on the trail but it's perfectly smooth and salty from sweat. My insides tingle at the taste, making me go for it harder. I bite and suck at his skin. If he's not going to break on his own accord, I will try my hardest to make it happen with my tongue.

He brings my face up, keeping his fingers under my

chin. "You're playing with fire, princesa," he hisses, his eyes roaming my face.

I can see his control about to snap and because I'm no fucking angel, I say, "I don't mind getting burned."

His mouth crashes to mine again. My words did their job; his control is gone and I'm finally getting the real Saint. His tongue invades my mouth, swiping and teasing my own. His hands that were once gentle are firm against my hips, pulling me so close his hard dick is pressing against me. It's giving me the most delicious friction, even over our gear.

With each taste, lick, and swipe of his tongue, my body becomes more and more alive. Reminding me of everything he did to my body on the tattoo chair, in the tent, and back to our first kiss at the bar. I've tried to fight this pull. I've tried to fight this lust and the need to be with him. To have his hands on me and his lips on mine. I've never needed anything or anyone in my life, but my body is craving Saint's. Everything I've imagined when I'm alone trying to find release has to deal with him now, and even then, I can't make it. He's taking over my senses; as if without him, I don't know what pleasure is anymore.

The way his mouth moves against mine, and how his hands touch my body has me spiraling out of control. He's cupping my breasts, pinching my sensitive skin, and if he keeps this up, I will come undone by this moment alone.

"You like to play with fire, princesa? You want to see what your beautiful body can do to me? Then show me." He unbuckles my pants as he pushes me down onto the handlebars. "Better yet, watch what I can do to you."

He traces the line of my panties with his thumb. I place my feet on either side of him, lifting as much as the position will let me, and he gets to work. He removes each boot and the pants, Leaving me in nothing but my jersey, full of desire.

"Open up for me, princesa," he says and at his command, I drop my knees open, allowing him to see all of me. He's not touching me with his hands but the way his eyes darken ignites more of me than anybody ever could with a single touch. He traces his index finger over my slit, opening me more to him. I twist my hips in a circle, trying to get more contact.

"Now, now, now, muñeca, let's not be impatient."

I drop my head back and close my eyes as he slides his finger lower, closer to my entrance. I bring my hands up, under my jersey and cup my breasts.

"Si, princesa, tocate así, pero mirame," he says, and I don't really understand what it means until he explains, "Eyes on me, Roe. Touch yourself just like that but your eyes stay on me."

Lost-in-the-moment Santiago might be my favorite, so I obey and train my eyes on him. His finger circles my entrance, and I know I must be dripping because he meets no resistance pushing in and driving me wild.

His touch is deliberate; he's giving me just enough to writhe beneath him, but not enough to let me come. I feel shivers down my spine and the hunger that has been fighting its way out is here, ready to be fed.

He adds another finger and I lift my hips to meet him. He uses his other hand to hold me on the bike, his rough palm pressing against the tender skin under my belly button. He removes his fingers and brings them up to his mouth, licking them clean.

"Fuck, Roe. For someone who's so feisty all the time, you sure as hell taste sweet." I'm sure my eyes darken by the sigh he makes. He smirks before asking, "What? You don't believe me?"

"I call bullshit," I say, but instead of sounding sure, my voice comes out breathy. Desperate.

"No, princesa, I'm the one calling bullshit." He brings his fingers back to my entrance, pushing inside in one quick motion and twirling his fingers before pulling them back out. He brings them close to his nose and smells them, closing his eyes and humming. This time he doesn't clean his fingers but instead hovers them close to my mouth and says, "Taste how sweet you are. Suck, Roe, like the good fucking girl you are."

I part my lips and let him slide his fingers in. I swirl my tongue around them, never dropping his eyes. Because if he wants to play with fire, then welcome to hell, my Saint.

"Where the fuck did you come from?" he asks, his breath catching the minute my tongue touched his fingertips.

"Your worst nightmare," I reply, unbuckling his pants and tugging at them, trying to pull them down.

He removes my hands from his pants and hisses. "I don't have a condom, Roe."

"I don't care, Saint. I'm on the pill and I've never fucked without a condom. However, I'm close to fucking myself if you don't fuck me right now. Condom or not." He stops completely and just breathes in my words.

He closes his eyes and shakes his head saying, "Roe, if I take you bare, all bets are off. You won't be able to push me away anymore because you will be mine."

"I'm nobody's possession, Saint," I snap back, crossing my arms like I'm not half naked in the middle of the damn trail in front of this man.

"But that's where you're wrong, princesa. You see, if you

were mine, not only would I be making you come right here, I would have you screaming my name every damn day until the day you die. I would make sure there wasn't a doubt in that pretty little head of yours how incredible you are and how fucking desirable you are. Not just your body but you, Roe, you," he says, placing his hands on my lap. "It's not possession, it's a claim. Let me worship you, Roe. Let me make you mine, but even more, let me be yours."

There's so much I want to say right now, but I'm lost between lust and this whispered confession. I don't have any restraint. I don't have any control. My body wants him but I think deep down my soul is longing for him. My heart is finding solace in this moment, in the man, and I'm not sure how to feel about it.

I guess I'm not dead inside after all.

PLAY WITH FIRE, Sam Tinnesz

SANTIAGO

"WHAT'S it going to be, Roe?" I ask her. After what feels like an eternity, she sits up and wraps her legs around my waist.

"I don't care what you say as long as you fuck me, Saint," she replies.

My dick is right at her entrance and coño, she's gonna kill me but I won't back down. "Say it, Roe; say you're mine."

She's fighting it. I can see it on her face. Her lips are closed tight and she looks away from me for the first time since I told her to keep her eyes on me. It's taking every ounce of power I have not to drive into her right now but I won't do it. I need to hear her say it.

"Say it, Roe."

"You stubborn man, I'm yours, okay? Is that what you want to hear?"

Yes, Roe, it is.

I take those four letters and show her exactly how much I mean them. *Mine.* I drive into her hard, her pussy clenching around my cock immediately and I groan. *Esta mujer me va a llevar a la locura*[1].

I use one hand to balance us on top of the bike, while the other one wraps around her back and pulls her flush against me. I slowly trace down her skin, causing goosebumps to form right under my fingertips. Her hands are around my neck, holding onto me and digging her nails into my skin. Her breathy moans next to my ear are driving me to show her exactly how much I want her. How much I need her.

My hand dips to her ass, lifting it and angling her better so I can hit that spot that makes her moan loudly against my ear.

"Hands above your head, princesa." She obeys my command and places both hands on the handlebar. "Hold on to the handle bar and don't let go. No matter what happens." She nods and when I lean over her, hitting a sensitive spot inside of her, I know I have her right where I want her.

"Yes, Saint, I think that's the…" she says but her moans stop her words and I know she's about to come.

"No, not thinking, just feeling. Feel how hard I am for you."

I drive into her harder, deeper, gripping her ass and digging my face into her neck. I can feel how close she is,

---

1. Llevar a la locura: Drive me crazy.

and to be honest, so am I but if she doesn't go, I won't either.

"Feel how good you fit. Feel how perfect you are for me."

She bites my ear and whispers, "Make me come, Saint, show me I'm yours." She's using my own words against me and damn it if I wasn't already gone for her, this might have done it. My fucking undoing.

I bring my hand to her clit, and press my palm against it, making her detonate around me while screaming my name. Her screams and her clenching pussy against my cock make me explode, too.

"Yes, fill me up," she begs, and could she *be* more perfect for me?

"Every ounce of my cum is yours, princesa," I growl as I drive in again and again until she's limp in my arms, draped over me. I'm spent, completely taken by the girl who has no idea the hold she has on me.

"THERE THEY ARE," Marco snarls when we make it back to the trailhead. All four of them are there waiting and some of the bikes are back on the trailers. *I guess we took longer than we thought.*

"We have six flags," Roe announces with pride, but Marco smiles at her and shows off four flags in each hand. They got us by two flags.

"It's fine, Roe, we didn't even get one," Joey says, smiling and waving us away when we all laugh at him.

We pack up and load the bikes and we're about to leave when Roe stops me right behind her Jeep.

"Hey, you can ride with your friend, I got it. Thanks for fixing Lola, I'll stop by to pay at some point tomorrow."

"Are you sure?" I ask, disappointed that I don't get to spend more time with her.

"Yes, see you tomorrow for the party?" she asks, walking backward toward the driver's side and I nod, standing there frozen in place.

"Good luck next time," Marco shouts from his truck and Roe shuts the door of the Jeep and speeds out of here, flipping Marco off.

We ride back into town in silence. When we cross the railroad tracks to Baker Oaks' town limits, Marco breaks the quiet by asking, "What's the deal with you and Roe?"

"No deal, we're just friends," I reply.

"But you want to be more?" he asks and I don't like his tone or the questioning. He's never been interested in who I see before.

"Yeah, I do. I'm not gonna lie," I reply. "What's the deal with you and her? You seem to be bothered by everything she does."

"Other than the fact that people like her are ruining the sport? This is a man's sport and we let them in on their own class so we could be inclusive, but now they want in with us too? Pathetic. And for the record, she doesn't do 'friends,' man. She's a man-eater and a loner, other than the people who work for her and maybe a couple of other people. I don't think I've ever seen her out with the same person more than once."

My hands are in fists over my thighs, and I can barely contain my rage. "Watch how you speak about her, Marco. I've told you this three times now. We might be just friends but she deserves respect, even when she's not around. Also, women in general don't need men talking like that about them. Grow up a little."

"Alright, alright, calm down," he snaps, lifting his hand off the steering wheel. "I'm just saying, don't get too attached to her."

My phone pings with an incoming text that has her name on it. Marco looks down and after seeing it snarks, "Speak of the devil."

> Roe: Saint, can you stop by my place?

> Me: Sure, what's up?

> Roe: I think someone was here again.

> Me: Get back in the Jeep and lock the doors, I'll be there soon.

> Roe: I don't like this at all.

> Me: Get in the damn Jeep, Aurora. I mean it.

"Drop me off at her house, now," I all but shout at him, and he knows better than to ask any questions.

I thank God and all the saints that this town is as small as it is. I It doesn't take long to make it to her house. I also say another prayer, thanking them for this girl listening to me for the first time in her life, when I see her sitting in the Jeep.

"Thanks, man, don't wait up," I tell Marco before he drives away. I walk over to Roe and she's physically shaking. Instead of checking out her house like I should, I open her door and pull her to me. She hugs me tightly, resting her head on my chest.

"I know I'm not crazy, Saint. It's not a lot but I know someone has been there," she says.

"What did they do?"

"My bed is made and I didn't do that this morning," she adds. Trying to pull away from me but I don't let her, I hold her tightly and show her that I meant it when I said that I was hers and that she was mine. Mine to comfort, mine to protect. She might be used to being alone but now she won't have to be.

"Okay, stay in the Jeep, I'll be back," I say and walk into her house.

I don't find anything out of place but it feels eerie; too tidy for the chaos that is usually in this house. I wouldn't call it messy, just chaotic. Roe usually forgets to put things back where they go. Sometimes I'm here for our running sessions and I'll find a fork on the floor. When I ask about it, she just says she sat on the floor to eat and must have forgotten to pick it up. Or finding towels on every surface because she walks out of the shower and just leaves it out. I call it the Roe trail, leaving marks wherever she goes, including my heart.

"Hey," I whisper to her when I get back out. She looks calmer but still not her usual self.

"Am I crazy? Am I making it all up?" she asks. Her voice is shaking and it breaks my heart in two to hear her like this. My girl, usually so confident and strong, but showing me vulnerability right now.

"No, princesa," I reply, bringing my hand to her face and touching it gently. "You're not. It looks normal but also is missing your touch. It's too tidy, not very 'Roe-esque'. Someone has been there."

She closes her eyes and cusses softly so I can't hear it. "Hey, hey, hey, it's okay. Tranquila. Let's call the police and go from there," I say, trying to be supportive but also trying to get to the end of this.

"And say what? Hi, my bed was made for me today," she states, definitely annoyed.

"Well, you have to do something about it, and just FYI, we're going to my place."

She pulls her arm from my hold and looks at me like I just killed a kitten. "I'm not going to your place. There's no reason for me to leave."

"Roe, someone has been coming to your house when you're not here. You won't lock the damn door and you won't go to the cops. Do you have a death wish?" I ask, frustrated as fuck but not wanting to piss her off more. The fact that I can be here for and protect her but she won't let me is more upsetting than she probably knows.

"Everyone dies either way, it's just a matter of time. If it's in the plans for me to die today, there's nothing we can do. You haven't watched Final Destination and it shows."

"This is your fucking life, Roe, not a movie," I all but scream at her and she flinches for a second before she scrunches her eyebrows at me.

"Do *not* yell at me," she says, pausing between each word. She might be tiny, but she's scary as hell when she talks like that. "I'm staying in my house and you can't make me do anything else." She slams her Jeep door and stomps past me into her house, and once again, I chase her.

"Roe!" I shout, stepping in after her and following her back to her room.

Walking into her room, I'm caught off guard by the view. She's already half undressed. I stop dead in my tracks, taken aback by her beauty. The windows are open and the natural light gives her a soft glow. She looks like she's straight out of my dreams. She's standing there in dark silky panties and a gray sports bra. Her straight blonde hair is falling down her back effortlessly. She catches me staring and smiles at me, hugging herself and grabbing the edges of her sports bra, pulling it up above her head and throwing it on the ground. Her perfect tits bouncing and her smile growing wider. *Fuck me.* She came to war and she's not fighting fair.

"Aurora," I hiss, my dick hard and straining in my pants. Twice today this girl has gotten me on the edge without even touching me.

"You know, *Santiago*, you only use my full name when you mean business. What business do you mean right now? Is that a plea or a curse? Is that a claim or a warning?" She pulls her panties down, dropping them on the floor and daintily steps out. She may be the one naked but she has stripped me bare. Bare of every wall that I carefully crafted for years. I met her with defenses that have protected me and my heart, and with every passing second we spend together, she has knocked them down.

Standing in front of her I say, "I already claimed you, princesa, and I think you might be the biggest curse. You came without warning and crashed into me, so what does that leave me with?" I bring my hand up to her face and tuck her hair behind her ear.

"A plea," she whispers, breathy and untamed.

"A plea for what? A plea for you to have mercy on my soul, or a plea to ask you to help me keep you safe? If you don't want to leave, fine, then I'm staying here. If you don't want to lock the door, then let me take care of that. If that's the plea, then I'm pleading too."

"Fine," she snaps and reaches for my face, searing my mouth with a scorching kiss, melting in my arms and taking my heart with her. I pull her to me by her hips, pressing my fingertips into her ass

Her hands grab my neck and I dip low, biting her neck and squeezing her ass at the same time. I bring my mouth to the shell of her ear and whisper, "You won't distract me from the trouble at hand, princesa, but if you want to play, let's fucking play."

I lift her up and she wraps her legs around my hips, lowering her arms to tug off my shirt as I walk us to her bathroom. I don't stop after that; kissing her deeply and getting lost in her.

The best part?

She absolutely lets me.

THIRTY

SWEET BUT PSYCHO

Sweet but Psycho, Ava Max

ROE

FOUR TIMES. That's how many times Saint made me cum in the shower. On his fingers, on his face, and twice before he was the one shattering alongside me. We had the whole protection conversation and he wanted to make sure I was sure we could have sex without condoms. After telling him three times I was sure and I was on the pill, he told me he could get tested next week, even though that was the first time he was intimate with someone without protection. He used the word 'intimate' and I almost wanted to fuck him again because why does he have to be the sweetest man in the world? Infuriating, yes, but sweet.

I did tell him that I was his or whatever, but I hope he knows I meant physically. While I'm seeing him, I am physically his, but that's all I can give him. That's all I have to give in general. Eventually, he talked me into letting him stay here until we could figure out some options like getting cameras and hopefully catching whoever was pranking me. Believe it or not, I *do* believe this is a prank. Nobody in their right mind would go out of their way to do the dishes or make my bed.

I took Saint home to get clothes last night. And this morning, I dropped him off at Baker Auto. Now I'm waiting for Jake to show up for his tattoo. I may not have a lot of friends but Jake is one of the few. We met a few years ago when I found myself arguing with the town committee over permits for the bar. They didn't want to approve it and were making me jump through a million hoops to get my permits —but Jake spoke up on my behalf. And since he's the town's golden boy who does no wrong, they approve everything. I told him his first drink at the bar was on me and the rest is history.

He also included me in his group of friends, even added me to the group chat. But I left as quickly as I could because the girls were talking shit about other people and I don't vibe with that. I may not be everyone's cup of tea but I'm not talking about someone behind their back, especially if I know they're supposed to be friends.

Cara's ex, Cole, is also in that group and I actually hate him. I hate him as much as someone can hate another person. In fact, I wish he was the one pranking me so I would have an excuse to punch him. He strings her along every summer until she goes back to Chicago and then breaks up with her and acts like she never existed. They're supposed to be high school sweethearts but I think that's only in Cara's head, and I don't know how to help her see it. She deserves so much more than being someone's afterthought. She deserves the world.

I hear the melody of my wind chimes, signaling that someone's here.

"Took you long enough," I say without looking up. But when I do, I see Jake walking in with a beautiful girl. They are both smiling, and if I wasn't distracted by the fact that Jake is holding someone's hand, I would say something about the fact that he's glowing. His eyes are bright as he introduces Allie to me, and it takes everything in me not to tackle her into the ground with a hug and thank you. He deserves to be happy and if this small interaction is any indication, she definitely makes him happy.

"Hi, nice to meet you," she says, giving me her hand.

"Likewise! You can have a seat over there," I say, pointing at the couch and the mini fridge next to it. "Feel free to grab drinks and snacks from the fridge. There's wine too if you want to opt for that, the glasses are right on top." That area of the shop is one of my favorites. Hanging plants and glasses stored upside down above a wine cooler. There's a box on top that says coffee and it has different things to make the best coffee you can think of and an espresso machine. It's right next to the mustard yellow couch that adds a burst of color by the grass wall.

Jake takes a seat on the tattoo chair and offers me his arm. Like I need to look at it again. We've been working on this owl tattoo for long enough that it's embedded in my mind. "You good?" I ask him.

He looks Allie's way and whispers, "I'm more than good." He smiles softly, and shit, if that doesn't make me a tad emotional.

"So, Allie, how do you know this knucklehead?" I ask, while I put my black latex gloves on. I wipe the area clean with an alcohol pad and shave the part of the arm where the tattoo is going. I clean it again with water and green soap, and once the skin is smooth, I inspect the site. I'm adding more details and colors to an outline of an owl tattoo we've spent a couple sessions on already. I start pouring the inks into their caps and unwrap the fresh needle I need, getting ready to put it into the gun while Allie talks.

"We went to high school together, kind of," she replies while sipping on some peach wine. One of the locals owns the winery that makes that one, and although I don't drink wine, I'm supporting my local people by getting some. It's always a hit with visitors.

"I went to Baker High my senior year and we knew each other then," she continues, pausing while she looks at Jake. "I came back for work and, as fate would have it, we met again."

Jake is also looking at her from the tattoo chair and I can tell by this whole interaction that they are *so* in love with each other.

"Mmm, so high school sweethearts rekindling their love? How 'second chance romance' of you," I say and we both laugh.

Jake looks confused, casting his eyes between the two of us and sarcastically adding, "You two already have a secret language… great."

We continue laughing and eventually I add, "It's a book thing, and judging by her reaction, she reads the same type of books I do. I like this one, keep her."

Jake replies to that without taking his eyes off Allie, "I'm trying Roe, I'm trying."

Allie furrows her brows and tilts her head to the side with a smirk, saying, "You know, the guy from earlier, what was his name? Oh yes, Santiago, he said the same thing."

I almost fall off my chair when she says that but I try to ignore it and see if they will stop talking about it.

Jake turns his head to face me and smirks while adding, "Yeah Roe, Thiago said the same thing. You two must be connected on a deeper level." Jake is not done with that sentence when my immediate reaction is to smack him on the arm with the disinfecting pad I was using to clean the site. I even forgot everyone else calls him Thiago because I've been calling him Saint since I met him.

I'm ready to start the tattoo but I see Allie grabbing her Kindle so I ask, "Do you mind music, Allie?" When she shakes her head, I start my work playlist and Sweet but Psycho by Ava Max begins to play through the speakers. I get to work. The sharp buzzing sound hums under the music and Jake closes his eyes and lays back on the chair. In no time, I'm lost in the art that I love creating, tuning everything else out including the noise about what Saint might mean to me and, even more, what I might mean to him.

About an hour later the owl is done. It looks perfect. The colors carry shade, contrast, and highlights, making it look almost three-dimensional. I love playing around with techniques and strokes. It's a creative outlet more than it is a job and I wouldn't trade it for the world.

Jake pays for the tattoo and gives me a side hug; he knows I hate them but he still does it every time. I punch him on the not-tattooed arm and ask him if I will see him at the party tonight. He shrugs, walking back to his gorgeous girl. Allie walks toward me to say goodbye and the sudden urge to hug her kicks in, so I do. It catches all of us by surprise, but especially Jake.

"Come by later, first drink is on me," I say as I wave goodbye.

"See you later, Roe," he says, draping an arm over Allie's shoulder and leaving the shop.

THE BAR IS CROWDED TODAY, like every Saturday. The line dance lessons are going. People are twirling and crashing into each other. The floor is sticky from spilled drinks after bumping into one another while dancing and laughing. This place brings me so much peace, purely because so many people come here to share their happiness. Some find peace in a beer, some on the dance floor, and some by the pool tables. I say peace because I can't feel joy again and if happiness isn't in the cards anymore, peace and contentment will do.

Nick's party is in the VIP lounge and everyone's there, including Jake and Allie. The animosity that group of girls is showing her definitely makes me feel like there's something going on there. I wouldn't be surprised if Allie is his high school ex that he never got over, considering who's in that group. But I'm so proud of Jake, who pulled her out of that situation and is walking her back my way.

They grab a couple stools, and Allie smiles at me as she waves.

"Long time no see, lovebirds. What can I get you?" I ask.

"The usual for me," Jake replies.

"Mm, surprise me," she says and it's music to my ears. My heart races every time someone lets me pick their drinks, just like when I'm riding. I rub my hands, smile at her and turn around to get her a flight.

Other than people-watching and owning a fun escape for locals and visitors, using my creativity to figure out people's favorite drinks is one of my favorite things about owning this bar. Saint said that music pops into his head in situations, like a live soundtrack. For me, it's things that will please people through art. Mixing drinks or matching a certain type of drink to someone's personality is art.

I can tell she liked that peach moscato today so I'm gonna go with fruity drinks, but I want to see if there's a wild side in there too. Tequila with lime juice, guava beer, a negroni, Aperol spritz, a martini, and an Angry Orchard are on her flight and I can't wait to see what she thinks of these.

Her eyes go wide when I hand her the flight. I smile before telling her, "My brain is too chaotic to pick just one drink. I choose drinks from a customer's vibes and my first timers get a flight so I can get an idea of what they like. After this, I'll never get your drink wrong."

"She's right," Jake says, sipping on his Old Fashioned.

"You are *insane*," Allie says, rolling her eyes at both of us.

"Maybe, but it works. Go ahead," I add, propping my elbows on top of the counter and staring at her while she sips on her drinks.

Her face reacts differently to each drink but the ones that are heavier on the sweet side with fruit added are her favorites. I smile before saying, "I knew you were a fruit girly." I grab the tray from her and return with a full glass of the guava beer she liked. Jake takes a sip too and they have a whole interaction that seems too intimate for me to witness, so I get busy cleaning and getting drinks for other customers. As I'm working, I see Saint sitting on the same stool he sat at the first time I met him and I smile at him. *I fucking smile*. I guess I tolerate him fine after all.

Shivers by Ed Sheeran starts playing in the background and this is the one song that I always want to dance to. I see Allie walking toward the exit but I feel in my soul that she likes to dance, so I run from behind the bar and pull her with me to the dance floor.

There's line dancing every Saturday here so we follow

the instructor, or at least I do, because Allie is dancing like she made the choreography for this dance herself. I'm not that coordinated so I just stick to the routine that I've learned from joining every time they play it. I run into another one of the regulars and we partner up, but at some point, we all stop and we just watch Allie kill it on the dance floor.

The song ends and we all clap for her. I run to her and hug her before saying, "Girl, that was impressive. I didn't know you could dance like that."

"I love dancing, Roe. The more we hang out, you'll see it's practically second nature to me." She looks at Jake and smiles at him, and that is my cue to go.

"Well, come back any time and we can dance some more," I say, giving her another hug before walking toward the bar.

I look for Saint and I find his intense eyes watching me while some girl sits next to him, talking and twirling her hair while she smiles like she wants to eat Saint for dessert. I suddenly want to kill someone because apparently the whole *I'm his* conversation decides to come to mind now.

THIRTY-ONE
BULLSHIT AND FIGHTING THIS

Love Lies, Khalid Ft. Normani

SAINT

"WHEN DID YOU MOVE TO BAKER?" the girl who has been babbling for the past five minutes next to me asks. How someone can be so clueless is beyond me. There's nothing about my demeanor that should be an indicator to her that I'm interested. If anything, my eyes haven't left Roe, dancing in the middle of the dance floor, having the time of her life.

She's smiling big and moving around, taking all the space she deserves. I can practically hear her laughter too; it's probably in my head because it would be impossible to hear her over the music. But my soul hums with the way she's smiling, like it's recognizing her laugh the same way my brain does with music. I get the instant urge to find out all the ways I can be the one to make her smile that way. To make her laugh that way. I want to be the reason for the joy she's showing right now and I would do whatever it takes to make it happen. As soon as I get rid of this person.

"What was that?" I ask.

"I said," she says louder and slower, like the reason I didn't answer the first time was because of the music drowning out her voice and not because I'm not interested in even a polite conversation with this woman. "How long have you been in Baker Oaks?"

"Not long," I say politely but short, sipping on my whiskey and trying to avoid more conversation. I notice the song stopped so I look for the beautiful girl that has a hold on my heart. No matter how much I want to deny it, I'm falling for Roe. I'm falling fast and hard, and I'm scared of what might happen if I let her know.

Roe's walking toward me with purpose. Her brows furrowed and her arms crossed. Her hair is in that high ponytail she loves that shows off her neckline. Her. Fucking. Neckline. It's sexy as hell, especially the way she holds her head up high and carries herself with confidence, paired with the low-cut tank top and the ready-to-bite neck have me rock hard just by looking at her. Thoughts of wrapping her hair around my fist while she sucks my dick invade me and my body is on high alert just thinking about it.

I think she will make it to me but instead, she goes around the bar and to the back, coming out a minute later with a seltzer in her hand and a mischievous smile. *Coño. Shit.*

"Hi, can I get you guys anything?" she asks nonchalantly, as if she's not annoyed by this girl like I am.

"I'll have whatever Handsome here is having. I never got your name," the girl next to me says.

"You're right, I never gave it to you," I say. I sound rude

as fuck but I don't know how else to get this girl to get the memo.

"Ooooh, mysterious. I don't need to know your name, Handsome," she says, touching my shoulder with a finger and dragging it to my elbow.

I pull my arm back and stand up. She does the same and says, "I just need to know what your plans are to get out of here and if you're taking me with you." She winks and I hear Roe act like she's gagging, so I scoff.

"Oh, I do have plans tonight, miss," I say, training my eyes to Roe, who is currently standing there looking like she's ready to kill little Miss Forward here. "I have plans with the most beautiful girl I've ever seen. So, if you'll excuse me, I've wasted enough time tonight not being near her."

I walk past her and around the bar, grabbing Roe's hand and pulling her to my chest. "Is this okay with you, princesa? Your eyes and your body are telling me that you want to claim me, right here, right now." I tangle my fingers with hers while my other hand caresses her arm, all the way to her neck, touching her chin. "But I need you to say it, Roe. You know I'm yours, but are you ready to let everyone know? Because I sure as hell am and I'm hoping you are, too."

She closes her eyes delicately, her long dark lashes brushing against her cherry pink cheeks and she nods, tilting her head toward my hand. "Why are you determined to make me lie to you?" she says like an assassin, stabbing my heart and killing every hope.

"Why are you fighting this, princesa? Why are you fighting us?"

"There's no fighting something that isn't real," she replies, and I hope she doesn't mean that. I hope that's just the fear talking, because I know deep down, she feels this too.

I bring a hand to her chest. "Bullshit. This, right here —" I say, pointing at her chest "—tells me otherwise. The way your heart's racing right now is calling your bluff." I look at her intensely so she knows that I'm not pulling back, that this time I'm not letting her push me away. "I bet it started racing the minute you saw her talking to me. Did you think I sought her out? Were you hoping to use that as another excuse? Another barrier between us?"

Her eyes darken and her cheeks grow brighter. I can see every emotion in those ocean blue eyes. Right now, they're telling me she's mad and I'll take it, because any emotion is better than numbness. She could mask them for annoyance or indifference but instead she's letting me see the fury irradiating from her. The anger rising from her pores. The confusion swimming between her eyes.

"You know I'm right. Don't lie to me; but most importantly, don't lie to yourself. Let me kiss you in front of everyone here, let everyone see that you belong to me." I want to kiss her senseless and maybe even spank her for not letting me kiss her sooner in public, but I'm waiting for her consent. As much as I know her heart, or hope to, she has to be the one to say yes. I can want us enough for the two of us but she still has to wave a white flag.

"Why are you so impossible?" she asks, grabbing my neck with her hands and pulling me down to her. "You're giving me the matches with that request, Saint."

"I already told you -- maybe I like playing with fire."

"You can kiss me, *Santiago*. Show me how much you want me," she says, licking her lips and closing her eyes. But before she can kiss me, she whispers, "Show them you mean it when you said I'm yours."

I don't hesitate this time and pull her to me, kissing her just the way I've wanted. Her lips caress mine; her hands grab my neck and her head tilts to give me better access to her tongue. My tongue swipes against hers eagerly but without taking it to the point of no return. I've never liked kissing the way I like kissing Roe. I've never thought about stripping someone naked just after one kiss until Roe. Nobody has driven me insane more than her and I think I fucking love it.

I think I love her.

Roe breaks the kiss, jolting back at the same time the other bartender, whose name I always forget, finishes saying something about PDA.

"You're fired," Roe yells, rolling her eyes just as the girl hits her ass with the bar towel.

"Like you could ever survive without me," she snarks, folding the towel and shoving it into her back pocket. "I'm glad you finally found someone to deal with your crazy ass, but keep the PDA away from the bar. We don't need a citation for contamination due to the two of you exchanging saliva here."

I laugh and Roe just shrugs, telling me to go back to the other side of the bar, where I wait until Roe's ready to go to her house and she takes me with her.

"BUENOS DIAS, MIJO," *Good morning son,* my mom says on the other line. Like every Sunday, I wake up to a call from her so we can catch up. She talks to her children one-on-one on a specific day of the week since Ana died. She says that her only regret in life was putting other things first. The house, cooking, working, and all other adult responsibilities that she had that stopped her from spending more time with us. No matter how many times we try to let her know that she's incredible and that she *did* spend quality time with us, she never believes it. She says that time is the only thing that you don't get back, so she wants to spend it showing the people she loves that she truly loves them.

"Bendición mamá," *Blessings mom.*

"¿Cómo te amanece?" *How's your morning?*

"Bien, bien. Salí a celebrar a un amigo anoche y estoy cansado pero bien. ¿Y tu? ¿Tienes planes hoy?" *Good, good. I went out last night to celebrate a friend so I'm tired. What about you? Do you have any plans today?*

"Vamos a la iglesia pero tu papá tiene que trabajar así que solo tus hermanas y yo vamos a ir. Dani tiene unos dibujos en la escuela y creo que vamos a pasar a verlos. Mi pequeña artista. Ustedes todos me enorgullecen tanto, Santiaguito." *We're going to church but your dad isn't coming, he has to work. Dani also has an art showcase at school that we might stop by to see. She's my little artist. I'm proud of all of you, Santiaguito.*

She stops and takes a deep breath and I can hear the sadness in her voice before she says, "Espero que lo sepas, mijo." *I hope you know that, son.* I know what she's trying to say. She's hoping Ana knew. I can't imagine what her pain is like, constantly worrying if Ana knew how much she loved her.

We keep talking while Roe tosses in bed and eventually drapes an arm around under her blanket. I'm surprised she slept in until 7:00am again today. I wonder if she's comfortable with me. I wonder if she feels safe, so her brain takes the time to settle when I'm with her and she sleeps. She's heard me talking on the phone so she stays quiet and just looks up and smiles at me. Her beautiful smile, just for me.

"Santiago?" I hear my mom say on the phone, forgetting for a second I was still talking to her.

"Digame," *Tell me,* I say.

"Santi, ¿Tienes a alguien ahí contigo?" *Is there someone there with you?*

"Si, mamá. Creo que tengo en mis brazos a la mujer con la que quiero pasar el resto de mis dias." *Yes, mom, I think I have in my arms the woman I want to spend the rest of my life with.* I look down at Roe and pull her so her head rests on my chest, while I stroke her soft hair.

"¿De casualidad tiene el nombre de Ru?" *By any chance is her name Roo?* I laugh at her attempt at saying her name, but it's still cute enough. It means the world to me that she's taking the time to learn her name, to ask about her, to worry if it's her that I'm spending my time with.

"Roe, mama, Roe. No Rooo."

"Eso, eso. Bueno pues te dejo, mijo, disfruta tu dia con tu Roe no Roo. Espero que nunca olvides que tu papá y yo te amamos mucho. Ven a visitarnos pronto."

Same thing, same thing. Let me let you go, my son. Enjoy your day with your Roe and not Roo. I hope you never forget that your father and I love you so much, and I hope you can come visit us soon.

"Te amo ma, pasa un buen dia." *I love you mom, have a great day.* I hang up the phone and set it on the nightstand, kissing Roe on the head while I say, "Buenos dias, princesa."

"You're so fucking hot when you speak Spanish, Santiago," she says, adding a sassy tone when she says my full name.

"You're always hot, but you saying my name in that tone makes you sexy as hell," I say, stroking her hair again.

She moves her body so she can straddle me, placing her hands on either side of my face, and looking at me with a devious smile. I can see her hard nipples through her tank top and in this position, her ass is rubbing perfectly on my dick, which is hard as fuck right now.

"Tell me something in Spanish," she says and rubs against me again.

"I can't think when you move like that," I add and close my eyes to keep me from bending her over and fucking her raw.

"Tell me," she says, lifting a hand from beside my head and running a trail from my throat to my navel.

"Eres perfecta," I say. She continues lowering her hand until it touches the band of my boxers.

"Más," she says. I lift my eyebrow at her at her sudden use of Spanish and she just adds, "I did pay attention a little bit in Spanish class." She traces the band, touching the sensitive skin underneath it.

"Si me sigues tocando así, no me hago responsable de lo que va a pasar, muñeca.[1]"

"Whatever that means, I like it."

"It means *doll*," I say, smiling at her when she realizes that I've been calling her that name she told me she hated.

"You've been calling me *doll* this whole time?"

"I usually just call you princess, but muñeca works some-times." I smile at her and she rolls her eyes at me. "One of these days I'm going to grab you, bend you over, and spank you so hard you'll think about me for days after rolling your eyes at me." She immediately rolls her hips at those words.

"Is that a threat?" she asks, lifting an eyebrow.

"No. A promise."

"Are you a man of your word, Saint?" she asks, pulling

---

1. Si me sigues tocando así, no me hago responsable de lo que va a pasar, muñeca: If you keep touching me like that, I'm not responsible for what will happen, doll.

my boxers down and biting her lips at the sight of my cock springing free.

"Try me and find out," I say, my voice betraying me, showing that I'm about to lose control.

She lowers her head, hovering above my dick, taunting me. She doesn't move to touch me, she just looks. But the sight of her on all fours, her ass up and her mouth inches away from my dick, makes me even harder. She sticks her tongue out and swirls it around the head, giving me a taste of what's about to come but not enough. She does it again, her eyes on me and her ass rolling every time she twirls her tongue around me.

"Roe," I hiss.

"No talking, Saint, just feeling," she says before she opens her mouth and slides it over my dick, sucking hard and twirling back up to the head. She does that a few more times. All the way down and slowly back up, swirling, twisting and sucking. She sits on her knees and grabs a hair tie from her wrist, quickly putting her hair in a ponytail. Her eyes are pure flame and fire, burning me from the inside out.

She then stands up and walks toward the bathroom. *What in the actual fuck?!*

"Roe!" I shout and she turns around, eyeing me deviously.

"I have a feeling that you're holding out on me, Saint. I know that you like to demand and take control, yet you're letting me do whatever I want with you. And fuck I like making you feel good, but I know the way you look at my hair every time it's up like this. I know you want to spank me every time I sass you. I have a feeling deep down you would rather see me sucking your dick on my knees. Tell me I'm wrong," she demands, putting her hands on her hips and tilting her head sideways, challenging me to call her on her shit.

"You're the caretaker, I know. Everyone around you knows it. You're not the only one paying attention, pretty boy. But I'm actually asking you to take care of yourself for once. Take what you want, how you want it. Show me how bad you can be, *Saint*," she adds, putting emphasis on the name Saint like I don't know what she's trying to do. The worst part? She's not wrong, I do put everyone else first, including her. Can I really be a little selfish and let go in front of her?

"Come on, babe," she pleads, and if I didn't know I was already lost in her, this did it. "I'm trying to let you in, but you have to do the same. I'm safe with you, so let yourself go a little. Live a little with me." She twirls her hair one more time and bites the inside of her cheek, before touching her neck and closing her eyes. A silent invitation if I've ever seen one.

THIRTY-TWO

MIRAME, MUÑECA

***UNRAVEL ME*, Sabrina Claudio**

ROE

I SEE IT, the moment he makes his choice. The acceptance to lose control and to tell me exactly what he wants, and if I wasn't turned on before, I'm a fucking goner now. His eyes darken the closer he gets to me. They linger on my neck with longing and intensity, and the fact that even a little piece of skin makes him this feral for me, makes me feel invincible. I grab my hair and twist it, pulling it to the side before clasping my hands behind my back, surrendering control. *Take me, Saint. I can't give you my heart. But this, this I can give you.*

He stops a few steps away from me and with a raspy, deep voice says, "Come here."

I walk to him and stop right in front of him, biting my lip and smiling, knowing exactly what my smile does to him.

I want to be his fucking undoing, in case he hasn't figured that out yet. I want to make him feel even an ounce of what I feel when I'm with him.

He strokes the hair above my ear and back until he makes it to my ponytail. He twists my hair in his hand and pulls my head back slightly, giving him full access to my neck. He kisses that spot between the bottom of my neck and my collarbone, opening his mouth and sucking. Is this man giving me a hickey? He does the same in another spot and then peppers kisses all the way back up to my chin and then my mouth. He starts kissing me slowly, tenderly; but when he tugs at my hair, he immediately deepens it. Kissing and licking. Biting and tasting.

"On your knees," he commands, his mouth still so close to mine. I drop to my knees and drag my hands up his thighs and around back, grabbing his toned ass. I hover my mouth over his dick, waiting for him to tell me what he wants.

"Mirame, muñeca," he says, his voice raspy and his hand stroking his dick. "Look at me, Roe." I peer at him through my lashes and smile. With a curse, he yanks on my hair, pulling my head back. "Open your mouth and suck," he pauses and then says, "hard."

I do just that. I slam my mouth onto him, twirling and sucking, hard. My fingertips are on his ass so I dig my nails into him, pulling him to me and he growls.

"Fuck, Roe, Fuck."

I pull back and say, "Fuck or suck, which one is it?" I smirk and he tugs on my hair harder. He shoves his dick into my mouth with force, making me gag and driving me into it, over and over again. *Yes, Saint, lose control.*

"Where did that smart mouth go, my little brat? It sure as hell looks good when it's full of my cock."

I moan into him; my release builds up more and more with those words.

"You like that, huh? You like when I take control?" He keeps driving in deeper, as if that's even possible. My eyes water and he groans louder when he notices. "Filthy fucking girl, choking on my cock."

I move my hand from his ass and drop it to my clit. He responds by pulling harder on my hair.

"You want to touch yourself? Do it, but don't you dare come. Touch yourself until you can't take it anymore and then stop. Got it?" he asks and I nod, earning me the praise I've been craving. "Such an obedient little thing."

I shiver at those words and continue to suck him hard. I can taste the salty precum and that makes my clit even harder. I touch myself in the same rhythm that I suck on him, and I can't tell whose moans are louder and deeper -- his or mine. I close my eyes because I'm so close, but then I remember I can't come yet. I stop touching myself and open my legs wider so I can sink lower and give his dick more attention from this angle.

"Fuck, princesa, if you don't want me to come in your pretty mouth you need to stop now," he demands and that just fuels me to continue doing what I'm doing. Sucking harder, taking him deeper, and humming. I bring my hand down to my entrance, sliding my fingers through my wetness, before bringing them up and rubbing them against his balls.

"Coño[1]," he groans before he's coming in my mouth, holding my face in place while I swallow everything he gives me. "You were fucking made for me, Roe. You're so perfect, such a good girl, swallowing every drop," he moans.

---

1. Coño: Shit

Once I've sucked him dry, he holds my hands and brings me up so I'm standing next to him. He pulls my tank top over my head, freeing my breasts and immediately lowering his mouth to one of them.

"You're killing me, Saint. I need some friction, to be touched, to come, I need something," I beg. I can feel how tense he got after I said something; I'm sure he's wishing that I said I needed him, and maybe I do, but I'm not ready to admit that. He picks me up, throwing me over his shoulder and spanking my ass. I jolt at the contact but before I can say anything, he brings me to the bed and lays me down, while he stands there, naked and perfect in front of me.

"I know exactly what you need, princesa, and right now, only I can give it to you. But let me be crystal-clear: I know you need a lot of things, but above all, what you need is me."

He brings his hands to my hip, dragging his fingers from my thighs all the way to my ankles. "Now open up for me and let me see that glistening, perfect pussy."

He grabs both my ankles, opening my body for himself and confirming what I already know—that he also likes to watch. "So ready and needy for me," he adds.

He lowers his head, swiping his tongue from my clit to my entrance, making me writhe under him. He does it again and again, until I'm ready to fuck his face if he'll let me. I'm so fucking turned on and I just want to come. I wrap my legs around his head, pulling him to me and not letting him off of my pussy. His beard scrapes slightly over everything and he moves his chin, making me feel it even more.

"Saint..." My voice breaks, an invitation for him to do as he pleases. He sucks on my clit and I'm about to come undone but I need more.

"More, Saint, more," I plead, moaning and rocking against him.

He grabs my ass and tilts me forward, pausing before he asks, "Do you trust me?"

Do I? Trust him? With my life, even if I'm too afraid to admit it. I nod.

He slides a finger in my ass, gently at first, but moving faster and faster as I moan louder. He pumps his finger in me, letting me move in the right amount that I need but I don't want to come down from this high. My hips move in circles and I let out a deep breath. I let my legs loosen so they fall on his shoulders. At the same time, he grabs a pillow and tucks it under my ass to keep me in that position.

"Feet on my shoulders, Roe, open up," he says with his finger still curling in and out of my ass.

"Fucking hell, Saint. That. Feels. Incredible. Don't stop," I gasp, opening wider to give him more access. His tongue goes in, sliding between my folds, while his other hand presses on my clit. "Make me feel full." My words come out breathy, my skin breaking out in goosebumps.

He slides his finger out of my ass, and gently teases with two. When he sees that I'm not backing out, he spits on them and slides them back in at the same time that two from his other hand go into my pussy. He licks and sucks on my clit and when I pull on his hair, pressing his face to me harder, I let out a scream.

"Holy fucking shit, that feels so good. Don't stop," I cry.

He lifts his head from my pussy, his beard glistening with all my arousal. "I wasn't planning on stopping, but now I think I want to hear you ask nicely, princesa. Beg for it; beg for me to make you come again all over my fingers and my face."

Gladly. "Please, Saint, keep going and don't stop until I

make a fucking mess all over you," I beg. And like the man of his word that he is, he lowers his head, scraping his teeth over my clit, pumping in and out of both holes, and sucking hard, making me unravel all over him.

"Yes, fuck, yes," I moan. He slides his fingers out of me and I suddenly feel so empty, I don't even know what to do.

"Do you use any toys, muñeca?" he asks, and even though it takes me by surprise, I nod and point at the drawers on my nightstand. He walks over and searches for something, bringing out a small butt plug. He brings it to my mouth while saying, "Suck, princesa, make it ready for your pretty little ass." I do as he says and when it's done, he teases my clit while sliding it into me.

"Saint," I moan, my back arching off the bed. He grabs one of my legs by the knee, brings it up at the same time that he slides his perfect cock inside of me. He lowers his mouth to mine and kisses me. Our kiss tastes salty and tangy, a mix of both of our arousals and it's fucking hot. Knowing that we both made the other one come undone and then kept bringing each other pleasure is hotter than I could ever think it was.

He bites my lower lip and kisses me all the way to my ear, sucking on my ear lobe while continuing to fuck me into oblivion.

"You're so tight and perfect around my cock, princesa," he whispers in my ear. His words make my body come to life, building me back up. "Fuck yes, I can feel you're close," he growls between his teeth, not letting go of my ear.

"So close," I say.

He moves his mouth from my ear to my nipple, and when he bites down, that's all I need to come again at the same time that he does. Both completely in sync, we're two bodies moving as one.

THIRTY-THREE

SHINS AND TEEPS

CONTIGO*, *Karol G & Tiesto

SANTIAGO

"I KNOW we missed our run this morning, so I have an idea about what to do instead," I say to this beautiful girl lying across from me completely naked. I've never considered myself a guy who could go several rounds, but I guess I just needed the right girl to make that happen. I grab her hand and pull her toward me, and with a yelp she splays a leg over mine. I take that as an invitation and pull her completely on top of me. She's limp on me, her pretty eyes closed while she lazily traces circles on my chest.

"I thought our workout session this morning was our training for the day," she groans, tucking her hands under her chin and looking up at me. She's stunning, even more now with her full lips and her sated face. After she said she couldn't come again, I still made her come one more time.

Her moans of satisfaction are like a drug. I got one hit, and now I want more.

"Although that was great, I've been meaning to show you something. Before we can even get into that, though, we need to eat, and you, my darling, have zero food in here. Want to go out for breakfast—" I look at the clock on the wall and notice it's already 10:00am "—I guess brunch?"

"You asking me out on a date, Saint?" she asks with a shy smile on her face.

"If I thought you were going to say yes before, I would've asked you a lot sooner," I quip, tucking a hair behind her ear and kissing her forehead before adding, "Is that a yes?" Can she see that I'm putting my heart on the line here? I wish I could just tell her that things have changed for me and although it's fun to be with her, I also want her all the time. The fun nights, the days of riding, and the times of just being with each other. Waking up late after an all-nighter, lost in each other and then a slow day of breakfast and talks. I want it all and I want it with her.

"Free food and a hottie to look at? Let's go," she says.

"Hottie, huh?"

"You're okay, I guess," she adds, sticking her tongue out and parading her body around until she puts some clothes on. In no time, I'm dressed too, and we're on our way to our first official date. I think to myself how we did this backward. How I fell in love with the girl before showing her the proper way a girl should be treated, but I guess there are no rules in love. Sometimes it catches you off guard and lifts you higher than anything in your life has before.

"TEA OR COFFEE?" she asks, on the way back home from brunch. She has made it a habit of asking random questions every time we're together. I take it as a small win that she's trying to get to know me more and not that she's trying to fill the quiet with surface level questions.

We ate our weight in cheese and bread from a charcuterie board that Roe ordered. After her second Bloody Mary, I stopped drinking and stopped keeping track of how many Roe was drinking. I figured if I had to drag her home, I would. She was having fun. Smiling and talking about life, racing, and the bar. I like a 'little out of control Roe,' her guard down and her essence shining through. I could always see through all of that but it's nice to see her let go for once.

"You've seen me drink coffee how many times now?" I say, continuing driving through town.

"I get it, but I don't know if you just drink it to look tough and shit," she adds.

"If I liked tea, that's what I would drink. I like café con leche and that's it," I say.

She makes a gagging face at the sound of that and I remember she had that reaction when I ordered it too.

"Do you have anything against milk, Roe?" I ask, and if this isn't the most bizarre conversation I've ever had, I don't know what is.

"No, I don't drink coffee at all, unless it's iced and with oat milk," she says.

"So you do like your coffee with milk, just not cow's milk."

"Can we be done with this conversation? Eggs Benedict or fried?" she asks.

"You started it, and neither—scrambled; you prefer them Benedict, right?" I say, knowing that I hit the nail on the head since she punched me on the arm. "When can it be my turn to ask the questions?" I ask, keeping my eyes trained on the road.

"Go ahead," she adds.

I know I have to ask her about this, but knowing this girl can go from zero to one hundred and lock me out of her feelings, I'm worried. I have to because I can't sleep or think straight when I remember that she's out there acting like James Bond without any of the skills.

"I've been thinking about something, and it's something that I enjoy doing, so I would love to show you."

"Where is the question in that?" she asks.

There's no easy way to ask about this so I just blurt out and say it. "How would you feel about learning self-defense?" I look over to see her eyebrows pinched together. "Hear me out. I know you have some knowledge and I won't take that away. I want to show you how to use your whole body and some moves that most people don't know. You won't lock your doors. And as much as I want to be with you at all times, I can't." I turn toward her house and lower the music. I feel like she needs the silence to be able to focus.

"I can defend myself, Saint," she snaps.

"I know you can. If I didn't think you were capable, I wouldn't offer to teach you other things." I pull up in front of her house, shifting the truck into park and turning my body so I can look at her. "I want it to be *my job* to keep you safe, muñeca but I realize that it won't always be the case. So let me teach you. Best case scenario, you won't need it and it just turns into a hot training session," I add.

"Hot?" she asks, her eyebrows raised with curiosity.

"You'll see. Come on, let's take some of these clothes off," I say, stepping out of the truck and giving her my hand. She won't stop climbing through the driver's seat to get out.

Might as well just help her out this way. *Cuando la montaña no va donde Mahoma, Mahoma va a la montaña.* A saying my mom always says that basically means when something is not happening on its own, you make it happen.

"KICK ME, as hard as you can," I insist, standing at attention in front of her. I'm wearing shin guards from a bag in the truck and she's currently wearing my extra pair, so even if she actually kicks me, I'm not worried about the impact. We've been training for the past hour; my muscles reminding me of how much work has gone into this session. We're both tired and ready to be done with this. But you never know when you're going to need to use self-defense, so we push through ten more minutes. A little past exhaustion is when you know what your body is truly capable of.

I'm dealing with the heat of the afternoon sun shining on us since she refused to do this inside her house. But I would deal with the heat anytime if my reward is the beads of sweat making Roe's body glisten. Her body is the definition of a masterpiece. You can see both her strength and her grace in every inch of her body. You can see that she's disciplined and works hard. Toned muscles on subtle curves. The perfect balance.

She kicks, showing me the move we've been working on. But I catch it, grabbing her leg and holding it against my hip, keeping her standing on one leg. I drop her leg, letting her stand on her own and say, "Again."

Her kick is fast and strong. If I wasn't prepared, it could do some damage. But it's not strong enough to take someone down unless she leverages her body. Her long lean legs square up to me again, and when I think she's going to kick with her right leg, she switches and kicks with her left, quickly and efficiently hitting me right in the rib cage.

"That's it," I grunt, grabbing my side and keeping my eyes on her legs as she goes back into a fighting stance. She's a fast learner. "Again." Controlling my breath, I bring my hands up. I wrapped both of our wrists before we started, in case she wanted to learn some punch combinations. And of course she did, so I'm ready to take a kick or a punch at any time.

She lifts her right leg in a fluid rapid motion, letting out a sound that could be both a battle cry and a scream of annoyance. Either way, it works when she tilts her hip and she lands her kick directly on my stomach. I hold her leg in place so I can show her what to do next.

"So now you have them right where you want them, what's next?" I ask, allowing her a moment to decide her next move.

"I grab my knife from my necklace and stab them," she says. *So stabby.*

"Using just your body, princesa, work with what you have at all times."

She brings her arm forward and tries to throw a jab that I block with my other hand. "That's risky, baby. I can get you off balance real quick." I move her back gently and she has to jump to stay standing. "Try again," I add, letting go of her fist.

"This is bullshit. Let go of my leg," she demands, looking pissed. I use that to my advantage, to try to use that as her driving force.

"Are you mad that I won't let go?" I ask, holding her leg higher and harder, making her balance stumble again. "Are you angry that I can control you like this and that you're at my mercy?" And that does it. I see the switch flip.

She grabs the back of my neck and pulls down toward her Using my body weight as leverage to hold her own, she turns her hips until her shin is pressing across my hips, which makes me break my stance and my hips go back while I let out a painful sound. She doesn't stop there; she pulls her leg back and teeps me right on my chest, pushing me back onto the ground.

She stands by my head, hovering over me before saying, "Nobody can control me, asshole." She walks past me toward the house, walking in and slamming the glass doors behind her.

"Roe, wait up," I shout, scrambling to my feet, struggling to catch my breath and catch up with her inside the house. The girl has a mean kick and an even better teep. When the session started and I taught her what a teep was, she folded over in laughter. *That doesn't sound like a real name,* she said, and funny enough, I also thought the same. A push kick, my Muay Thai instructor taught us. A kick that nobody sees coming, and she used my own words and knowledge against me.

I grab her hand, pulling her toward me, and it's the first time that I see how out of breath she is too. It must have taken a lot of strength to pull that move off and to successfully kick me to the ground after training and learning for over an hour in this heat.

A little past exhaustion and you'll see what you have left. That's something that I learned from Ana and I always keep it at the forefront of my mind. She fought hard, and even when she was exhausted, she kept fighting. In the end she may have died, but she never lost the fight. I strive to do that every day of my life.

"Hey, hey, hey," I say gently, pushing a piece of her hair behind her ear and brushing other pieces away from her face. "I'm sorry if I pushed you too hard. I wasn't trying to get you this upset."

"Yes, you were, don't back off now," she snarls with fury in her eyes.

"Yes, I was, but just to get you to snap and show me what you could do. You never held out on me before; why now?"

She looks down and closes her eyes, and this might be the most vulnerable she's ever been with me. I don't want to push but I do want her to open up to me.

"Roe," I whisper and she shakes her head. "Mirame, princesa. Why were you holding back?"

That does it. She looks up with teary eyes.

"I don't want to hurt you, Saint," she whimpers. And before I can do anything, she walks into the bathroom and locks the door, quickly starting the shower. As much as I would like to join, I think she needs her space. And I can respect that.

THIRTY-FOUR
LET ME IN

REWRITE THE STARS*, *James Arthur & Anne-Marie

ROE

THERE'S something therapeutic about washing my hair. Like the water takes away all my worries and sins. Like it can cleanse away the pain. If I wasn't hollow inside, if I could pour any emotion out, I'm sure this would be the place that would see me cry–letting my tears blend with the steady stream of water. But you can't pour out of an empty cup, and that's what I am. Empty.

Except right now, I feel more alive than I have in years. I'm not sure what to do with this feeling of joy and pride coming out of my pores. Not sure how to handle the fact that I think I'm actually happy, or how I hesitated to hurt him just now because I care. He asked why I was holding back, and what was I about to say? *Because I care about you?* I can't say that when I know he deserves better. He deserves someone who can lift him up, not drag him down with a shit load of trauma. He deserves someone who can feel and let him in wholly. I've done a lot of stupid shit in my life but keeping Saint close when I know I'm not what he needs, what he deserves, comes in big as first place.

I hit the cold tile wall in the shower while letting out a scream. I'm so annoyed at this whole situation and at myself for allowing it to happen. I have to tell him that he needs to go. I have to find a way to get him to save himself even if it breaks me further in the process.

I step out of the shower with a newfound purpose: make Saint understand that he's better off without me. Wrapping a towel around my body, I quickly blow-dry my hair before heading to my room to dress. Walking into my room, I grab a pair of shorts and a tank top but before I can go find Saint, I look at my phone and see I have a few new messages from Cara.

> Cara🔍: I hear you two met.

> Cara🔍: I guess I should say, Roe, I heard you met my bff.

> Cara🔍: Now we can all be best friends and the world will be a better place

> Me: Who is this bff that you talk about?

> Cara🔍: Allie. Jake's girl <3

I save the other number in this group text as Allie and add a little plane emoji next to her name since that's the tattoo she has on her wrist. A little plane with a dotted heart. I started adding emojis next to people's names on my phone in an attempt to connect with them deeper when I try to remember which phone number and name matches which face. Cara has a little fried egg because we met at the diner.

Me: Hey Allie, it was so nice meeting you. Didn't know you knew Cara.

Allie : Same! Cara has been my best friend since we were kids. What I'd like to know is how did she keep YOU from me?

Cara : You said, and I quote, "I don't want to know anything about Baker Oaks." Roe was part of that. Sorry bestie but those were your rules. Now that you're all up in people's business over there, we can all be friends.

Cara : The whole reason for this convo is to talk about the hottie mechanic that you're banging

Allie : I knew it!! I knew you and Thiago were more than friends like you both said.

Me: We're not even friends so don't get too excited. We're just having a little fun.

Cara : Roe, I love you but you need to stop lying to yourself. I don't think I've ever seen you with the same person more than twice and it's been weeks of you two hanging out, or more according to the peeps

Allie : I'm pretty sure I saw them at Nick's party together too

Me: Allie, whose side are you on here?

Cara🔍: She should be on my side but either way I'm actually on Roe's side here. You deserve a good man in your life and from what I hear and see, Thiago is as good as they come.

Me: It's too late for this conversation

Cara🔍: It's like 7:00pm

Me: I don't really care. Have a good night you two.

Allie✖ : Bye!

Cara🔍: When you're ready to talk, we're here. Don't blow us off.

I put my phone down on the nightstand and walk out of the room. I can't pay too much attention to those messages right now. *I deserve a good man.* That's if I actually deserve anyone. I don't deserve the friendships I have with Cara and Jake – hell, even Allen makes the list at this point – but no matter how far away I try to push them, they just keep coming back. I'm not sure being close to someone is worth risking their life over.

He's sitting shirtless on the couch, reading the American Motorcyclist Association (AMA) Magazine, with his feet up on the coffee table. *Fucking hell.* He's so damn hot and yes, I like him for more than his body, but what an incredible work of art his body is. And the ink just adds to the appeal. He's not playing fair at all. *Can he tell I'm about to break his heart? Does he realize I'm about to tell him that our time together is up and I have no way of fixing this?*

I stand in front of him, and without looking up he says, "Looks like Jerry Britner is done for the season." Jerry is the top rider in our class. He has been the reigning champion for years and he suffered an injury last round, which is probably the main reason why we both placed so high. He's been managing injuries on-and-off all season and it sounds like he's dropping. This means that we might have a shot at qualifying for regionals next summer.

Saint looks up, showing me the page that has a picture featuring the two of us at the last race with the caption, "Could Sorelle and Cruz go head-to-head to win it all?" I snatch the magazine from his hand and jump when I look at all the spotlights they did.

"We might have a chance," I all but scream, and Saint gets up and grabs me in his arms. He picks me up by the back of my legs and spins me around. "Put me down," I kick and shout in the middle of giggles as he grabs my ass and keeps spinning. We probably look like two teenagers, not like two whole-ass adults.

He finally puts me down, a mix of our heavy breathing and excitement filling the air. His eyes roam my face as he tucks two pieces of my hair behind my ear, whispering something. I really hope I heard him wrong. I ignore it. If I ignore it, then it won't happen, and I don't have to worry about breaking his heart more than I thought I was going to already. I try to turn, to get out of here, but he grabs my hand and stops me.

"Don't walk away from me, Roe," he pleads, his voice breaking with every syllable. He doesn't even know what's going through my mind but he can sense that whatever it is, it's not great. "Please, don't do this," he adds.

Turning to face him, I look into his eyes and I know I've already lost the battle. Before the words come out of his mouth again, I know I'm screwed. I don't only like him. I think I actually care about him which makes breaking his heart the shittiest and hardest thing I've ever done.

"I love you, Roe, in case you didn't hear me the first time. Hear me loud and clear now." His other hand holds mine, his attention exclusively on me. "Life's too short not to tell and show others how you feel. And damn it if I don't love you, princesa. I think I've loved you since the first day I met you, with your witty sass and your challenging eyes giving me a hard time over a beer."

Against my will, my body is melting into him. Every word is a sweet caress to my soul. Healing the little parts of me that have shattered through the years. In this moment I wish I could just let him in. Especially when he brushes his lips against my forehead, kissing me gently, or when his soft chuckle reverberates through every inch of my body and soul at the end of his sentence.

He brings a hand up to my cheek and rubs small circles, adding, "I know you've been hurt. I don't know exactly what happened but I can feel it in my heart. I can see it in your eyes. I know you want to push me away. But I'm here to let you know that you don't have to hide from me. Let me see the hurt. Let me help you heal. Or at the very least, let me carry the load with you."

I shake my head no and whisper, "There's nothing for you to help heal, Saint. There's no saving a soul that doesn't exist anymore." The tenderness of his words, his sorrow-filled eyes, and his touch burning my skin and reaching what I have left of a soul… it's too much. I feel the last piece of the dam on my emotions break and for the first time since I was sixteen, a tear falls down my face.

THIRTY-FIVE
UTTERLY BROKEN

When September Ends, Green Day

SANTIAGO

"YOU DON'T UNDERSTAND, Saint. I am utterly broken. Way beyond repair. There's no kindness, no tenderness, no love that will fix it. That will fix me," she urges with tears rolling down her face. It's the first time that I've ever seen her show an ounce of emotion beyond anger, happiness, and lust. It breaks my heart to see her like this, but I'm finding it hard to move past my thoughts of how lucky I am that she's opening up to me. That she's letting me in, and her trust will mean more than words could ever explain.

She tries to get out of the hold I have on her. My arms are wrapped tight around her, my hand rubbing her back. Where she would shy away to the slightest touch when we first met, now she melts into my arms, her body speaking to mine before her brain can catch up. *This is what she needs.* My body knows it and my heart knows it, too.

"Don't run away anymore," I say carefully, my voice barely above a whisper. I need her not to flee. I need to be the one thing that grounds her in this moment, even if that means reassuring her that she's safe with not only my body but with my voice. "This, what you're feeling right now, give yourself the permission to feel it. Let me hear it."

She lets out a sigh and her shoulders drop. I can hear her soft sniffles and feel her shaking her head. When I think she won't say anything again, she speaks.

"I got tired of feeling. Feeling lost, feeling sad, feeling abandoned. I got tired of wondering *why me* and *what I could have done to make them stay*." She pauses, taking another deep breath and wiping her tears with her hand.

"I was eight when she died. That's when I started wondering what it would take to have my mom back. What it would take for the big bad wolf named cancer to be a nightmare and not the reality that took my mom from me. And guess what I learned? That nothing would make it happen. Not wishing upon stars. Not blowing out the candles with my eyes closed. No wanting with all my heart. Not eating my vegetables. Not blowing on dandelions." She sniffs and rests her head against my chest, finally stopping her fight in this embrace. Finally letting me be the support she needs but has been too afraid to ask for. Too afraid to show.

"I used to hunt those down, you know? I would run across fields, gathering them in my hands and wishing one at a time to just have my mommy back. But we all know that life doesn't work that way. Good things only happen in movies and real life is haunted. My rose-colored glasses had to come off.

"My dad tried his best. But he was also mourning the love of his life and trying to raise a child whose brain didn't work the same as other kids. A child who forgot her homework on the bench outside of school. A child who was so in the clouds trying to think of ways to bring her mom back, that she started failing school. A child who would cry herself to sleep every night. He tried his best but he was also broken beyond repair. Have you ever heard of broken heart syndrome?" she asks and waits a beat for me to answer, but I can't find words to talk right now without my voice breaking. She doesn't need sympathy right now. She needs strength. So I just shake my head, hoping that she can feel the movement and continue.

"It basically means that the heart is hurting so much that it weakens. People supposedly recover from it after a while, but I don't think he ever did. We were both in a hole of despair together, both mirroring each other's sadness, slowly drowning in sorrow and grief. Except I was a little kid and he was an adult and we entered this vicious cycle together, both without the proper skills to cope. Me because of age and him because he never thought he would have to face life without his other half."

Her skin is sticky with sweat but I refuse to let go. I pull her soft gold strands up and hold them away from her face. Now that I can see her face, I notice her eyes are closed and her cheeks are flushed. She's letting me in and it seems to be the hardest thing she's ever done.

"After a couple of years, my teachers were seriously concerned and my dad finally sent me to therapy. I was diagnosed with ADHD and a sensory processing disorder, on top of grieving for my mom and my dad, all at once. He wasn't dead yet but he wasn't himself anymore. Therapy worked for a while, until my hormones kicked in and I hated the world, including the therapist. By fifteen, I was barely tolerable. My dad had healed as much as he was able to but he didn't want to parent me, he wanted me to like him. He wanted me to have the same relationship with him that I had with my mom. But I was not that little girl playing with dolls anymore. I was an angry teenager ready to give him hell. But here's the thing, Saint, I didn't need a friend, I needed *him*. I needed him to see how much I was suffering and how much everything hurt, all the time."

Roe stops suddenly and wiggles out of my hold. This time, I let her. She sits on the couch, placing her hands on her lap. She dries her hands on the fabric of her shorts before bringing them up to her face, then brings her knees up to her chin. I move but she raises her hand, signaling me to stop.

"Please, Saint, let me finish. If you hold me for the next part, I might not be able to tell you everything and I really want to. I think I really need to. I need to let you know why you can't love me. I can't be the one to hold your heart when all the hearts I've held eventually stop beating."

Just like her emotions pouring out of her, the rain starts to fall, tapping on the porch windows. Gently at first, and then like drums of war.

"One day, I was yelling at him to get a grip and to understand that his little girl was never coming back. He got so upset, Saint. You should've seen his eyes. I could feel the disappointment and the guilt behind his eyes. He started coughing"—she lets out a deep breath and peeks at me with her storm-filled eyes—"and there was blood, so much blood. I started losing it, called 911, and after the longest ride to the hospital and days of tests and doctor's appointments, he was diagnosed with cancer. Unlike my mom, there was nothing they could do and they said he could live for another four weeks to four years. He lived for nine weeks. Eight of those he was at home with me, basically living the fullest bucket list life you could imagine."

She tilts her head to the side, closing her eyes, letting the tears fall.

"Those eight weeks were the best of my life. I didn't complain once. I was the perfect child for him. Whatever he wanted I said "yes" to, because the little girl in me still believed that if I truly tried my best, maybe he wouldn't be taken away from me too. But we both know it's only in books that the girl gets the happy ending, and in the end, he left me too. He didn't really leave me though; he took the rest of what I had left in me with him. The sliver of hope. The little pocket of happiness. I have been this shell of a human ever since."

She gets up, walks to the front door of the house, and turns to look at me.

"What are you doing, Roe?"

"And this is why I can never give you what you're asking. I can't let you in, because everything I love dies. My parents died, my grandma died, and I refuse to kill anyone else. It should've been me, Saint. It should've been me instead because you think they had cancer but no, the cancer is me. Turning everything I touch into sickness and darkness. Making everything I let in die and suffer. And you don't deserve this fate."

Her eyes finally snap up to mine, to deliver the last sword straight in, leaving me without wondering if she means these words or not. She does, and her eyes are the proof.

"You're so good Saint, so fucking good. But this is not

the trail I often cross. This is the one I'm in all the time. The one that will lead me to my grave and I refuse to take you with me."

She walks out into the rain and starts running. And like the man in love I am, I run after her, again.

THIRTY-SIX

AURORA

LET ME LOVE YOU, *Glee Cast*

ROE

DESPITE THE OMINOUS sky and the chill from the rain hitting my skin on this hot day, I'm running. Running through the feelings, the emotions. My old therapist used to say that crying was good for processing emotions. That it's needed every now and then so as to not get clogged up in our systems. Well… I don't even remember the last time I let myself feel so much, and it fucking sucks. I'm tired of this numbness inside but feeling this deep is breaking me apart. I'm tired of the black hole that consumes me every day but this flood of emotions is not any better. I just want to shut it all off.

A shower and now the rain, both to match my tears. It's like the force that's ripping me from the inside wants to be heard. Even the sky feels it. I let out a guttural scream and

273

keep running, hoping the rain will wash me away with my tears.

Big, calloused hands take hold of my wrist from behind just as a broken sound leaves his mouth. "Aurora, please stop." Not Roe or princesa. *Aurora.* He only calls me that when he needs to get his point across. When he needs me to hear him.

That's the thing: I hear him loud and clear. I always do. I need him to understand that's not the issue. *He doesn't have to say more for me to know that I'm hurting him. But I don't know how to make it stop.* How do you stop your heart from shattering completely? From losing the last piece of hope it has left at a life of contentment? From taking with it one of the purest souls you've ever met?

"Sh, sh, sh, it's okay, princesa, let it out. Lean on me, let me help you with the load." That's when I notice that my silent tears have turned into agonizing sobs. I bury my face in his chest, letting him console me; once again giving up on trying to fight whatever this is that I have against him helping me, because it's just not working.

I don't even know where my brain is at until the words come out of my mouth cascading into a desperate fall. "I can't, Saint," I say in a broken supplication, "Don't you get it? You will die, too. I'd rather not have you at all than lose you too. I wouldn't be able to survive that." I cover my mouth in an attempt to stifle my sobs. "I won't survive you dying, too."

"Nothing you do can harm me more than you pushing me away, amor." *Love;* four letters that I am terrified of and that I swore I would never say again. Can I actually be in love with him? Is this what this is? Love?

"Let me in. Let me show you I can hold you. Hold both your joy and your pain. Hold your wins and your losses. Let me prove to you that you're worthy. Give me time to convince you that I can love you the way you should be loved. The way you deserve. Your past doesn't scare me, princesa. If anything, it just makes me want to hold you tighter. What you've been through. It doesn't make you less," he urges, kissing my head before continuing, "it makes you stronger. Una guerrera[1]. Una campeona[2]. Una muestra de que todo se puede[3]."

I have no clue what any of that means, but it sure sounds like he believes in me; like he truly wants to be a part of my fucked-up life.

I wrap my arms around this gentle giant. The solid rock of a man who I somehow hated only a short time ago. He rubs my head gently and has not moved an inch, no matter how hard I squeeze. The rain falling over us, soaking us both, and his body flushed against mine is helping me settle. He's helping me ground myself and is making me less and less overstimulated. Like this is all the sensory input I need to be balanced. Just his arms and the rain, in the middle of the damn trail.

He grabs my face with his perfect hands, tilting my face to look at him, but I keep my eyes closed. This is too much. Too much to feel, too much to handle.

"Mirame, princesa," he says. *Look at me.* My favorite phrase from him. He rubs his knuckles against my chin, kissing my forehead, eyelids, and temple. And when I open my eyes, his beautiful whiskey irises are full of an emotion I have not seen looking at me in so long.

---

1. guerrera: warrior
2. campeona: champion
3. Una muestra de que todo se puede: living proof that everything is possible

"I love you, Aurora. Loving you won't kill me, but you not letting me in might. Please don't shut the door." Saint's eyes are trained on mine as both hands cup my face. His heartbeat under the palm of my hands is steady, settling mine down. Grounding me again. He lowers his head and brushes his lips against mine. His breath a soft caress, making me break into goosebumps while he whispers, "Te amo, princesa. I'm not going anywhere."

Saint's lips crash to mine, but not with the same hunger that he usually has for me. This kiss is slow and tender, full of emotion. He takes his time, his lips molding against mine, perfectly in tune with my heart. I really hope he means what he says because I don't think I could survive after him; not with the way he's kissing me and the way his hands are holding me. Like I'm made of porcelain and he's afraid he'll break me. Like his lips have all the secrets to my worries and like his soul is gently caressing mine. Suddenly there's too much space between us and the rain that was soothing one minute ago is now making my shoulders tense and my eyes roam on the space. He must sense that tension and picks me up, not breaking the kiss once, and walks us backward under an oak tree in the middle of the Saint Mary's trail to shield us from the rain.

"Promise me you won't leave me," I plead between peppering kisses, not letting go of this man.

"I promise, princesa. If I could show you my heart I would, so you can see that it only beats for you," he replies without hesitation. And I don't know when we went from rivals to fuck buddies to this– whatever it is. I don't have the brain capacity to figure it out. But tonight, I want to feel safe, loved, and cared for. I want to let this man in and let him show me how much he means those words.

"Then show me that you really mean it. Show me that

you love me," I insist. But when I think that he'll just fuck me senseless, he does the unexpected and picks me up. Good thing I live a few blocks from the trail because this man knows going home is exactly what I need as he walks me there.

After we get in the house, he dries me with a towel, puts one of his shirts on me and places me on the couch delicately. He goes to the kitchen and comes back a few minutes later with hot cocoa. *The fuck?* He even added marshmallows on top. And maybe I don't need a man. But Saint bringing me my comfort drink without knowing it? On the day all the tears that my body has been hoarding for almost a decade come out? Yeah. That might be exactly what I need.

"You know, when I said show me you love me, I was expecting you to rail me against the oak tree, not bring me home, wrap me up like a burrito and make me hot cocoa," I joke, sipping on my drink and placing my feet on top of his legs.

Saint smiles lazily at me as he sits with his feet propped on my coffee table. "I always want to be inside of you. But when I told you I love you, Aurora, I didn't mean I just love fucking you."

I raise my eyebrows at him, and Saint laughs, raising his hands in surrender. "Don't even start," he quips, not dropping my gaze. "I didn't say I don't want to. We've talked about this; there's not a minute in the day where I don't want to be holding your body to mine. Not a moment passes that I don't want to be inside of you, hearing the sweet sounds you make when I push you to feel everything."

Well then, boy, okay. My whole body reacts to that statement and he's only *talking* to me. *Great, Roe, you're more fucked than you thought.*

"But what I need you to understand, princesa, is that

you're so worthy of love beyond your body. In case nobody has told you lately—and God I hope nobody has so I don't have to punch a motherfucker—you're sweet, funny, and kind. I know you mask your tenderness with...what is it that you call it? Badassery?"

I nod with a smile when he says that because I guess he pays more attention than I thought.

"I know you don't want to hear it but I fell in love with you, Roe. Your little outbursts, random questions, lack of sleep, and the way you need very little from others yet you give wholeheartedly. I fell in love with your taste in music, your willingness to push through hard things to be the best you can be at everything you set your mind to, and yes, I fell in love with your body too."

Saint reaches for my hands and brings one to his mouth, kissing my knuckles. "I fell for your artistry."

He peppers kisses up my arm. "Your creativity and your tattoos too."

He kisses my shoulder, neck, and my chin. "I fell in love with your soft skin, your heart, and how you don't take shit from anyone."

He kisses my temple and adds, "I fell in love with your beautiful blue eyes that remind me of my second favorite place in the world. I fell in love with your brain—" he taps on my temple and kisses my forehead "—even when your neuro-spiciness makes you forget to eat or to lock your door."

Saint brings his hand to my chin again and rubs my bottom lip with his thumb. "I fell in love with your lips and the way you respond to my kisses." His hand lowers to my chest as he continues, "And I fell in love with your heart. You're not hollow, amor. You just have a tall wall, keeping your heart hostage. Protecting it after going through more pain than anyone should go through, let alone as a little girl."

I set the mug down on the table, making it thud louder than I expected, and crawl over the couch to Saint, who's surprised by this as much as I am. I sit on his lap and lay my head on his chest while saying, "Thank you, Saint."

"For what, princesa?" he asks, his hand falling immediately to my back.

"For loving me, I guess," I reply, my voice shaking. This is why I hate crying. One tear leads to a fucking series of emotions that I hate dealing with. "Saint, I—" I start but he stops me.

"I don't want you to say something you're not ready for, amor. Just be with me right now and promise me that you'll try to stop pushing me away every time I'm getting closer to you. Let me love you."

"But what if you—"

"No ifs, buts, or maybes, princesa. Just," he sighs, "let me love you. Everything else, we can figure out a day at a time, okay?" He kisses my head again and I don't know why, but that gesture alone means more than he could ever know. Maybe he's right, too; maybe I can just let him love me and we can try this a day at a time, and hope that he doesn't get taken from me too.

THIRTY-SEVEN
I WILL ALWAYS COME BACK, AMOR

YELLOW, **Kinna Grannis**

SANTIAGO

"CAN we talk about the fact that we might be going head-to-head for the title this weekend?" I ask Roe. We got back from our run and are eating a couple of yogurt bowls in the kitchen. We're sitting on the floor because that's where she sat and I won't let her sit by herself.

"Ha, speak for yourself. I'm actually taking the title, Saint," she snaps back.

"You're so full of yourself," I add as I watch her scrunch her nose at me.

"I'm confident. There's a difference," she says. And she's not wrong. She's more confident than a lot of people I know, but I know she hides her true feelings behind the front she sets up. "I can't believe we were published in a magazine;

can we talk about that?" She emphasizes the *that* and points at the magazine on top of the breakfast bar.

"Yeah, that's cool, but it just adds to the challenge because every single rider will be coming for you and me now, especially if they want to qualify."

"They have to catch us first," she says, winking at me and getting up to put her bowl in the sink. She looks delicious, the way she walks around with her tight workout shorts and her tiny sports bra. Just looking at her, my dick goes to attention. I get up, setting my bowl on the countertop, scoop her by her legs, and throw her over my shoulder.

She yelps. "Saint, what the fuck? Put me down," she says, kicking her feet, or trying to, and squirming in my hold.

"Oh, I'll put you down. Let's make it to the bedroom first so I can lay you down exactly where I want you." The little minx stops kicking the minute I say the word 'bedroom,' and we spend half of our day off exploring each other and pushing some more boundaries.

"SO ARE you two living together now?" Jake asks while we're all sitting on his back porch.

Jake and Allie invited us to come over for dinner tonight and I was surprised when Roe said yes, too. She said, when I first met her, how she didn't love hanging out with people and she would rather be with her books. But I knew she was friends with Jake, so I asked and she was excited to come. She and Allie have been giggling for the past hour or so and neither have paid any attention to us.

"I don't think so," I answer, taking a sip of my drink.

"I'm staying with her until this shit with her house blows over but we haven't talked past that." I look at Roe, searching for any indication that I'm lying, but we both know that's the truth. I don't know where we stand. If it was up to me? I would be attached to that girl's hip 24/7 but at the end of the day, it's taking baby steps for her to feel comfortable sharing her life with someone and I don't blame her. She has been through so much and she's resilient as fuck. She needs time and she deserves someone willing to give it to her, and I'm going to be that man.

"What about your house?" Allie asks, tuning in to the last part of the conversation. The sun is dipping behind the trees, casting purple and orange hues in the sky. I look up and notice the sunset, closing my eyes briefly before looking back at the girls. Roe looks at me expectantly but instead of talking to me, she answers her friend.

"Someone's breaking into my house. They're not taking anything, just moving things around," she answers and Allie gasps.

"Go to the police," she tells her.

"And tell them what? That someone moved my plants and did my dishes?" The same argument she gave me. We installed cameras and nothing has happened since. It might be a pesky teenager just pulling a prank but it doesn't make me feel any better.

"How are they breaking in?" Jake asks.

"Funny you ask, Jake. They just walked in," Roe says.

They both look at Roe with a puzzled expression, before Jake just shakes his head.

"Do you not lock your house either? I thought it was just your Jeep," Jake says.

"Apparently, she trusts everyone," I reply.

"Alright, alright. I get it, I should lock my doors, *yada*

yada. It's done, and now Mr. Self-Defense over there is all up in my business about it. I don't need to lock my door all the time."

"Mr. Self-Defense, huh? And no, you don't, because I lock the door every night now," I snap back and she smiles at me.

"I thought you two were *'just friends,'*" Allie says with a big smile on her face, walking to Jake and sitting on his lap.

We both reply in unison, "We are." We all laugh.

We keep talking about how weird everything is about the house and how nothing else has happened since the last race weekend. We talk about Allie and Jake, and about how funny it is that Cara is Allie's best friend. Roe and Allie Facetime her at some point and they all coordinate to get together in the winter. They both want Cara to move back to Baker Oaks, but something happened with her ex and Cara doesn't want to live in the same small town as him. I don't blame her; everyone is in everyone's business here.

We discuss the upcoming race, the expected outcome, and what will happen after qualifiers. Allie says she wants to come watch us race and we exchange information.

The drive back to Roe's house is serene. The full moon bright in the sky casts a glow over the road that glistens after the light rain we got earlier today.

"Hey Saint?" she asks.

"Si, princesa?" I reply, looking over my shoulder at the girl who stole my heart and is keeping it hostage.

"Can I ask you something?"

"Always, amor, always."

"Why do you look at the sky and close your eyes?" she asks shyly. I don't think I knew she had a shy bone in her body.

"My sister," I say, taking a deep breath before continuing. "When she got sick, she started appreciating the little moments in life more because she said she never knew when they would happen again." I make a right turn around the dirt road, with its own bumps and roots, just like my heart right now.

"It wasn't always the sky that she would stop to look at. Sometimes it was family dinners or my mom reading a bedtime story to the little ones. She would just stop, close her eyes, and take it all in. Her words, not mine," I tell her, pausing to hold my emotions in and not open a can of worms that I don't want right now. "So now, it's the best way to honor her memory, pausing to appreciate it all."

She nods and reaches over, holding my hand and squeezing it gently. "You know? I don't know if I believe in fate or whatever, but what are the chances that we both lost someone with the same name and who believed in basically the same thing?"

"What?" I ask, dumbfounded at this.

"My mom, her name was Anna too," she says, taking a deep breath and letting it out gently. "My mom used to say that too; 'Miracles happen every day'. She would tell me if I only stopped long enough, I would see them too. I'm not ready to talk about this more, but yeah, Anna was her name. I guess they both believed in little miracles. I almost called you a liar the first time you said your sister with wings was Anna too."

"My angel sis," I add and she nods.

The empty roads surrounded by stillness are making me aware of the fact that I consider going to the house with Roe a home. *Our home.*

I try to get out of my thoughts, so I ask Roe, "My turn?" I've been wanting an answer to a question that has invaded my mind since she gave me that damn nickname that I love so much.

"Shoot, but don't kill," she says and winks at me. *Dios, la amo.* [1]

"Why do you call me Saint?"

She almost spits out the water she was drinking. She laughs, full force, and loudly. I'm talking about the type of laugh you would hear if you went to a comedy show or how a little kid freely giggles when you tickle them.

She settles down and says, "At first, it was because everyone seemed to like you, and I figured only a saint could manage that. It was close enough to your name, so it fit." She stops and I think she might be done, but she pulls her feet down from the dash and under her body while turning to me.

"Now, I keep calling you that because only a saint would put up with my chaos and continue to stay by my side. So far, you keep coming back and you've never left me, not once, even when I pushed you away."

"I will always come back, amor. For as long as you'll have me and then some. I'm yours to keep."

"Mine to keep?" she asks and I smile at her. But her smile fades, her eyes skimming the road, and when I turn to face her, I see all the lights in her house are on and I know we turned them off.

---

1. Dios, la amo: God, I love her.

THIRTY-EIGHT

LET THEM HEAR IT

DIE FIRST, **Nessa Barrett**

ROE

"OFFICER, respectfully, either figure out what's going on or get away from my house," I tell the cop who has been asking me the same questions for the past hour. After parking the truck, Saint rushed in to sweep the house, but immediately backed out when he realized the entire place was trashed. We called the police, who arrived within ten minutes. They've already taken pictures, dusted for fingerprints, and filed the report. Just like before, nothing is missing; but this time instead of just moving things around, they broke plates and cups, and some plants were on the ground with the dirt spilled all around them. All my clothes were taken out of the drawers and closets, pillows were thrown on the floor, and torn books were everywhere. The creepiest part? They wrote in the mirror, *Don't do it.* Don't do what? Were they trying to get themselves to stop? Are they trying to get me to stop from doing something? Is this part of a prank too?

We looked at the cameras, but whoever did this was wearing a hoodie so you can't see their face at any point. The police concurred that it was a man around six feet tall who's doing this, based on their evidence. He used gloves and with the minimal visibility of his face, we don't have a lot of information to use. He left with a bag but we can't figure out if there was anything in it. We have no other identifiers and have been instructed to call back if anything changes.

They leave and I plop myself on the ground, exhausted and emotionally spent from dealing with this shit. I can't think of a single person that would do this.

"Princesa," Saint whispers. I look up and see his hand wide open, held out to help me up.

"I'm so pissed about this. Who would do this?" I ask, letting him pull me to my feet.

"I know, and we will figure it out, but right now it is late. Let's go to my place and we can deal with this tomorrow."

"Let me grab a bag and some clothes," I say, walking to the linen closet where I keep my overnight bags. Opening the door to grab one, I let out a yelp when I see it.

"What? What is it?" Saint asks, running to me the second he heard me scream.

"My trophies are gone," I whisper. I didn't think to look in here because what were the chances that someone would break into my house and steal my trophies? I don't even like displaying them -- they're a reminder that I have no one to share my wins with. A reminder that strangers think I'm worth having something to celebrate but nobody in my life to actually celebrate it with. *Until now.* I don't know when that changed in my brain, but now when I think about who

I would want to celebrate with, Saint comes to mind immediately. Front and center.

"What do you mean your trophies are gone?" he asks.

"Exactly that. I keep them in this closet but they're not here anymore. That's a pretty odd thing to steal," I add and he hums. "I'll call the cops tomorrow and tell them; maybe now that they know that something was stolen, they'll put some effort into figuring out who did this." He nods and we proceed to pack my stuff.

The ride to his place is eerily quiet. No music is playing and he's not saying anything which isn't like him.

"Are you okay?" I ask, snapping him out of whatever stupor he was in.

"Si, amor," he replies, glancing my way and smiling at me. His smile doesn't reach his eyes but it's still a smile just for me, and I take it. I want to take them all. Take whatever he'll give me. Keep him.

"Then why are you suddenly so serious?"

"Something about this thing is not settling right with me," he answers, running his hand over his face.

"Yeah, Saint, nobody wants their house broken into."

"It's not my house, princesa. But that's not what's unsettling." The AC is blasting in my face, making flyaway hairs become more apparent.

"You practically live there," I say, and wait to see what he says. Again, he barely reacts, and that's how I know something is clearly wrong. "What is it?"

"What if they are asking you to stay away from me?" he asks with a frown and his jaw tenses.

"That's ridiculous. You're not the first guy I've ever been with. Besides, it's too late, we're already together. Also, they asked me not to do it and if you think about it, I already *did* you," I say, wiggling my eyebrows at him and smiling, trying to break his sour mood.

"I guess you're right," he adds.

I gasp and bring my hand to my chest. "Can you say that louder for the people in the back?"

He chuckles and keeps driving. In the blink of an eye, we make it to his place. It's when I see another car in the long driveway that I remember he has a roommate.

"I guess you're not fucking me tonight, huh?" I ask.

"For fucks sake. What?"

"Just saying, we don't want to make your pal jealous."

He gets out of the truck, holding the door open for me, allowing me time to climb over the seat and get out on the driver's side. Not once has he questioned why I like to climb through. He just keeps holding open whatever door I decide to climb out of.

"For the record, princesa," he says, as soon as he closes the door behind me. "I don't care if I make anyone jealous." He closes the space between us, placing his hand on the truck's window, caging me in and whispering in my ear, "If you're screaming while I'm buried in your sweet cunt, then let them hear it. I'm dying for you to let me scream at the top of my lungs that you're mine. And if the best way for people to know that is with you yelling out my name while I devour you whole, then I'm okay with that too." He kisses the shell of my ear and pulls me toward the house.

This man didn't even touch me and I'm instantly wet, just from his naughty words against my ear. This is fucked up and I need to figure something out. I wish I could say before it's too late. But truthfully, I'm already in too deep. He's already cracked the shell and my heart is wide open for him.

We walk quietly when we notice that Marco is in his

room. He might be already asleep and we don't want to be rude.

Walking into Saint's room, I'm surprised to see mementos and pictures everywhere. I know pictures were important for him, since he has them in his truck too, but he's usually so neat and tidy, I expected his room to be white walls, a bed, and maybe a desk. Instead, I find art on the walls, family pictures on tables and desks, a colorful pillow on the bed, and even drawings hanging on a poster board. His comforter is sage green and his bed is neatly made.

He notices my eyes exploring and he says, "Sometimes all you have are memories. If you can capture them, maybe they'll last longer."

I can't believe I've never shown him my own collection of pictures. I open my goose backpack and grab my own box of pictures, handing it to him, and say, "I believe in that, too."

We climb into bed together and look at the pictures. Some are so old that you can barely tell who's in them. And I've taken some new ones recently so Saint laughs when he notices one of him, sitting on his bike, looking into the distance.

He traces his fingers over one from when I was six and I was sitting between my parents on a pontoon boat. The wind is blowing my blonde hair and my toothless grin is front and center. My mom was already sick, with a bandanna over her hairless head and my dad's eyes are focused, not on the camera, but on her.

"This picture right here reminds me that life is fickle. I was so naive and didn't even notice my mom's life slipping through our fingers, or my dad's heart breaking with every passing day." I lay down, lifting my feet and taking my socks off. "A vivid example that life is not always what it seems." I close my eyes as my head hits the soft pillow and after a minute of shuffling things around, Saint joins me too.

"Aurora, mirame," he says. When I turn my face to look at him, I see many emotions in his eyes. His hand comes up to gently touch my cheek, making small circles until his thumb is under my chin.

"I wish I could promise you that I won't die. But I can't, because that's the one constant we all have. But I can promise you that I won't leave you. You won't ever have to worry about me leaving physically or emotionally. I'm here, amor, you've got me." He smiles and suddenly, my world seems safer again.

"You do mean that, right? You're mine?" I ask.

"I do," he says and reaches over grabbing my hand and pulling me to him. "Yours to keep, remember?"

"Does that mean that you're only mine? You're not seeing other women, right?" I ask and I want to gag at how needy I sound.

"Roe, I've been with you every minute I have off and every second I'm not, I'm thinking about you. You're front and center in my mind and my heart. I'm. Yours. To. Keep. Only yours. That's what love is."

"Okay, got it," I whisper, biting my smile with my teeth.

He looks at me and raises an eyebrow, silently asking a question.

I don't even bother trying to suppress my immediate eye roll. "Yes, Saint, I guess you can keep me too."

I don't know how we got here but I think he does have a hold on something that's mine.

My heart.

I close my eyes and with his ocean smell and his warm body, I drift away into sleep.

THIRTY-NINE

BEFORE IT'S TOO LATE

The Cello Song, The Piano Guys

SANTIAGO

FOR THE FIRST time since I met her, Roe didn't want to go running this morning. She's stayed in before, but today she openly chose not to. She said she wanted to read her books and take it slow. We leave Baker tomorrow morning to go to the last race and I think she's finally letting her body rest the way it should before a big event.

I ran out to grab some breakfast, with an uneasy feeling that I haven't been able to shake since last night. For some reason the whole situation with Roe's house feels odd. It's not only the fact that it escalated so quickly from moving things around to then destroying things, but taking trophies also feels so strange.

I walk into Ronnie's and run into Jake who's also grabbing food. He's having a conversation with some dude and

293

if I didn't know Jake, I would think he's an asshole. His tone is spiteful and although he's not yelling, anyone who gets close enough can hear the conversation.

"Why can't you just be honest with her?" he asks.

"I don't owe her anything, Jake. We broke up months ago," the other guy says.

"You've been with her all your life, Cole. The on-and-off thing has always fucked with her and you know it. But this time you went beyond that. Why did you keep her hopes up if you were just going to tell her *never mind* when she offered to move here? Do you even love her?"

It feels wrong to eavesdrop but there's not much I can do. They're sitting at the bar, and so am I.

"Of course I care about her," Cole says.

"I didn't ask if you cared about her, asshole. I asked if you loved her, because if you did, you wouldn't want to hurt her like this."

Cole doesn't reply but he sets money on the table and grabs a bag of food before standing up. "I'm done with her and with this damn town. Can't do anything without having people talking about it. You wanna know the real reason why I told her I couldn't date her, Jake? Because I'm marrying the one girl that nobody sees in the right light. And I guess you out of all people would know, considering she's *your* fucking ex. We're both out of here as soon as the school year is over. Hell, we might not even make it to that." He gets up and walks toward the door before turning around and saying, "I'm done with everyone here."

"What can I get you, hon'?" Miss Jane asks me, breaking my eavesdropping. When it's not one of the Thompson's here, Miss Jane takes care of the restaurant. I don't know her well but all the locals love her and treat her like their own grandma. Ronnie's is my favorite place here in Baker because of the 'at home' feeling, and I'm not the only one who embraces that.

"Can I have two Baker's to go, one with scrambled eggs and one with two benedicts?" I ask without having to look at the menu.

"Coffee while you wait?" she asks. I nod, and before I can open my mouth she says, "With milk, not cream." She pats the counter and smiles, like a mom does to their child. We're all Ronnie's children after all.

I turn to Jake who looks ready to kill someone. "What was that all about?"

"You know Cara, right?" he asks.

"I do. I met her here a few months ago. She's close with Roe."

"Yeah, the girl is a pure ray of sunshine. She's close with Allie too and that douchebag, who used to be my friend, is her ex."

"Ah, Cole," I reply. Not that I know much but I've heard some.

"Yeah, he's lucky Mr. Ronald wasn't here to witness that. We've been telling Cara for years to cut her ties with him. But the heart wants what the heart wants. Anyway, enough about town drama. How are you? How's Roe after the break-in?"

"She's Roe, you know. Tough as nails no matter what happens."

"What about you?" he asks, paying for his food when Ms. Jane brings the bill and my coffee, just how I like it.

"Me? I'm fine. It's just weird and has left me feeling uneasy. They started by just messing with things, but now they added a message and actually took some stuff. It's like they're trying to mess with her head," I explain. I don't know why someone would feel the need to do that. Roe doesn't mess with people unless—*Coño*. It dawns on me the one time that Roe was spiraling and bitching at me before she even knew me. The one thing that other people don't think she deserves.

"Jake, I gotta go." I pull money out of my wallet and slam it on the counter before rushing out of Ronnie's and hoping I'm wrong. And if I'm right, I hope I make it back to her before it's too late.

FORTY

WHO THE HELL IS SAINT?

9 *Crimes*, *Damien Rice*

ROE

I WANTED to stay in so I could finish doodling some new art. When inspiration strikes, you have to take the opportunity because you don't know when it's going to happen again. I'm sitting on the back porch, drawing on the iPad when I hear the squealing sound of the sliding door opening. I turn around and see Marco standing there, his eyes throwing daggers at me.

"Hey, sorry if I woke you up, I can go back to his room," I say.

He snarls at me. "You couldn't just stay in your female class, could you?" he asks. And it takes me a minute to realize what he's talking about, but when it does, everything makes sense.

"What are you talking about?" I ask calmly, trying to

mask my feelings as much as I can. I look at his clenched hands and see a magazine in one hand and a bat in the other one.

"The race, Roe. I've been watching you for years and I knew you were good, but I didn't think you would be stupid enough to race with the men. Then this year, you had to. The one year I had scouts asking about me but they all ran away as soon as pretty little A. Sorelle took over," he spits, stepping forward with his eyes narrowing on me.

"Marco, it's just a race, no need to get serious."

"TO YOU!" he shouts. He throws the magazine on the ground and rubs his face with his hand. "It's just a race to you. But this could have been the out I needed for my parents to finally let me off the hook. If only I can show them that I can do it, they'll let me follow my own path and get out of this shit hole town."

"Marco, you're a grown-ass man, just move," I say, though maybe not my brightest moment considering this man has a bat in his hand.

He clenches his jaw so tightly that I can see a vein bulging in his neck. "I won't get my inheritance unless I have a career by twenty-five. Riding has been my passion for years and they placed this ultimatum when I turned twenty-one."

"And you still haven't made it? Sounds to me like this might not be your path, pal." *Damn it, Roe. Hush.*

"I've been sick. This year I finally was able to make it through most races to get the needed points. But this isn't about me, Roe. This is about you dropping out of this weekend and getting your boyfriend to drop out too."

"What? No, we're not doing that. Marco, move over," I urge, trying to push him away. I'm getting out of here.

He puts his hand up and stops me from going into the

house. "Oh, but you are. Dropping out, that is. Let's go," he snaps, grabbing my arm and walking me into the house.

This fucking man is acting unhinged over a god damn dirt bike race. It's not that serious. I try to yank my arm from his hold but it's futile. "Let me go, you jackass," I snap, pulling and trying to hold my weight back without any luck.

We go through the house and out to the garage where his truck is parked. He pushes me forward, in between him and the door, and lets go of my hand as he opens the truck. "Get in," he snarls, showing me the bat he's still holding in his other hand.

I obey for once in my life and climb to the front seat. I don't think he's going to hurt me, but I also don't want to find out if I'm wrong.

He drives quietly, holding on to the steering wheel with white knuckles; every time I try to talk, he tells me to shut up. I don't have my phone or watch, so there's no way to let anyone know. If this happened a year ago, I wouldn't have anyone to contact. But right now, I have a couple of people in mind.

One in particular comes to mind and I hope he hurries up and finds me missing from his home. I hope he doesn't think I just left him without saying anything. It does cross my mind that he might think I just took off. It's not like I've told him how I feel about him, though. So how would he even know?

We pull up at my house and this dude pulls me by my arm out of the truck on the driver's side. Funny how this is my preferred way to get out, but at this moment, I just want to crawl out of my skin. He drags me by the arm until we make it to my front door. Then he grabs keys from under the mat that I completely forgot I had and opens the door to my house. MY HOUSE.

"Where is it?" he asks.

"Where is what?" I snap back.

He walks into the garage, leaving me in the living room. "Don't play dumb. Where's the bike?"

"Which bike? Mine?" I ask, like I'm not talking to a man that has a bat in his hand. "If that's what you're doing here, then you're out of luck. Saint has my bike."

"Who the hell is Saint?" he asks and I forget that only I call him that.

"Santiago. Santiago has my bike in his trailer."

He slams the bat on the ground, pounding at the tile floor over and over again. The front door of the house slams shut and after a loud, "Roe?" comes from Saint, Marco walks toward me and grabs my arm.

"In here!" I shout as Marco yanks me to him. *Who does that?* "Let me go, you asshole," I scream at him.

"Do you really think you're in a position to be talking to me like that?" he asks at the same time that Saint walks in, stopping in his tracks when he sees Marco grabbing my arm.

"Woah, woah, what is going on here?" Saint's hands go up, raised in caution toward his roommate and friend.

"Stay back, Thiago," Marco snaps. "I'm finally putting an end to this stupidity of letting a *girl* race in our class. I was sure you'd feel the same way but then you went and chose pussy over bikes."

I choose again to speak over keeping my mouth shut. "Maybe you could use some pussy too to fix your mood."

"SHUT UP!" he shouts. I might be going insane but I laugh, because what else can I actually do? He drops my arm and shit escalates quickly because in the blink of an eye, Marco's hand is on my neck and my back is against the wall.

His eyes are fury-incarnate, burning into me as he squeezes my neck.

He's lost his mind but so have I, because instead of trying to get out of this fucked up situation and try to see if Saint can help, I say, "What Marco? You jealous of Saint? Are you trying to show me your daddy side?" He pounds on the wall by my head at the same time that I sass, "You gonna spank me too?"

If this is how I go out, I might as well go hard.

Little Bit Better*, *Caleb Hearn & ROSIE

SANTIAGO

"ROE, for once in your life, be quiet," I snap at her. She keeps babbling back and forth; her smart mouth, the one I love so much, is going to get her in serious trouble this time. The first thing I did as soon as he turned his back to me was call 911 and put the phone in my pocket so they can hear this bullshit and hopefully come quickly. I'm not waiting for them, though. I've already waited long enough since walking into her house and finding him manhandling my girl.

"Marco," I say, lowering my voice and walking calmly and steadily to him. The garage is bright, letting the morning light shine through, so I can't see anything he can use to hurt me or her. I approach him carefully, trying to keep this situation under control. "Take your hands off of her and back away." It's a command. Not a suggestion. Because this is not up for discussion.

It's taking everything in me not to let all my inner anger out on him. I want to give him the benefit of the doubt because we've been friends forever but the second he put his hands on her, he lost that chance.

He must hear my steps approaching him because he puts a hand up before saying, "Stay back, Santiago, or I will hurt her. Don't try me."

Roe snaps, "I'm nobody's-" and he must squeeze her tighter because the sudden gasp that she lets out makes my heart pound in my chest. There's no more trying to calm him down. There's no more holding back. He's hurting her, and I'm going to kill him.

"Get your hands off of her!" I charge forward, kicking him in the ribs. He immediately drops the hand from Roe's neck, and holds his side, coughing.

I block his body with mine, putting space between Roe and him. I look to the side and see Roe breathing hard and shaking her head. "Are you okay, princesa?" She doesn't reply, but her eyes go wide and I see Marco trying to charge at me. I bring my foot up and push him back with it, keeping the distance between us before following it with a punch straight to his jaw. I grab him by the waist and take him to the ground.

He tries to bring his hand up to my face so I grab his jaw and push it to the side. "Not so tough now that it's not a girl you're fighting, huh?" I ask. There's clear tension in the air and he's trying to get out from my hold, but it's futile. I'm bigger, stronger, and trained. He's just a mommy's boy who thought he could scare a girl away with his nonsense, not knowing that Roe was the wrong girl to mess with.

"Roe, princesa. Talk to me. Are you okay?" I ask,

needing to make sure that she's alright. I don't want to take my hands off of him but every fiber of me screams to go to her.

"I'm fine," she answers with a cough, grabbing her neck and stepping back away from him.

The minute he hears her talk, he spits and screams at me to let him go. Despite me pinning him down with his face in my hands, Marco's not backing down. He's still moving and squirming, trying to fight me. This makes me even more upset, but it's when he says, "You've ruined my career over a girl who could be everyone's flavor of the week," that I lose my shit and punch him hard, a splatter of blood coming out of his mouth.

"Shut the fuck up, Marco. Watch how you talk about my Roe and actually, now that I think about it? Don't," I shout, stopping to tilt his face my way. "Don't talk about her. Don't think about her. If I ever see you or hear that you're talking about her, I will fuck you up. Do you understand?" Nobody should talk about women like that but nobody is going to talk about my woman like that.

"Nod if you understand, asshole," I command and he does. The sirens wail in the background and Marco tries to say something but I tell him to hush. I wait for the police to walk in and after the all-clear, I walk to Roe.

She's standing with her back to the wall, a police officer talking to her while she squeezes her hands and shakes her head no.

"Excuse me, officer," I say and pull Roe to me. With her head on my chest, and her sweet floral scent engulfing me, I breathe for the first time.

"Took you long enough," she sasses and I don't have a choice but to laugh.

"I love you, princesa." What else is there to say? We stay

there until the cops give us more instructions and then we follow them outside.

The police take Marco to the station, and they ask us to meet them there so they can take our statements. Hours later, we're finally free to go while they figure out what the hell is wrong with Marco. There's not much for them to tell us, but they did inform Roe that he was the one breaking into her house. It was clear after he told them how much he wanted her to drop out of the race, but apparently, he said where the trophies were too, so they're closing that case. I'm tired from dealing with the day and I bet Roe is feeling it too.

I rest my hand on her lower back, guiding her out of the building and toward my truck. Unsurprisingly, she tenses at the touch. I don't blame her; the girl has had more going on today than most people do in all their lives. I could stop right here and ask her about it but knowing Roe, she needs privacy and probably silence.

I open the door for her and help her up. "I'm going to buckle you up, princesa. I won't touch you." A promise. I want nothing but to touch every inch of her skin and her soul but she needs her boundaries respected right now, not crossed. She nods and I reach over and buckle her. The loud click settles her and her eyes instantly close.

I walk around to the other side, climb up, and shift the truck into drive, leaving the police station and hopefully part of this nightmare behind.

"Yours or mine?" I ask. She doesn't answer. At least not with words but with the slow shake of her head I get my answer. *Neither.*

I drive in silence until I find a hotel. Baker Inn is a small mom-and-pop place right by the highway. It has the same small town feel as the rest of Baker Oaks, but it's far enough away from the center of town that it feels less close to home. More people passing through stay here than locals, making it the perfect place for this.

"I'm going to get a room, I'll be right back," I tell her and go to the hotel lobby.

After getting the key to our room, I get Roe and we walk toward it. Stepping into the quiet and quaint room, I help her slip out of her shoes and guide her to the bathroom. I turn the water on hot and help her remove her clothes. I usher her in, letting the water fall on her before stepping in with her.

"Saint, take your clothes off," she whispers, her voice breaks.

"Sh, sh, sh, this is not about me. Come here," I say, pulling her to my body.

She wraps her arms around my waist laying her head on my chest and sighing. Without moving she lets me later soap all over her body; lets me take care of her. In this moment, I realize she loves me, whether she's ready to say it out loud or not. I know now that she has let me in, and she trusts me to the point of complete surrender, allowing me to show her how much I want to be here for her.

Turning the water off, I bundle her in a towel that swallows her whole. I twist another one on her head and carry her to the bed, laying her down gently and covering her with a blanket. After I remove my wet clothes, I wrap a towel around my waist and sit on the chair across from the bed.

Roe's eyes are closed but when she senses me near, she opens them and looks at me. The short distance between us does nothing to dampen the way her gaze is burning right through my soul. She holds my heart in her hands and I pray to God and todos los angelitos that she will keep it.

"Saint, I won't bite," she jokes, patting the spot on the bed next to her.

"I want to give you space, princesa."

"What if I don't want space? What if I don't need it?" she asks.

Her eyes are sincere. She looks tired and spent but she wants me there. She wants me next to her and I've never wanted anything more than that. "Then maybe I can fill it."

"You already have," she whispers and if it wasn't as quiet as it is, I would've missed that. I would've missed the pretty little sigh she let out after she said that, and I would've missed her shoulders tensing as she waits for what I'm going to say next.

"I've already filled what space?" I ask, walking toward the bed and sitting down next to her.

She turns her body so she's facing me and she lays a hand on my chest. "The space missing in my heart, pretty boy. I haven't been afraid of being hurt or dying in a long time, Saint. But somehow, today I realized that I was scared," she says.

I raise my eyebrows at her and she raises her hands in surrender.

"I wasn't scared of what would happen to me. I was afraid of getting hurt when I feel like I've finally started living again. I was afraid I might never get the chance of going through the what-ifs with you," she adds, letting out a sigh and bringing her hand up to my face.

"I think I might love you, Santiago Cruz, and I don't really know what to do with that," she admits, and all she can see is the giant smile on my face and nothing else. A smile that stretches all the way to my heart.

"You might love me?" I ask, pulling her flush to me, her legs locking around mine and both of us lost in this moment. I wish I could stop the clock right now and let time engulf us forever. Forever wrapped in her love is where I want to be.

"I think I do. I'm terrified, though," she says.

"Of what?"

"Of loving you. I don't want to lose you." Her voice shakes. As her lashes flutter against her cheeks, I bring my hand to her face, tilting her chin toward me.

"You won't," I whisper, afraid to break the spell if I speak louder.

"You don't know that for sure. You don't know if you're going to walk out of here and drop dead, leaving me in shambles."

"Well, I hope I don't," I chuckle, bringing my finger to her cheek and touching it slightly. "I can't promise you I won't die, but I can promise you I'll stay for as long as you'll let me. You won't lose me, amor. I'm here for the long run. I'm here until the finish line. I'm here to help you carry the load and I'm here to remind you that it wasn't your fault."

Two tears run down her cheeks and her nose turns a soft pink color. I know she's fighting all these emotions at once. Feelings that have been bottled up for years. Feelings that have turned to anger for a lack of a safe place to land. And man, how fucking lucky I am that she's letting herself fall on me.

"Thank you for leaning on me, Roe. Thank you for letting your guard down."

She sucks in a breath at my words and when I smile at her, I know that she feels it. She feels my whole heart opening up to her, embracing every part of her, and never letting go.

"You tore all my walls down, with your pretty face and your beautiful heart. Promise me you won't leave," she whispers. "Promise me you won't give up on me. Promise me you can love all my broken pieces."

"There are no broken pieces, amor. Just a beautiful chaotic masterpiece. But I do promise, princesa. I promise I will always be here and I will always remind you how incredible you are. I promise to give you space when you need it but to be your blanket too." I bring my lips to her forehead and kiss her gently, her body instantly melting into mine.

"I love you," she says and if those are the last words I ever hear in my life, I would die a happy man.

"I love you too, amor and I always will. Never forget that."

She closes her beautiful blue eyes and falls asleep, safe in my arms.

FORTY-TWO
THE FINISH LINE

THUNDERSTRUCK*, *AC/DC

ONE MONTH *later*

ROE

"I'M ROOTING FOR YOU, ROE," Allie shouts from the starting grid. I'm not used to having someone on the grid with me holding my bike. Other than Allen when I race near home, it's usually just me over here. My bike is usually on a stand for me to hop on after the run and take off. But today, Allie and Jake joined our race. Jake's holding Saint's bike and Allie's holding mine. She's so loud, I can hear her above the noise; until it's time to start the bikes and the revving sounds drown out *all* of the noise. It's nice to have someone in my corner. This is the first time that I don't look like the loser with nobody on the grid for me. The first time

311

I have eyes to look for on the other end of the starting line and the first time I have someone rooting for me. Other than Allen, that is.

I walk across the fifteen steps between my bike and the starting line. I'm about to start my pre-race mantras when I feel a hand touching my shoulder. Looking to my right, I see Saint standing there, pulling his helmet up so I can see his pretty smile. He brings his hands up to my face, and with his visor touching mine he says, "Good luck, princesa. Show them how badass you are."

"Don't go easy on me, Saint," I reply and he shakes his head. I know he won't. I know there's no way Saint will back down and let me win this just to prove a point. He knows I would riot. I want to win this. I know I can do it, but I want to win it fair and square. I want to know that at the end, I gave it my all, and I came out the other end victorious. With Marco and Joey out of the race, first place is really up to Saint and me. We're talking about what could be a second's difference on who will make the best time per lap. Between winning it all and losing. Because let's be honest, second place is not winning at all. It may be good enough to pass to the next round, but I want first place or bust.

"I love you," he shouts with a smile. Three words that would make me want to crawl out of my skin before but now soothe my soul. I know he does and I know that he'll keep the promise of staying with me, for as long as he can. Will it be easy dealing with my chaos? No, but I know that he will be there with me, despite it all.

"I love you too," I shout back. He scoops me in his arms and bumps his helmet with mine. The vibrations from the tap go through my body, reminding me he's here with me. That for the first time I'm not alone. We take a deep breath together and he steps to my side.

"Give them hell, Saint," I say.

"You too, amor, you too," he shouts.

The countdown begins at the same time my breathing deepens. I can feel the pressure against my chest and the world closing in. The noise muffled under the engines roaring. Everyone disappears from my view, with only the bike and the end in sight.

"FIFTEEN SECONDS," the announcer shouts at the same time that I feel a hand on mine, squeezing, and grounding me. I turn and see Saint, his eyes boring through mine, offering me reassurance that I didn't know I needed. I nod and turn to face my bike.

The horn goes off and I run fast, mounting my bike and kicking hard. It's time to race one more time and show all these assholes who rules this track.

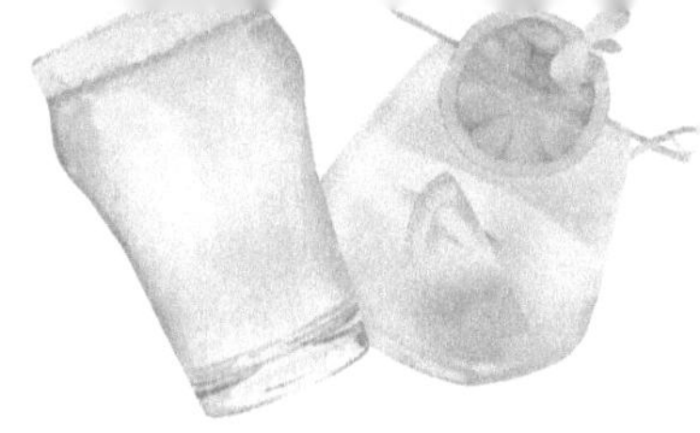

EPILOGUE

EVERYTHING, Lifehouse

TWO YEARS **later**

ROE

"Hurry up, amor, the wedding is going to start in an hour," I hear Saint shout from the other side of the door.

We had a race today that I couldn't miss. Once you're the reigning champion of a class, especially a class mostly run by men, you go to every event they invite you to. Even if it means changing clothes in a tiny bathroom by the racetrack.

Two years ago, Saint and I raced neck to neck on the AA hare scramble classifiers, and I won by two seconds. *Two seconds.* That's how much faster I went than him. We both made it to regionals but didn't make it to nationals. Last year, I took the title in both. Saint dropped out of regionals,

315

not because of will, but because of an injury. Old man couldn't keep up.

The whole Marco situation shook the organization. People didn't realize how many riders felt the same way as he did about women racing in men's classes. His case made it to court after we both pressed charges, but instead of being sent to prison, Marco pleaded insanity and was sent to an inpatient institution. His parents took him somewhere outside of Florida for this. They sent letters and emails apologizing for their son – or so Saint has said, because I couldn't care less what any of them have to say. As long as he's out of my life forever, I don't care. I hope he gets the help he needs and if he doesn't, that he stays locked up forever. The one positive thing that came out of it was the awareness and the protection needed to make this a healthy environment for girls.

Today, SMX ran an event for girls who wanted to race in the boys' class. We had a group of ten girls, little Emma being one of them, ready to show everyone that they were capable of winning both the girls and the boys class. Saint, of course, was by my side, holding my bike like he has since he stepped out of racing. Even though today we have our friends' wedding, he still stood there, supporting me.

Allie and Jake have been planning this wedding for months and we wouldn't miss it for the world, even if it means arriving late. But we might be late because when I open the bathroom door, Saint's eyes find mine with pure fire behind his gaze.

"Damn, princesa," he growls as he scans my body. I'm wearing a red strapless dress with the biggest cleavage you could imagine. It frames my body before flaring open. I drag my hand up my leg, showing him how much the slit on the skirt shows and he licks his lips.

"Are you trying to kill me here?" he asks.

I roam my hands all over my body while I tease, "You like?"

He steps into the small bathroom, closes the door with his foot, and grabs me in his arms. No matter how many times this man has seen me naked, he's never satisfied. He can't keep his hands to himself and he sure as hell makes sure I know how he feels about me and my body.

He presses me against the sink and brings his hands under the skirt, skimming my thighs all the way to my ass. When he finds that I'm wearing a thong, he hisses.

"We don't have time, Saint," I say, letting out a whimper when his mouth finds my neck and he bites.

"We'll make time. You look like a whole damn meal, and I'm a starving man, muñeca. I'm ready to feast." Unhinged Saint is my favorite, and through the years he has allowed himself to chase what he wants. He has allowed himself to put his desires first, and I'm here for it.

"I'm yours to do as you please, just make it quick," I say and that's all the permission he needs.

His hands are frantic. Pulling my underwear down and touching me everywhere, he yanks them over my shoes and sticks them in the pocket of his suit. "For later," he says, winking before his lips are on my neck again. Licking, biting, nipping. I let out a moan and he covers my mouth with his hand. "Shh, someone's going to hear us. Can you be quiet for me, princesa?" His eyes flare with lust and it's all I need to know that I will be very happy if I can just comply with his one request, so I nod.

His mouth goes back to my skin, blazing a fire across my neck, leaving a trail of sensations. Biting, sucking, and kissing to alleviate the sting. *Staying quiet will be more challenging than the fucking race.* He cups my breast, lowering the top of my dress to expose a nipple, and his mouth sucks over it. His other fingers work the other one and twist the hard bud in between his index and thumb with the rhythm of his flicking tongue, making me see stars.

I'm grinding on him over his dress pants. Even though he's fully clothed, his hard dick presses against my center, teasing me, unraveling me. I pull his hair while I continue to grind on him, and he takes that as permission to go rougher. Saint bites my nipple while pinching the other one. Just when I think I can't feel more pressure, he takes his free hand and slides two fingers into my already-drenched pussy.

"Fuck, Roe, you're so wet. So tight," he groans with his mouth still close to my sensitive nipple.

"Always for you. Always wet for you," I say, gasping for air as he lowers the rest of my dress, making my breasts spill out from the top without apologizing.

He leans back slightly, just enough to take me in. His eyes flash with a dangerous lust as he murmurs, "You're so fucking gorgeous, amor." I never get enough of this.

He brings his mouth back to my nipple, not stopping his hand from pumping in and out of me. My back curves against him, pulling his hair and pressing my breast into his mouth to find my balance and ride his fingers. He hooks his fingers, sliding another one in and I'm about to see stars. He looks up at me with a cocky smirk on his face, watching me catch my breath, because all this man does is leave me breathless. No matter how many times we fuck, he manages to make me feel more each time.

He curves his fingers, dropping his other hand under my ass and squeezing, helping me move up and down. *I can't take this much longer.* My breathing is heavy; my hands claw at his back as he continues to drive me wild with his tongue and his hands. He takes his fingers out with one quick swoop, but before I can complain about feeling empty, he turns me around. Ass up, face practically hitting the sink.

Before I can ask what he's doing, he slides his fingers back in, making me feel deliciously full again. His thumb is rubbing my clit while his other fingers tease me mercilessly. I hear him spit and shortly after he says, "Breathe for me, princesa."

I take a deep breath in as he slides his finger into my ass, gently rubbing the puckered hole before pushing it in, little by little.

I hiss, and he drops a kiss on my ass cheek, before biting and kissing it again. Pumping his fingers in and out of both places. *This is too much.* I know I'm going to scream soon if he doesn't make me come, or maybe even when he does make me come.

"Saint," I whisper.

"Stop holding on, Roe. Give it to me," he commands at the same time that he curves his fingers and bites my ass.

"Now," he demands and that's all it takes for me to let go and pulse against both his hands. This is euphoric; I can feel it everywhere. My skin is covered in goosebumps; my pussy and ass clenching against his fingers. I drop my head onto the sink and bite on my arm because it's either that or I'm going to scream, and we really don't want that.

When I'm finally done, spent and sated, he turns me around to face him as he licks the three fingers covered in my arousal like a caveman, and shit was that the hottest thing I have ever experienced. Even after two years with this man, he still finds ways to keep me on my toes. He licks his lips, and then kisses me, pulling my dress up and smacking my ass.

"We have places to be, princesa, let's go."

ALLIE AND JAKE'S wedding is beautiful. The tree canopies surrounding the arbor with the lake shine as the backdrop. Family and friends are sitting in their own chairs. Allie had petitioned for all her friends to bring them; a group of mismatched chairs, she said. Cara's currently sobbing while she stands with her flowers listening to her best friend say the sweetest vows I've ever heard. I'm not very emotional but these might make it to the cry count of the year.

After the ceremony, the reception is hosted in a ballroom with floor-to-ceiling windows overlooking Lake George. The sun starts setting, lighting the room with soft orange hues. Their first dance is like a fairytale. The couple is surrounded by the warm tones from the sun and 'To Make You Feel My Love' by Adele is playing softly while they sway around, looking happier than ever.

Saint wraps his arms around me, kissing me on my cheek and pulling me toward him so my back is resting on his chest.

"Are you sad that won't be us one day?" I ask. We've talked about not needing a wedding, and even though his mom wanted to kill me when she found out her only son wasn't getting married, it's never been something I wanted to do. Yes, now I have friends that are like family in my life, but it doesn't negate the fact that my side of the room would be empty. I don't want to do that, and Saint understands and is okay with that. We moved in together after the whole Marco fiasco and we're happy the way we live, but sometimes I wonder if maybe he's compliant to keep me happy.

"No, amor. I can dance with you any day of the week. I

don't need an audience to know how I feel about you and to know that you love me." He kisses my forehead again and lowers his mouth to my ear. I can feel his warm breath before he says, "I love what we have, Roe. No need to do something just because others do it. As long as you're happy, I'm happy too. All I need is you. Everything else is negotiable."

I turn my face slightly, catching his lips on mine and kissing him gently. "I love you, Santiago," I say and he smiles against my lips.

"I'm never going to get tired of hearing those words out of your lips, princesa."

"Good," I reply, "because I'm not planning on stopping anytime soon.

"I also won't get tired of looking at these beauties," I add, touching his arm, the one that's full of beautiful butterfly tattoos that he made me do on him after a year of being together. He said there was no anniversary gift or anything like that, but he wanted something permanent. Something that reminded him that when you think life will be over, it can transform again, like a butterfly. He told me how much he loved that I had so many on my arms even without knowing that meaning because deep down I knew, I could love again. I could live again. So now, our matching butterflies remind me, more than him I'm sure, how beautiful life can be after you've been in a shell for so long. Or a cocoon, if we want to be technical.

"These are my favorite tattoos," he says.

"Nah, I think the cityscape on your back is bad ass."

He laughs and grabs my hand and pulls me to the dance floor at the same time that the DJ announces that all couples should join Allie & Jake, to celebrate with them. We all slow dance to a song about endless love while the DJ calls out years together. First, he calls out six months. *If you've been together for six months, step out.* Then he moves on to one year and two years. Saint and I step out during this time, and this goes on and on until Allie's grandparents are the last one dancing with fifty years together. *Impressive.*

I never thought being together with someone for fifty years was a goal I'd have, but after being with Saint for two, I don't think a hundred years will be enough. I don't think a lifetime will be enough to be with him. I feel sorry for the people that don't get to experience this kind of high and I'm so fucking thankful he never gave up on me when I pushed him away. Because these last two years? They have healed every single part of me that needed mending. Every part of me that needed saving.

"Are you okay, amor?" he asks, tucking my hair behind my ear and pulling me flush to him.

I inhale his salty, breezy scent, find the spot where I belong right next to his heart and say, "Never better."

WHAT COMES NEXT?

Not ready to say goodbye to Baker Oaks? Make sure to preorder TRST, book three in The Baker Oaks series, to read Cara's story.

Preorder TRST NOW

BAKER OAKS

IF YOU HAVEN'T READ Allie & Jake story, a small town, second chance, football romance, you can start today!

READ The Truth Never Spoken for FREE with KU!

ACKNOWLEDGMENTS

Hi, friend!

You made it 'til the end and I wish I could add a little recording here of me screaming in gratitude. I'm still in shock that people want to read my words and what I have to say, and I will be forever grateful because of it. This book is one in a million of books out there and you decided to pick this one up today and my heart couldn't be fuller.

Writing this second book was such a different experience than the first, and somehow, I have even more people to thank, so here we go.

To my husband, my number one fan. I will never have enough words to describe how thankful I am for you in my life and for your support in my authoring career. Thank you for picking up the percentage that I'm dropping at home to be able to chase this dream. You are the true meaning of support and I still can't believe you're mine.

To my friends, alpha readers, and ultimate hype girls: Adriana, Jen, Beth, and Colleen; what would my author life be without your feral support for my dreams? Sometimes I don't think I can do it and that's the day that one of you chooses to send me a message about my gift. Some days, I wrote because you told me I could and I will never get over that, thank you. Adriana, specially you who let me use your friendship, personality, and badassery as inspiration for Roe.

To my editor, Kendra. I'm writing this as you're actively editing another portion of this book. I really wish I had enough words to describe what you did for me with this book. How your support, comments, suggestions, and little videos to teach me things on track changes may have changed my life. I could cry right now (actually crying) on how much your work on this book means to me. You are one of a kind and everyone needs you to edit their books (maybe not everyone because I might need you to myself sometimes) and in their corner. Thank you, thank you, thank you!

To my beta readers, ALL OF YOU are pure gold. Jayné and Rachel, I still can't believe you didn't give up on me and this manuscript. Thank you for all your hard work and for understanding my gibberish and helping me form it into better sentences. Michelle and Nora, you two came to beta at a time in which I needed feedback to feel like I could write again and you delivered. Mandy, ILYSM, I loved your feedback and the fact that you devoured this book in a day will forever be a favorite memory. Brittany, Wren, Erica, and Malu, thank you for being the extra set of eyes I needed to have this book be the best version of itself it could be.

To my author friends who went above and beyond: Nicole, Bella, Sarah, Veronica, Emily, Shann, Hailey, and Rachel; I don't know where I would be without you girls today. I hit the author-friend jackpot with you guys and I hope you know how grateful I will be forever.

Thank you to Motocross Moms, Wives & Ladies Facebook group for being my sanity while my little ones were riding. The countless hours I spent reading and learning about motocross safety or track-friendly foods was amazing. Special thank you to Diana, Kaylea, Tammy, Ava, Morgan, Lauren, Cherri, Ashlee, Brittany, Kelsie, and Tammie (and daughter) for letting me use your pics for promo!

I also want to take a moment to say thank you to some

of my friends who read my first book to support me (sometimes not even liking romance in general) and then were ready to read this book as soon as they could. Amber and Diane, Thank you!

To Ever After Cover Design (Discreet) for taking my thoughts and putting them on a gorgeous cover. More than I could've asked for. The tears of joy I shed when the final design came were infinite. Aliyah, you were incredible to work with, thank you so very much!

To Kim from KBG Designs. I don't know how you do it but you nailing the illustrated cover on the first try and making me cry two times in a row should be a record. You are stuck with me forever.

To my street and ARC team. I don't know what I did to deserve all of you but just know that I am so grateful. Thank you for being the ultimate hype babes.

To YOU reader, for giving me a chance and making my wildest dreams come true.

Now, off to cry in author tears and on to the next book.

143,

Ambar

BONUS EPILOGUE

Want more Roe & Saint?

SCAN HERE FOR A BONUS EPILOGUE!

ABOUT THE AUTHOR

Ambar is a multicultural romance author of the Small Town Series: Baker Oaks. She writes emotional romance that brings raw emotions and butterflies to her readers. Ambar is a wife and mom of two who has been living in Florida since 2015, and who loves the small town where she currently lives. Born and raised in the Dominican Republic, she embraces cultural differences and brings that to her books. When she is not writing, she is enjoying time with her family, traveling, and reading.

instagram.com/acordovabooks

facebook.com/acordovabooks

SPICE GUIDE

Here are the chapter including explicit or open door spice.

- Chapter Three
- Chapter Fifteen
- Chapter Nineteen
- Chapter Twenty-eight
- Chapter Twenty-nine
- Chapter Thirty-one
- Chapter Thirty-two
- Epilogue